THE
BROOKLYN
BOOK OF
THE DEAD

THE
BROOKLYN
BOOK OF
THE DEAD

—— A NOVEL BY ——

MICHAEL
STEPHENS

DALKEY ARCHIVE PRESS

Parts of this book, sometimes only fragments, and in slightly different form, first appeared in the following magazines and anthologies, for which the author wishes to express his thanks to the editors: *Adrift, Fiction, Hanging Loose,* and in Wesley Brown and Amy Ling's *Imagining America* (Persea, 1991) and Jerome Klinkowitz's *Writing Baseball* (Univ. of Illinois Press, 1991).

Library of Congress Cataloging-in-Publication Data
Stephens, Michael Gregory.
    The Brooklyn book of the dead : a novel / by Michael Stephens.
    1. Irish American families—New York (N.Y.)—Fiction. 2. Irish Americans—New York (N.Y.)—Fiction. 3. Brooklyn (New York, N.Y.)—Fiction. 4. Family—New York (N.Y.)—Fiction. I. Title.
PS3569.T3855B76   1994   813'.54—dc20   93-36135

ISBN 1-56478-037-6
First Edition

Partially funded by grants from The National Endowment for the Arts and The Illinois Arts Council

Dalkey Archive Press
4241 Illinois State University
Normal, IL 61790-4241

Printed on permanent/durable acid-free paper and bound in the United States of America.

To
Rosie & Stevie & all the kids

CONTENTS

"Heirs are cruel"
　　　—Thomas Bernhard

"Moon Mullins has lived through it,
the lout. So why not he,
the question."
　　　—Gilbert Sorrentino

FIVE JACK COOL

1

HE'S DEAD. THE OLD MAN'S DEAD. POOR OLD BASTARD.

His sons gathered in the old neighborhood. In this funeral parlor across from the shrine church of Our Lady of Lourdes, the elevated subway train rattling past every couple of minutes. A few blocks over: the abandoned bocci courts and Eastern Parkway, the ramshackle Long Island Railroad station, the Canarsie Line. The old ghetto in Brooklyn. East New York. That mythical land between Bushwick and Bed-Stuy, between hell and Brownsville. High crime, low rent, none of the buildings more than a few stories except the projects—and not a familiar face on the street. This neighborhood hadn't seen their kind since Kennedy became president, two or three junkyard dogs' lifetimes ago.

Five of Inspector Coole's children were present and accounted for. His namesake, the oldest son Leland, was there, aka J. L. Coole, of the shock treatments and lockups on the flight decks of countless hospitals, VA and otherwise. Emmett was there, too, of the medallion cab leases, and the rubber hose jobs in back streets around the Gowanus Canal, Emmett of a little muscle. Then there was that pretentious litterateur, the notorious Mickey Mack, the Manhattanite, the bon vivant, the pickled herring. He was followed by Paddy, Sir Patrick, small and muscled and blond, he of gesso and the canvas stretchers from

Pearl Paint on Canal Street where he used to maintain an illegal studio in an abandoned building near the Holland Tunnel but was now a rural gentleman of leisure and a purveyor of fine antique furniture (slightly used) and Adirondack Blue, a marijuana that he and his lovely companion, Dr. Molly Millarkey, developed in those northern straits. Finally, there was Terence, a boy of psycho dreams and perpetual noogies, the scourge of his clan, the homeless derelict who slept in abandoned vehicles at the edge of golf courses on Long Island.

The list was equally long and illustrious of the brothers not present: Wolfe, Brian, Parnell, Rory, and Francis Xavier, not to mention the six sisters in Samantha, Oona, Deirdre, Mary Grace, Eileen, and Elizabeth Ann.

Paddy added his two cents: "He looks like he did when he stepped off the boat back then. . . ."

"Way back when," Terry chimed in.

Those near Terry stared at him maliciously.

"You psycho," Leland shouted.

"Sorry," Terry said.

"Shut up," Emmett grunted.

"Quit fighting over there," Paddy called out, next to his brother Mickey Mack, who stood silently and, as usual, full of grudges.

"But he does look good," Paddy said again.

"Like he did back in the old country," Terry piped up.

"How would you know?" Emmett asked, kind of nastylike and punky. And he repeated the words just to punctuate how nasty he felt. "How would *you* know?"

When they were kids, Emmett looked like an angelic blond-haired, blue-eyed altar boy. Now he had a gnarly countenance, bald like the rest of them, but parched and dehydrated and belligerent, almost like he was still a juvenile delinquent, not a man approaching fifty years old who drove yellow cabs through the boroughs for a living. Emmett had made an art out of his bad attitudes and tempers, out of his revenge fantasies, and his killer dreams. Protégé to the Irish gangsters of Long Island and Hell's Kitchen, he was his own one-man crime wave.

Leland got them back to the business at hand.

"I don't care what I thought about the old man or what you still think of him now. Even we have our obligations and duties."

Leland liked to tell whoever would listen that Emmett was just like Grandpa Coole, a hell-raising, boozy ne'er-do-well, and like Emmett, Grandpa Coole drove a cab at the end of his life, and before that drove a lorry, steering a workhorse that looked as shabby as he did through the gaslit streets of old New York, a pint bottle of hooch in his back pocket, collecting rags from the curbside, his head full of booze and immigrant resentments.

"It's just a thought," Paddy told him.

"You weren't even born when he came from wherever it was he came from, though I know it wasn't the old country. It was Brooklyn," Emmett said.

"Besides, I don't think he ever did come from the old country," Leland said, in a rare moment of agreement with his eternal adversary Emmett.

The two of them were like Stan and Ollie, only the game was more serious, played more for the hurt than the comedy.

"I think maybe he was born right here in Brooklyn, and that everything else he said was a lie: where he came from, who his father was, and how his mother died," Leland went on in that lofty stage-Irish voice he sometimes had.

"Why do you think he wants to be waked and interred here?" Emmett asked, keeping up his agreement with his oldest brother in this eerie, almost dangerous, unpredictable way, as if at any moment he might contradict himself and go for a baseball bat to settle things the old way. But he didn't; he went on speaking civilly and in agreement with his antagonist Leland.

Their father's death had made each of them behave differently.

"Why do you think he wanted it?" Emmett asked. "Why here and not in goddamn Florida next to his wife—Lord have mercy on her because she's our mother—but in those tombs at the fuckn Brooklyn-Queens border?"

"Why?" Mickey Mack asked.

Emmett drilled his brother with the evil eye, staring him down until that bookish Mickool shut the hell up.

The old man left instructions in his will that he was *not* to be buried in Florida next to the marker for his wife, their mother Rose Moody Coole, whom all of them thought would outlive him by decades. Instead he lived to make a widower's codicil that stated he was to be laid out, waked, and buried in the old neighborhood in Brooklyn. Another one of his demands was that the funeral parlor where he would be laid out had to be the one across from Our Lady of Lourdes, and afterward they would wake him in the bars along Broadway underneath the elevated subway train—how was he to know that all the bars would be boarded up and replaced by crack houses and bootleggers and numbers parlors?—and then inter him in a plot across from his beloved Tromer's Brewery (long gone but a good corner at which to buy heroin) up on Bushwick Avenue, into that land of cemeteries beyond the eerie reservoir and park system which was a several-miles-thick buffer that separated East New York, Bushwick, and Bed-Stuy from the more gentrified world of Ridgewood and Ozone Park, and the outer borough to the city limits, outside of which he raised them in Nassau out on Long Island, supposedly a decent interval from these urban rookeries.

In other words, he asked to be buried with the family he so detested all his life—his father, his stepmother, his stepsister Aunt Augusta, and his emaciated corpselike cousins (even in life) from counties Mayo and Clare, those banshees of the Gaeltacht and former galoots of Riis Park and Breezy Point barbecues. He never did stomach the exceptions that Florida allowed, how those of the faith could be cremated because the ground was marshy and not deep enough for a coffin, and so the ashes could be scattered over the Gulf of Mexico, then to float, as no doubt Rosy Coole's did, into the gulfweed currents of the Stream, out of the Gulf and up the coast, past the Coney Island jellyfish—scumbags to you *shabbes goy* who don't know Brooklyn; whitefish to those who do—past the islands off Cape Cod, Nova Scotia, and clear across the continental drift and the mid-Atlantic rifts, right back to the primordial soil of the ancestral past; to be absorbed into the seaweed harvests, planted over the potato plot, be eaten by a toothless wonder and come back another Keltic bandit to haunt the land once again, making so many children, as Rosy did, or maybe become a monastic creature, doing penance for sins forevermore and a day until the cycle starts again.

The old man would have none of that megillah about the hereafter, forbidding that there be a Mass for him, or even a priest to say the Our Fathers and Hail Marys at the wake; everyone knew the only world Inspector Coole acknowledged came out of these intestinal streets. It would be East New York or it would be nothing.

Even though five brothers attended their father, more than twice that number of Coole children were missing. Less than half the family were women, the men always in the ascendancy number-wise in the household. Regardless of the number, their father rarely remembered any of their names. Sometimes, like Charlie Chan, he referred to his Number One son or his Number Two daughter. At other times he called you Jack or Mack or shithead, no matter what your name was. He called them all such names that sometimes they forgot why they even bothered to come here in the first place. But then one of them told the other that the old man was your father, Jack or Mack or Emmy or Paddy or Mr. T, and these are your siblings. They are all you have left.

All of this got complicated further by the fact that the oldest son, the dead father, and the late grandfather all had the same name—Leland. But they also were called James and Jems and Jack. One Jack could remind you of a thousand others or none at all; one Jack was enough to make a mess of anything. It reminded you of other Jacks, real and imagined, living and dead, from near and far, of the old and new countries, who come to mind when the old man got conjured.

One way or the other they were all Jacks here. But specifically there were five Jack Coole any one of them might spout about from the top of his head.

The sons of Inspector Coole stood in the main room of the funeral parlor before his coffin.

Their father, he art in his pangs, a hollow little fat man full of terror and that most Brooklyn of things—dentalized *t*s. It was a habit he picked up after he stepped off the boat from the old country with his own old man, not to live in this outermost post of civilization in Brooklyn, but on the Upper West Side in Manhattan, first in Hell's Kitchen and later up in Irishtown in the Eighties, a rundown tenement between Broadway and Amsterdam, just half a block from where Zabar's is today. Back then, there was no Zabar's, no designer bagels and salmon salads, no espresso machines and lingonberry jams. It was a new land, the promised land.

"What did you guys say over there?" Emmett called.

"Nothing," Mickey Mack said.

"Quit poking me," Terry shouted.

"I'll put a hot poky up your ass," Leland called out.

They all laughed.

"I'll put a hot poky up you, ya dirty Irish bastard," Emmett sang out, getting them all to laugh again. Their father used to say that when he was angry at them when they were kids growing up here.

So it could be said that they were joined together, not so much by a name or blood, the imagination or revolution, family ties or familial obligations, as by the terror and misery their father inflicted upon them, and their own individual and collective abilities to conjure it away by a sense of humor.

"There's still time for the others, it's early," Mickey Mack said, "still time for the others to pay their respects."

"Ha," said Leland, a bearish and aging bachelor.

Really, though, it was difficult seeing who made the remark because three of them were on one side of the coffin, and two of them (Paddy and Mike) on the other, but if you put two and two together, hearing those words, it was easy to think, ah, yes, Leland, also called Jackie Wackie, one of the three brothers on the other side of the coffin. His voice alone set off all the old post-traumatic shock syndrome (the explosions of memory and the implosions of denial and therefore forgetfulness) of being back with family, and then being present here in East New York, back in Brooklyn, that ancient ground.

Now it was back to the imperfect present. Sitting shiva with this fallen gentile who was turning to dust. This old *borracho*. The crazy man, the old Italian mobsters from Eastern Parkway called him, *doozy potz*. Little Lee. Jackie Ducks (don't ask how he got that one). Crazy Jack. Mr. Kool. Kool and the Gang, their black neighbors called him later. Papa Bear. Mr. Yentzer (the interminable copulator). The man, like the old woman who lived in a shoe, who had so many children, he didn't know what to do. But besides his children, each one of these innocents expected other relatives to show, even in this neighborhood. An endless stream of aunts and uncles. Not the old man's relations, though. They were probably either dead or out of town or out of their minds somewhere. The relations were all Moodys from their mother's side, still living in Brooklyn, though not in East New York; the Moodys were out in Flatbush, further out on

Eastern Parkway—separated by Crown Heights and the Luba-vitchers—or over the hump from the Reservoir and Highland Park in Ridgewood. Some of these relatives might show. Then, too, a long list of the old man's gin mill cronies might appear. Also his dockside partners, reprobates, priests, and friends to say a prayer over his wilted form, despite his wishes.

How wilted was their father?

When he was a boy, Jackie could tell you, he remembered his father as a huge man, not tall, but wide, no more than five and a half feet tall, but nearly that wide, too, weighing in at 220 pounds in his boxer shorts and stockinged feet. Now he was no more than a featherweight. Maybe a bantamweight or no more than a light-fly. In that sense, their father's size was accordion-like; sometimes he was huge (in memory), sometimes he was as small and fragile as an eggshell (in reality and the funeral parlor).

One of the people from the father's past showed up and came over to the sons.

"Good old Jack," the man said, though none of them knew who he was. "He looks better than ever."

It was Emmett who first realized it was his father's old friend Stanley, another bluebearded black Irishman from the neighborhood, but also a fellow dockworker, a customs inspector like the old man himself. Several times a year, throughout their childhoods, Stanley showed up at the house on Long Island with a cheesecake from Junior's in downtown Brooklyn or, more often, from Jack Dempsey's in Times Square, but never the day-old kind the old man tried to foist on them from Horn and Hardart. He rarely spoke, but simply sat, drinking coffee and eating the cake, sometimes sipping a beer or an Irish. None of the children ever understood his connection to the family.

Before Paddy or any of them had a chance to say hello and talk with Stanley, the man had crossed himself while genuflecting and scooted out the door, and the Jackster realized that he had never spoken with the man and that he had never heard him speak more than one or two sentences in his life.

Whether the old man looked better or worse was moot. What was less controversial was the fact that none of his typical anger and spite—the knitted black eyebrows, the scowl lines along his cheeks, the intense madness of his eyes—was apparent in the corpse. In that sense, he may never have looked better than he did that day.

Their mother, Rose Moody, was less ambiguous, having been born not too many blocks from here on Madison Street in Bedford-Stuyvesant, sprung in a birthing room of the twenty-six-room house—today it was a Carmelite convent—of her lace-curtain father, William Moody of Albany and Brooklyn, and her equally lacy mother, Elizabeth Moody née McGillicutty, the daughter of Richard Mojo McGillicutty, the radical newspaper-man, and Solange Cold-Veal (a loose translation from the French). There was no question that their mother was a Brooklyn blueblood and a Brooklomaniac, like all of them but Mickey Mack, born as was his wantonness in Washington, D.C., at the close of WW II. But don't let these retrograde brothers bore you to death at their own father's funeral; after all, this is their father's show, and it is a mockery of the father to speak of gene-alogies, because the man had none to speak of, whether he was born in the old country as half the brothers claimed or here in Brooklyn as another contingent of them liked to pronounce. Probably his name wasn't on any of their birth certificates be-cause he was an illegal and didn't want anyone to know. Or more likely, he probably was out drinking with his colleagues—the deadbeats from the local gin mills—after each of them was born, and had no time to do the paperwork at the hospital.

The funeral was a low-budget affair for a backdoor-type man who drank in shot-and-a-beer places on Broadway underneath the el or drank out of paper bags as he played snooker with his fellow East New Yorkolinos, Jackie Gleason just one name that comes quickly to mind.

Poor Jimmy Jack Leland Coole looks fine just where he is, a man without lineage to speak of but for these vagrant sons attending the cortege.

"Dad looks fine," Terry yapped.

Then Leland or Emmett mocked his plaintive voice and spat back, "Dad looks fine."

"Give us a break, ya little hard-on."

"Ah, shuttup!"

"Who said that?"

"Ya fuckn moron monkey-faced mick bastard ya."

And so on and so forth.

They went on like that, even after they sat in the chairs near the coffin, niggling, needling, taunting, despairing, and even finding little moments of grace. And all of them dressed like undertakers themselves in dark-colored suits, white shirts, and even ties, not exactly the way you'd picture any of them outside this funeral parlor. Dungarees, sneakers, and a work shirt: that was their standard uniform. The snappier dressers in the family had maybe a pair of Wellington boots and a corduroy jacket from the old Robert Hall's off the rack. Once, though, Emmett was a clotheshorse, but not since he discovered drugs, where all his money went these days. Paddy sometimes dressed like a country gentleman, in his L. L. Bean hunting boots and a thick plaid wool shirt with a Filson wool hat with earmuffs. Occasionally, when playing the ponies, Jack the Wack wore a leisure suit of Dacron polyester. Terry was hopeless in his Pittsburgh Pirates jackets and caps, but Mickey Mack might dig out a tweed jacket and twill shirt with a knit tie and do the town in his loafers and khaki pants.

For the wake they would dress like gentlemen, or what they thought was a gentlemanly way of dressing, though none of them had a clue what exactly that word *gentleman* meant.

After they had lugged his deathless form into the main room

and sat around moaning and keening, Paddy Boy was reminded that their father called him Jack too, though his name is Patrick J. Coole. He called Paddy terrible things. Some of them Paddy remembered bitterly. Others he cast away as so much childish experience. So much cargo that ain't worth dragging into his grown life. He'd left Brooklyn a long time ago. Then he left this family out on Long Island when he was still in his teens and went off to art school in the city only to wind up busted on a drug charge, but got the charges lessened by taking a parole upstate with a friend of Leland's who was a social worker and who got him a job working with wolves in an Adirondack forest preserve, and he never returned to the city again except for his periodic runs of selling grass and used furniture at the flea markets downtown and on Sixth Avenue.

But wherever any of them went they brought their bad attitudes, the grudges, the you-push-me-I'll-break-your-face kind of moodiness that so perfectly suited their own bad intentions in those days when love children ran through Tompkins Square Park stoned out of their peace-loving minds and Charles Manson sold smoke on East 10th Street, and where Mickey Mack had a crash pad and some of the brothers came by to get drunk or high and tease him for being a stoned-out hippie and unregenerate degenerate, but then again, if he was a Coole, what could they expect of their brother? What did they expect from Paddy or even Emmett who lived down on the Lower East Side for a time, too, or even their sisters, Sam and Oona, both of whom had places down there? Emmett used to drink a six-pack of beer in his rundown railroad flat on Avenue A with the bathtub in the center of the kitchen, smoke a wad of Nepalese hash he got from Mickey, then go out to get more fucked up in the bars on Avenue B (the Annex, Stanley, and Old Stanley), and get his teeth loosened up and his lip fattened some time after midnight when he tried to pick up some motorcyclist's old lady, his own wife at home watching the kids.

When Terence saw the old man there, earlier in the afternoon, supine, flowers about his head, rosary gnarled between his pudgy alabaster and rubescent fingers, fresh new white shirt and plain black tie, he thought of all those Cooles before his father.

Each one of them had that hawk nose. Each was small and stout. If a Coole was not short and stout, then he was tall and stout or short and thin. But no matter his morphology, no matter the physique, a Coole always had that bird beak. Old Hawk. Mr. Shooks, the Kelts called it.

"It's no bed of roses if your name is Jack Coole," Leland said.

"What's that supposed to mean?" Emmett asked.

"I'll tell you what it's supposed to mean," his brotherly companion Leland (Jack the Wack) answered, shoving him in the chest. It was almost as if that companionable exchange earlier between them was only an aberration. Now they would return to the old way. They never got along, should never have been in the same room, even now when both of them were over the hill and had one foot in the grave.

Now they sat around the parlor, drinking, snorting, sniffing, sniffling, shuffling, mumbling. . . .

"The old man used to say there were three strains of blood in our family," Mickey Mack said, hoping to diffuse the tension.

"Cro-Magnon via Europe and Africa," Emmett laughed. "Long head, long-limbed, try that blood on for size." Then he added: "Hey, you're not the only one who went to college. I got a fuckn BA in anthropology from Saint Jude's College upstate on the Hudson when I was doing time. Cro-Magnon blood."

"That wasn't it," Mickey Mack said.

Jackie Wackie said, "How about the long-limbed, short-bodied Iberni?"

"The fuckn micks!" Terry shouted.

Everyone stopped and stared at him, giving him stinkeye.

"There you go," Paddy said, again trying to be the mediator, one of his roles in this family. "That's what he called them. He called them that all right."

"The fuckn micks," Terry shouted again, as if their collective *mal occhio* hadn't fazed him in the least, though he had to know that even at their advanced ages, Leland and Emmett were capable of slamming him upside the head and putting a world of hurt on his body.

Mickey Mack thought of what his father called the ghoulish Kelts or the salty Gauls.

The old man wasn't much for history.

And yet Jackie Wackie recalled him, in his cups, calling out other names that made no sense whatsoever, whether he had a sense of history or not. These were more curses than appellations, and yet nonetheless all relations, the bloodline as it were, of the Coole family. He once told the oldest son in a saloon down the block from here—probably Featherstone's or Cunningham's or maybe it was Grim's tavern near Marion Street—that it was the Caspian where the last group came from, in the valley of the Danube, herdsmen, some even descended from sheep, he said, and from there they journeyed across the Rhine, no doubt drinking much wine, and then later to the Seine and Marne, and so on and so forth, until they entered the Valley of the Black Pig. Of course, it might not have been the old man who said any of this. Perhaps James Leland Coole imagined it. For he'd imagined a great deal in his life, Brooklyn lending itself more to the imagination than facts, more to feelings and drifts than actual truths.

The imaginative possibilities now were all Afro ones, with a sprinkling of *jibaro* dreams from the Hispanic fringes of the neighborhood. In their time it was all Irish, with the Italian gangsters at their taxi stand on Rockaway Avenue. But more than a few Moodys and Cooles identified with the Jews, not so much of East New York, because it was only a smattering of merchants (pickles, candy, baloney) who were Jewish, but it was the Jews that gave a voice to East New York from their pushcarts in Brownsville on Pitkin Avenue on Sundays with Aunt Augusta, but also in Grandma Coole's mouth: so many words they thought were Keltic from County Mayo, her birthplace, were really Yiddish words she picked up on the streets before she lost one of her legs and became housebound on Macdougal Street.

Of the crazy old lady Mamie who lived on the second floor, she said: "That lunatic, all she talks is *mishegoss*. That foockn *meshuggeneh*."

"Jack-in-the-Box," she said, "come inside and put a schmeer of peanut butter on this soda bread and have yourself a good nosh before you catch your death of hunger."

When Emmett wet one of her beds, she called him "the little *pisher*."

And she called Emmett the little pisher until she died and he had become a big pisher.

Of Aunt Augusta's Jewish boss in Brownsville, she declared: "That Mr. Shane, he's a real shlemiel."

And when one of the aunts' beaux strutted about the railroad apartment like the great King I-Am, she called him "a bloody foockn *shaygets*."

Not that he acted like a gentile but like a rascal. Though none of the boys or girls would learn any of this until after she died. When they were children, any words Grandma Coole uttered that they didn't understand were from the old country, Keltic kernels of delight, not nougats of Yiddish from the bowels of Bed-Stuy, Bushwick, Brownsville, and East New York.

Grandma Coole drank her beer by the quart, and from out of the bottle. The three oldest Coole boys smelled the stuff, and knew it as a familiar odor. Their father smelled like this when he came home from work. The gin mills on Broadway smelled like this when they walked by them.

Once, Emmett asked her for a drink of beer.

"You're too young, pisher."

"How old I gotta be?"

"Older than five," she said.

"I's five and a half, Grandma."

(He had picked up a black Southern accent from playing with Charleston and the other black kids in the schoolyard of P.S. 73 across the street.)

"Bejaysus," Grandma said, apropos of nothing. Then, growing more international, more Brooklyn, she said, "What a fine *shnook* this little one is."

"Come on come on come on, Grandma," he begged.

All day Emmett Coole pleaded.

Each time he saw Grandma Coole suck on her quart of beer, he asked her for a sip. Later that afternoon, just before Eileen came home from working at the sweater factory on the other side of Eastern Parkway and Augusta came back from working in the dress shop on Pitkin Avenue in Brownsville, Grandma Coole poured him a jelly glass full of beer.

"Here, little pisher," she said, "knock yourself out, Emmett the *Shmegegge*."

Emmett could discern her resignation, but also her disapproval. He had not won; he had worn his grandmother out by unfairly annihilating her resistance, her good nature, and her big heart.

Emmy got good and high, happy and silly, and when Eileen and Augusta came home, he was jigging and reeling around the apartment with batty Nora, who never went outside, and whom Emmett rarely if ever spoke with because he considered her cursed and damned, a kind of damage that was not really human but otherworldly. You might touch Nora and catch whatever it was she had, that Stan Laurel grin, her Charlie Chaplin gait, those strange Buster Keaton eyes. But she was other things that were not appealing to a young boy; she looked like Clarabelle the Clown, and she was as crazy as Krazy Kat in the funnies. That was it: she was crazy, and you might catch it from her.

"What's with Emmett?" Aunt Augusta asked, because he was known as a somber kid up until that point.

"He's a touch *shikker*," Grandma Coole said, using the lingua franca of Brooklyn.

Years later, Emmett's girlfriend exclaimed when he came home drunk from some dive in Queens after driving a car all day in the city: "I'm going out with an Irish shikker!"

His girlfriend kvetched, moaning and groaning as Emmett reeled and caromed around the tiny room, looking for the bathroom to pee and vomit.

The next day he asked his girlfriend why she used that Irish word *shikker*.

"Irish?!" she laughed. "Are you crazy?"

Later Emmett would protest; he was no shikker. His brother Mickey Mack—darker and more serious, and so therefore easily mistaken for a Jew when they were kids—he was a shikker, one of those black Irish from the lost tribe of Israel, like their father, too, but not blond-haired, blue-eyed Emmett, not the apple of his grandmother's eye, the altar boy and saintly looking sinner, the quintessential Irish drunk and hoodlum. No shikker this boy. Yet to Ruth Wollinsky, the belly dancer and proofreader whom Emmett Coole came home to stinking drunk, he was nothing more romantic than a goddamn shikker.

"What a crazy little shmuck," Aunt Augusta said, removing her sweater and walking around the apartment in her slip and bra (tough and sexy) with a glass of beer in one hand and a Pall Mall cigarette in the other, looking for a copy of the *Daily News* to read in the bathroom while she took a crap.

Grandma Coole prepared a dinner of potatoes and boiled cabbage and ground beef in the tiny kitchen which had a door that led out into the backyard, where Emmett stood vertiginously in the late afternoon sunlight, the smell of the sour grapes hanging from her trellis (oh Dermott of the Love Spot!) sickeningly powerful. She sang as she chopped the cabbage:

"Shikker is a goy
Shikker is a ligner
Gonif is a goy."

Emmett would later learn what his grandmother had sung: the drunk is a non-Jew, the drunk is a liar, the crook is a gentile. Is there any wonder that Emmett Coole, the little pisher, spent his life dreaming and thinking about this place even as he escaped from it, or any wonder that his father chose East New York over the Gulf Coast of Florida to be laid out and then buried? What an ingenious, clever gonif that Emmett Coole was!

One last thing Grandma Coole said as he stumbled about her backyard: "God watches over drunks and children."

"But a drunken child, Ma?" Aunt Augusta asked, refilling her beer glass and lighting another long, strong, unfiltered cigarette. "Jackie is going to go apeshit when he finds out ya got the kid drunk. I don't think God's watching over this drunken kid."

"Especially drunk children."

"I don't know, Ma."

"How do you think you survived to talk back to me?"

2

The last time Leland was in the old neighborhood was when they had the funeral for the old man's mother. Then a year or two later the funeral for his crazy Aunt Augusta, she of the flaming red hair and the temper tantrums, of the knuckle sandwiches on Pitkin Avenue, shopping for bargains from the carts of the Jewish merchants on Sunday; Aunt Augusta of the brawls at Rangers hockey games at the old Garden, where they asked her to behave or leave—at a Rangers game!—and Aunt Augusta of the brawls in the boardwalk bars of Coney Island, knocking out drunken, obnoxious sailors who came on to her.

Aunt Augusta and her funeral, that's the last time he set eyes on this hole in the borough of Brooklyn. He was eighteen years old, newly graduated from high school, and just about to enlist in the army, from which he would return, broken and electro-shocked, two years later, a military casualty. Emmett still had the pink '55 Ford convertible; Mickey Mack had not yet run away from home; Samantha was going out with Johnny Stiletto; Paddy was hidden away up in the attic, getting high on airplane glue as he constructed Messerschmitts and the *Spirit of St. Louis* from model kits; and the other children were infants or not yet formed, or maybe just developing inside Rosy O'Coole's belly. It was that long ago.

Still a kid but thinking himself a know-it-all, a man of the world, he resented Aunt Augusta from a few years earlier when she came out to Wilson Park on Long Island, right after Jack graduated from eighth grade at Saint Aidan's. Her boyfriend Gene the Bean was with her, that skeleton of a man who sold subway tokens in downtown Brooklyn and who paid the kids nickels to open his beer cans because he was too wasted to exert enough force on the church key to pop two triangular holes in the can of Piels or Rheingold.

After seeing the graduation ring, Augusta decided that it was hers after all those years of buying these damn kids of her step-brother Jackie all kinds of junk like Mickey Mouse puppets, baseball gloves, toy guns, erector sets, Leggos, and pogo sticks —why if she didn't buy these damn kids toys and presents they would have gone through childhood without ever receiving a gift, and that was not right, she decided—and collect a payback.

Payback was that crummy grade-school silver ring. The only problem was that her nephew didn't want to give it to her; he balked because he had promised the ring to his girlfriend Mona Murphy (real name Mary Beth, but she was reputed to moan a lot when she made love). But when Aunt Augusta was drunk, there was no brooking her passions; she would keep the ring whether the kid liked it or not.

This was the woman, as the old neighborhood changed and became more dangerous because of drugs and guns, who got robbed, beaten and tied up, and left for dead in a closet of the dress shop where she worked in Brownsville.

"Those fuckn black pig nigger bastards," she screamed many times over the next couple of weeks, nursing her bruised head and ego. "When I get my fuckn hands on them—forget it!"

The point is this: she would kick their asses if she ever found them.

Stupidly, they ran out of money, and remembering Shane's Dress Shop as an easy target, entered and pointed a sawed-off shotgun in her face. What they hadn't counted on was Aunt Augusta's history; she had nothing to lose. Literally nothing. A beautiful monkey-faced ghetto goddess with an alcohol jones and an anemic boyfriend who sold tokens, that was the hand dealt Augusta. Remember: this is the redheaded woman who got kicked out of Rangers games for fighting; got thrown out of Coney Island boardwalk open-air saloons for punching out drunken sailors. This is the woman who wore Jackie's school ring as if it were an engagement ring that she kept on until her boyfriend Gene won enough money at the numbers or ponies to buy her a diamond and get married. Get them the hell out of East New York, if not Brooklyn entirely, move, not to Long Island like her brother Jackie, or even out to Hoboken, but maybe South Brooklyn, Red Hook, or Gravesend. Who knows, after a couple of years, maybe they would skedaddle to Jersey. Yeah, Jersey, or maybe fuckn Pennsylvania.

She clocked the gun-wielding robber with her fist. Being a fighter, she knew where to hit and how to do it. She stepped to the right, creating "an angle," as fighters call it, and pulverized the black man's jaw with a right cross, cutting downward, turning out his lights.

With the butt of the shotgun, she clubbed the other robber,

but he did not fall unconscious. Rather, he sprinted out the door and down Pitkin Avenue and into the pushcarts and the Jews in their beaver hats and fancy-shmancy silk coats, their ear curls and their yarmulkes.

Augusta tied up the robber with hemp rope used to gather empty boxes neatly in a pile for the garbage man, and she called the cops to come gather this bit of suffering humanity off of the dress shop floor.

When the felon revived, he said, "What the fuck. . . ."

But that's all she let him say before she ripped open a package of nylons—Mr. Shane would forgive her this extravagance later—and stuffed them down the man's throat to shut him up.

The last thing in the world she wanted to hear was this man's version of what had happened, the dirty little black pig.

That's how long it had been for James L. Coole, better known as Jack, aka Jack the Wack, Jackie Wackie, Crazy Coole, The Big Guy, The Great One, Reginald Van Coole III. Leland, the family's bardic oral historian, never saw his aunt again after she stole his eighth-grade ring until that moment they laid her body out in this funeral parlor, her brother and sisters fighting with each other in the corner. Eileen and Nora would disappear into the mishmash of Williamsburg with Jorge Panaqua shortly after this, then wind up years later in a nursing home in Ojai, California.

Leland could not mark the distance he had traveled from East New York in ordinary time, say, years, but only by lifetimes. A lifetime ago he had last been here. The last time he was still a kid almost, and certainly had his innocence. Now he was a double veteran, of the military and countless hospitals, of shock therapy, group therapy, and his own alcohol treatments. His crazy aunts had nothing on James L.; his own father was a mere novice at going bonkers if you compared him to his oldest son Leland. Now here was a real loony, an authentic card-carrying certifiable as they say.

The last time he had been to East New York was an era before
he heard his first folk singer in the Village, before he ever heard
of Bob Dylan or Dave Van Ronk, even before Mickey Mack tried
to get him to listen to this simpy Joan Baez. His sister Oona had
yet to have her ears polluted by the Beatles. Kennedy was in the
White House, and though you would not know it from the
streets of East New York, it was the age of Camelot. Leland had
yet to hear Van Morrison sing "Crazy Love," and U2 weren't
even a shining possibility in their Dublin parents' eyes; Lee
hadn't listened to Them sing "Gloria," and the phrase *Tet Offen-
sive* meant nothing to him, or the friends or cousins who would
get shot up in its gorge, some to die, some to live disabled. The
Sunday funnies were still pretty good, though Dondi was a
skank, and even Uncle Willie of Moon Mullins had worn a little
thin, though Denny Dimwit still was sufficiently banal and
weird for Leland's taste to be effective entertainment when he
had no money for the movies. Malcolm X was a living man,
spreading his black gospel according to Islam; Robert Kennedy
was the quintessential kid brother to Jack, and all their mothers
were named Rose.

O Rose sad rose proud rose red rose of all my days.

It's been that long since Leland had been home.

In this world of grief-stricken fraternity and even evil-inten-
tioned fratricidal madness, brother fume to cockeyed belliger-
ence: Big Lee was taken ·from his own miserable reveries by
Terence at the coffin.

"Tell the one about Fenian Jack Coole," he said to the Big
Kahuna.

Terry was a boy eager for the old legends.

"It's not his time or place to eulogize," Emmett objected,
slamming his fist so hard on one end of the coffin that their
father's head popped up from his pillow. "He spoke already
and now it's time for the second oldest to have his say, his

prerogative if you catch my drift."

Still, Paddy couldn't resist putting his bit of salt into the wounds before the floor was relinquished completely.

"It goes back deeper than Fenian Jack," he said. "All the way back to King Cormorant in the Land of Tantrum."

That got them quiet, for a profound respect of the legends ran through them all on occasion, especially as they came upon the full domain of the half-lit main room of the funeral parlor.

Evening was upon them. Sparks blew down from the elevated train outside the broken and patched stained-glass windows. Mounds of empty beer and whiskey bottles from the afternoon were stacked in a corner, still not removed by the funeral parlor director. Suddenly it dawned on Emmett that their father never did much for any of them, and he wondered what the hell he was doing there. King Cormorant be damned!

If the family had a gift, it was this art of the pontificating knuckleheaded know-nothing—a specialty, you might call it—especially to a roomful of brothers who could not verify anything he said, could not prove the veracity of any historical or imaginative facts Emmett of the crime waves cared to put forward to them in their grief and cups. They did not call him Stone Cold Coole for nothing, and yet even Emmett felt that he failed already to render unto Jack Coole the things that are Jack's and to render unto the tallow merchant the renderings that are his.

Let him get back to the present. Let him dwell a little longer on the past as he sat in the present. Let him escape the present entirely.

3

One bare light bulb in the center of the ceiling lit the main room of the funeral parlor. Business had not been good here, the assis-

tant director told them. For one thing people died younger and
younger, and therefore poorer and poorer, each year, from gun-
shot wounds, from stabbings, from drug overdoses, from the
broken bottles to the neck of irate lovers, or even from children
dismantling avenging parents on drug and alcohol orgies of
death and destruction.

"East New York is not a happy place," the assistant director
said.

His name was Sean Carlos Padilla O'Brady, and he should
know. The Spanish used another funeral parlor up the block; the
blacks went to the parlor over on Gates Avenue or down the
block on Stone or over by Rockaway Avenue and up on Bushwick. The Jews had fled Brownsville and were now only in Flatbush (the reformed) or in Williamsburg or Crown Heights (the
orthodox), and the Irish and Italians were gone for good from
the old neighborhood, he said, and they were the last to use the
parlor. When the last of Mother Teresa's nuns died, Sean
Carlos's boss's business shrunk to the size of a pea, and soon,
he said, the owner intended to close up the place and move to
Miami.

Even the smells in the funeral parlor were not those overly
floral ones masking the stink of death. The building and its
rooms had a more primordial smell; the funk was more atavistic
and prehistoric, like the draft coming from a gaping hole in the
festering universe that needed stitches to close its wound. More
than once on this day James Leland Coole III had gone to the
wash closet and tossed up his cookies.

The radiators clanked, but they were regularly drowned out
by the subway train sparking and screeching overhead, the elevated train tracks weaving and shaking above. The panes of
glass that were not mottled by rocks and bullets were smashed
by fists.

They sat in chairs at various angles around the coffin. There
was Leland, of course, the brother-familias, all 350 pounds of

him, the joke being that it was a good thing Jackie Wackie was Irish because if he was a bambino working the underworld and then went into the federal Witness Protection Program, where would you hide this man? Jackie was okay. He hadn't had a drink in years, was on the wagon, and a lot of the insanity of his youth had disappeared, the avenging disabled veteran home to wreak havoc on his family. He was even a touch mellow, at least for a Coole he was.

Then there was Emmett of the crime waves and the sorrows. As Jackie expanded over the years, Emmett shrank. Now he could not weigh more than 120 pounds, even though he was six feet tall. The boozing had never stopped, and now he was determined to become the oldest crackhead in history, pushing his luck beyond anyone's idea of that evil concept. His physical and emotional bottoms had trapdoors, and his trapdoors had trapdoors, so that Emmett now inhabited a netherworld even unknown to the lumpen of East New York. His eyes had that thousand-yard stare that combat soldiers get, and his bad mood was like foul odor. He assayed the room, looking like a felon checking for exits and getaways in case The Man arrived. Then he cased out his brothers, as if trying to remember each individual grudge he had against them since childhood. Maybe it was even simpler than that; perhaps Emmett tried to remember their names, and who they were and what was his own connection to them.

Mickey Mack was the third of Jack Coole's sons. He was the poet manqué wearing the dark sunglasses, telling anyone who asked that if only he had a little time and money he could write that book he had promised everyone he would write, about the family and growing up in this world and all that. Once, you might have said that Mickey Mack did not fit in with the rest of them; now he was just another Coole, balding, with a fatty liver, complaining about his teeth and hemorrhoids.

Patrick and Terry took up the slack, though the young end of the family was underrepresented, which went against all the folk wisdom of the clan about the oldest brothers having the worst grudges toward their father and the youngest ones getting along with him best. The theory was that Leland, Emmett, and Mickey Mack would never show for the old man's funeral because each of them had felt his wrath worse than the little leaguers, who only got smacked around occasionally, not every night, because the old man was on a short candle burning out, and all those years of work on the docks and at the airport, followed by the hours spent decompressing in bars, had taken their toll on the old badger.

"He's still as fat as ever," Emmett said of their father, nodding toward the old boy.

"Fat as ever!" Terry said. "He's emaciated. He's all skin and bones."

"You know what I mean," Emmett corrected himself, "he's as fat as ever and emaciated too."

"He looks good, though," Paddy interjected.

"Good," Leland said, "and not so good."

"He looks terrible," Mickey Mack said. "I've never seen him look so bad."

The truth was more complicated than all the brothers' contradictions. Up until the end, the old man was a big little man, short on height but broad in the shoulders. But age and illness and alcoholism wasted him eventually, and the old codger in the casket was a shell of the man who antagonized these galoots.

Along the way from the back room, along the vestibule and into the main parlor, their speech had been garbled, with such likeness of tone, of emotion, inflection, cadence, of drunkenness, and their words were like each other's, flat and nasal, lazy-tongued like the old man's. Thick with alcohol, in the half-light of the parlor, its shadows playing with their vision, they seemed to speak in tongues. It was a kind of city babble that blended with the radiator and the elevated subway, with sirens, honking

horns, gunshots and firecrackers, popped bottles, flick of cigarette lighters over the clear white coals of crack in glass pipes,
the new high of the ghetto. The street outside was full of holler
and yell and colorful plastic lids to the crack vials, rattle and
hum from the passing trains so appropriate to this Keltic ruin.

Earlier, during a lull in their aggressive denouncements of
each other, Emmett and Leland reminisced, recalling for their
younger brothers how this neighborhood was one long under-
current of Mother Macree and John McCormack singing scratch-
ily from an old 78 record. Now the sounds were—Fight the
Power!—Public Enemy, Willie Colon, salsa, meringue, the old
guaguanco of the *jibaros* and their slick counterparts in the next
Spanglish generation, *muy típico* sons and ruby-lipped daughters. Yet the dominant strain was the old blues of Broadway, the
rhythm-a-neeking of the rattlepat of trains above, the early rock
'n' roll of Brooklyn, not the Brooklyn Fox or Paramount, not
Alan Freed and Flatbush Avenue, but a kind of James Brown
scream—I don't need nobody open the door I'll get it myself—a
mood as black as pitch, as black as starless night.

This blackness was not indigenous to the Afro-Americans
here either, but rather a blackness of Brooklyn itself, the pitch of
East New York and its rattling subway cars above that legislated
and dominated the backbeat of the village.

After all, the Cooles were once the black Irish of this burg, the
black pigs and green niggers of Marion Street, and the musical
strains of this hellhole fit their temperament—and maybe still
did—as much as any ethnic group that ever commandeered the
broad vistas of these ramshackle streets.

But no matter what the beat, East New York was always dangerous and raunchy, dirty and violent, sexual and down. The
street smelled of backed-up sewers and drains, and the gutters
reeked of plucked chicken feathers from Santeria rituals and
Haitian voodoo, of old mango skins, papaya peels, rotten and
unripe green bananas; the vestibules smelled of greasy meat and

burnt vegetables in old cooking oil that had been refried too many times, the kind of oil that invaded the skin and hair and didn't leave even after a good shower; the foyers reeked of underwear and sweat, Tiger balm and old cabbage gone bad. There was a dampness that was perpetual and evermore, as nagging as an erratic heartbeat.

Sparks flew down from the elevated train again, another passing subway in the night. Spaldeen high bouncers whanged off the chipped brick of the funeral parlor's outer wall, and Leland pictured a kid practicing his pitches for the summer stickball season. Stoopball was the old man's game. That and pool. While Leland's own recreational proclivities were shuffleboard—Go white boy, go white boy, go!—and paddleball, once the Jewish intellectual's game at the schoolyard on Macdougal and now the sport of Hispanic lovers.

East New York: not really New York and not east of anything. Really just the heart of Brooklyn, its heart and soul, a place without pretense or hope. An uncle by marriage to the Moodys had a sister who used to live above this craphole funeral parlor, their kids Evie and Harry, runty and bent and thin as reeds and carroty-haired. At any moment Emmett expected Mamie—the *farpotshket* street lady who rented the top floor of their grandmother's two-story house down the block—to walk in, wearing her five or six dresses, sucking on a quart of Rheingold beer or Ballantine ale, cursing God and Saint Francis and even Our Lady of Lourdes.

If Emmett had not attended his aunt's and grandmother's funerals in this very parlor, he'd even expect them to come in the door, telling his father to knock it off, get sober, that he had a wife and sixteen children to support.

Some of the brothers got up from the folding chairs around the coffin. One day soon each would hop inside that odd-shaped box, hands folded with rosary beads entwined in the pudgy fingers, plain black suit, white shirt, single-colored tie, etc.

"I wonder," Emmett mused aloud, "if the funeral director had put Dad's beat-up brogues on his feet."

"His calloused, pain-spattered feet," Mickey Mack said, as though writing a poem, and trying to find its measure.

"Huh?" Emmett responded.

"His feet weren't exactly like other people's feet," Big Leland opined. "They were like duck's fangs."

"Duck's fangs?" Paddy asked. "Ducks don't have fangs. They got webbed feet."

"Well, his feet were a cross between duck webs and eagle fangs," Leland went on.

"Eagles don't have no fangs," Paddy said, the naturalist in the bunch. "They have claws and beaks. Dogs, wolves, and lions have fangs, big teeth in their mouths."

"Maybe that's how he got the name Jack Ducks," Terry said, musing on his brothers' observations.

"What?" Emmett shouted.

"Who asked you?" Jack the Wack called out.

"Sometimes his feet were like cleft hoofs," Paddy observed, "sort of ungulate."

"Stumps he stuffed into his old brogues," said Emmett. "Then out the door he waddled to his job on the docks."

Paddy sat down next to Jack and demanded to know what had possessed him to mention King Cormorant earlier.

"I don't know," he answered as honestly as he could. "I'm under a lot of stress."

"Yeah," Terry wanted to know, "what made you say that earlier?"

Jackie Wackie tried to shoo this young one away, the time being inapposite to legend.

"Later," he said.

"It's Jack Coole we should talk about."

"He's dead," Mickey Mack said.

"Dead?" Terry asked.

"I'm all right," brother Jack said, mishearing what was said and presuming that the brothers were speaking about him. "I'm just a little under the weather, as who wouldn't be. Once the event sinks into my thick skull, I'll be able to talk."

Poor old fart, Jackie thought.

They sank into their chairs, the keens growing, at times, into gnashing. Questions were asked.

"Why was I born?" "Who is he?" "Why am I here?" "Will the Knicks win the two-game series?" "Will I get towed from the street meters after seven?" "Will my car be there if I parked it on a side street?"

Then these questions were answered: "I don't know." "I don't know." "I don't know." "I don't care." "I don't know." "Maybe." "Yes." Etc., etc. Et celery.

This receded into the babble of brotherly tongues, the cursing and remonstrations, the years of misunderstanding, each to the other, the despicable moments of childhood they spent in those crowded rooms, bodies flopped on top of bodies, five sons to each double bed.

"Perhaps the others were wise not to show," Jackie said.

It was his attempt to make conversation with a few of the gentlemen who surrounded him and whom he hadn't seen in years. The last time he spoke with, say, Mickey Mack was more than fifteen years ago when he was on a dry-drunk bender culminating with a murderous appearance at Mickey's door on Saint Patrick's Day, threatening to murder the third brother for the good of the family name, Leland said, whatever that meant. These things made so much sense when he thought them, but then he would come around again, see the light, and wonder what had possessed him this time.

Leland hadn't seen Emmett for a decade or more, and only then by chance as he crossed the street near the 42nd Street library where he had been reading about Fenian Jack MacCoole, the great Irish revolutionary, a man whom Leland liked to claim he was related to, especially when he approached the delusional, and when the madness really kicked in, he'd spout Sean Cumhal's poetry, calling him Johnny Coole, and the greatest poet in the English language. Emmy was in his cab, honking, while Jack the Wack fomented and thought, What a stupid fuck this taxi driver is honking like that at me, maybe I'll go over and wring his neck for him, until he realized it was his brother Emmett, grinning toothlessly at him.

"Ya fuckn bum ya," Emmett shouted. "How the hell are ya, Wackie?"

"Don't call me that name," Jack said.

"Ya make ya first million yet?" Emmett asked.

"Get out of my face, Emmett."

And then the brother obliged him because the light had changed to green and the cars behind Emmett honked their horns for him to go and his passenger, a man in a pin-striped suit and wearing a Borsolino, said he had to get to his appointment, and so Emmett sped away without another word until Leland saw him again this evening.

Paddy he spoke to on the telephone and even saw him once or twice a year when he drove down from upstate New York where he lived on a farm with horses and cows and raised vegetables and grew marijuana and his girlfriend processed psilocybin. Several times a year Paddy came into the city to sell antiques.

Terry had been homeless on Long Island for as long as Leland Coole could remember, living off the largesse of his girlfriends, barflies who got progressively less good-looking as the years went by. Usually at Christmastime Terry could be expected to call up and plead to come to a brother's house or apartment to visit. "For the holidays," Terry said, because he was only on the corner and he wouldn't stay long, but usually he wound up drinking all the liquor and eating all the food and not leaving until the next morning.

"You know what they say about our race," Terry piped up.

Everyone turned and stared at him. But it didn't stop Terry because he was both in his cups and in his grief.

"Sad in life, happy at death, we are known for songs, for dancing, for great cheer in these moments of stress."

"Stuff it!" Emmett snarled.

Terry did.

Whiskey (the breath of life) was poured. If one clocked their various stages of intoxication now, it was possible, at eccentric moments of brotherly silence, to interject words and perhaps sentences and maybe even a monologue of sorts. It seemed never long enough for truly eulogistic rhetoric, but there were these gaps in which one might attempt conversation.

"Christ rest his weary bones," Patrick said.

The other brothers stared at Paddy the same murderous way they stared at Terry for talking out of turn.

Even in a crazy household like the Cooles, all of them long gone from it but still a part of it, because they carried the old house on their backs like a knapsack filled with old socks and emotions, there was a protocol, a way things had to be done, even amidst the seeming and often verifiable chaos. This was never a situation where the last shall be first and the first last, but rather the oldest and usually the toughest had his way, and when finished, if time allowed, or when a Jackie Wackie or an Emmett felt a sense of noblesse oblige, then some younger twerp like Wolfe or Terry or Patrick—or even a Mickey Mack Coole—was given the floor.

Though the God of the New Testament had instructed them to turn the other cheek when struck, the Cooles had a nasty Old Testament streak that ran through them, almost a point of identification with the old Hebrews in Brownsville, and that was the biblical injunction of an eye for an eye, a tooth for a tooth, probably the only thing from the Bible they consistently practiced in their daily lives.

Yet there was a protocol here.

Even in this frayed surrounding there were precedents that had to be followed, forms of decorum, ways of speaking, the moment for individual suffering, the arc of the day's flight from morning into night when the oldest spoke, then the next to the oldest, and so on, and it happened to be brother Jackie's turn, only his throat was choked up with phlegm—he'd never call it emotion or feeling—his mind disoriented, and that allowed some runt further down the ladder to attempt colloquy.

There was a bellyful of roars.

"Our father," Mickey Mack said, nodding toward the coffin. "He's dead."

"*Your* father?" Emmett said.

"Ours," Mickey Mack corrected his older brother. "I didn't say mine or yours, I said 'our father.' "

"That's not what I heard," Emmett snarled.

"He's dead."

"Dead?" he asked.

"Dead," Mickey Mack said, feeling the alcohol hit his head like a punch to the jawbone, a shock of electricity going from head to toe.

"I'm sorry," Terry sniffled.

Jack looked at Paddy and shouted, "Shut up!"

"I didn't say anything," Paddy answered.

"It's your brain," he said, "spinning and twisting and reeling out the old tales." Shut it up, Jackie seemed to say, I can smell it burning rubber even across the room.

But that was easier said than done. If any of the Coole family knew how to shut off the brain, there would be no need for any of these words, Jack thought. There would be no need for any of this, for he'd be relaxing under a palm tree, sipping from a coconut, contemplating the great void and writing B-movie scripts for oodles of dollars.

But then Jack the Wack became more conciliatory.

He said, "You were saying, Mackey?"

"Mack?" Emmett asked.

"He was speaking," Jackie said.

It is true that Mickey Mack was speaking, although he didn't really have much to say. His conversation with Daddy had been restricted to a quick belt in the mouth or slap in the face, a punch in the stomach, or more often than not, lower still, right in the groin. That was an area he liked to kick, Mick wanted to say, usually employing a deft kung-fu snap of his leg at the kneecap, the entire leg extended high in the air, parallel to the ground. He resembled a dog peeing on a hydrant. That made Mick want to laugh, except that as he was about to guffaw, his father's swift-footed brogued kick slashed into his midsection. He was left unconscious or in great physical pain.

Paddy poured another drink, sitting back in his chair. He faced the brothers now. His turn at eulogy still upon him, he realized, once Jackie had backed off with his aggressions. He decided on the legends as opposed to the chronicles to reveal what it was the father told him. But then Big Jack reclaimed the territory once again.

Though it didn't mean a damn thing to his brothers and sisters, Jack Wackie persisted in this imaginative genealogy for his family, or, if not for his family per se, then for the family name. The Cooles. Jack often ascribed these observations to his father, but then he had to admit that his father usually didn't have a cogent thought in his head once his workday came to an end and he entered one of the local bars in Hell's Kitchen, usually on 49th Street, to let off steam, or stumbling further east from the docks, and then south through midtown to Penn Station, he rolled off the suburban transit, stumbling his way into one of the watering holes on Hillside Avenue in Wilson Park, there putting back shots and beers with the bakers, caddies, postal workers, and other lumpen that were his friends and enemies alike, though usually the friends and enemies one and the same person, depending on what stage of intoxication the old man arrived at.

It was really only James L. Coole III who acknowledged the legends, like that of King Cormorant in the Land of Tantrum, those warriors with aluminum spears and plastic helmets. Our first king's name was Cormorant, he liked to say, also a man with the bird-beak nose of our forebears, and that Finn Mac-Coole was in this cadre, and that all the knights lived in the Valley of Tantrum. Cormorant was the high king of everyone and thing, and where his hawk nose cast a shadow, there he claimed that territory as his own.

"He had many sons, my father said," Jackie told them, "just like himself, and each son was a little bit more a bastard than the last one, and in that way they each resembled their father, the biggest bastard of them all. Their patron saint was Saint Killumkleen."

But this nonsense seemed so hollow in the face of his own father's annihilation and end. It was merely a story, whereas the dead father was beyond that, not an imaginative fact but bold reality amid this equally bold place, another kind of reality, this one hyperventilated and cardiac alert.

"I don't find any of this amusing," Paddy said, looking dour and full of a woeful intelligence. "This is your father you're mocking here. His blood runs through you. His gene pool is your own. All of his ailments will be visited upon all of you, whether you make fun of him or not. You'll all die the same way he did, unless you fall to the violence on the streets."

"Is this going to go on much longer?" Emmett asked.

It was almost too close for comfort.

The old man's face seemed to melt in the steamed heat of the room. His forehead beaded with sweat. A blue-black shadow covered his jowls and cheeks, almost as if his beard had grown overnight. Tears flowed from his eyes with feminine luxury. The tears reminded Jackie Wackie of his sisters, Samantha and Oona and Deirdre of the Sorrows and the Weeping Marya (his name for Mary Grace), Lizzie Ann, and Little Eileen.

"Where are the girls?" Jack asked. But he could just as easily have asked, "Where are the guns, gringo?" None of them paid him any mind.

"How would I know?" Emmett asked, shrugging his shoulders and behaving like a Brooklyn wise guy.

Emmett's behavior was often out of a time warp, the world forever in the fifties, and everyone a punk.

"None of them have showed," Terry said, blank and scared.

Not Terry or even any of the others—not even the literary Mickool—ever seemed to get the gist of Jack's previous remarks. Or maybe they decided to ignore him out of a stubborn and playful antagonism, the subtle push and pull of brothers in their filial tensions, Jack thought, just like the lines of dialogue in a play, the conflicts there with every word and syllable, even with every silence between the words and syllables. Then Jack said to himself, So what, they are only acting like brothers, and since they are your brothers, how else would you have them act?

The brothers were too hardened by years and disappointments to care whether any sisters came or not to their own father's wake. Maybe if he had requested burial in Florida, it might have been a different story. Then maybe there would only be sisters present, and no brothers. Isn't that what almost happened when the old lady passed away?

Why they mourned their father, Jack did not understand, because none of them liked him one bit, and all of them, including himself, used to say that it would be a bright day when the old man passed on, and who would miss him? No one, he thought. Proof being that few, if any, of his barfly associates had bothered to drive over from Hell's Kitchen or from out on the

Island. The most you could expect from them, he thought, was a salute—"Here's to old Lee," a slug on the whiskey, and forget him like that—a snap of the fingers!

Jackie went back to thinking about his sisters, or if not thinking about his sisters, then thinking about their absence.

Their father was like his daughters in that he was always talking but not saying anything when he was talking, and when the sisters say that Leland—or for that matter Emmett or Mickey Mack or Paddy, etc.—is like the old man, they are wrong about one thing. None of them could talk like the old man except maybe his daughters; none of the sons were talkers. Never were. Never will be. Which is not to say that someone like Jack didn't appreciate the talkers in the family or didn't bullshit the night away with his yabber. If it was his job in this clan to be the silent one, then it was also his job to listen to them talk. But the trouble was that they were always talking and saying nothing and at a certain point—"Get to the goddamn pernt, you little shit," their father used to say, not mincing his words—Jack drifted off, no longer listening. Listening was not a strong point in the household, everyone talking, but few of them listening. You might say that listening was a dead art in the Coole family, and Jack was no exception to that theorem, as he wasn't exactly the family historian—I made up too many details, he liked to say, when I drifted away from pure listening—and so was better suited to the imaginative arts, the doggerel in honor of his mother, the grudge haiku—a form of his own invention—against his father, the bitter dirges he rolled off his pen about his brothers when he found himself sitting in all-night bus depots, writing on empty milk containers and cereal boxes because he ran out of notebook space, or the homages to the fair colleens that were the girls, which he wrote on subway ads in the bowels of the transit system.

Facts were too slippery for Leland Coole; he wasn't here to write his father's obituary, nor to mourn his family and the neighborhood. All he could do was witness this world in its endgame and feel it. Posterity didn't care what Jackie Wackie Coole had to say about himself or his family, East New York, or Brooklyn. Posterity was as indifferent to the rhythms of this experience as the police and firemen were to this neighborhood. All was lost, so why bother? Thus, one of the family mottoes: Fuck It!

"Oh that Jackie, he sure had a way with the words," his mother, God bless her, used to say. But usually she said this when Leland was in one of his manic phases, the stream of consciousness turning into a hurricane of vowels and consonants pouring out, not for sense or even sound value, but to relieve the pressure on the brain which the accumulation of syllables had engendered.

His newfound silence paid off this evening, though. Every time he opened his mouth, the brothers listened, expecting that he would do something different from what they did, that is, not mince the words, not parade them out for mere sound value without a thought to their content, but might in fact give them details, lay down a tissue of information—in the manner of a newspaper account or a magazine article—about the old man and his life and even his death.

All James L. Coole III could utter were the wooden refrains that had overtaken the entire family.

"The old man's dead," he said.

"Tell us about it," Emmett said.

"Let's be done with him, 'sisters or not," Mickey went on, "though I am surprised that none of them have showed yet in this his last hour. They depended on his unkindness and meanness. I thought the girls would show," he said, "maybe just one or two of them."

Emmett stared at Mickey Mack, wondering whether to punch him out now or later.

"His liver," Jackie Wackie said, apropos of nothing.

"His liver?" Emmett asked.

"It was the size of a watermelon," Jackie said.

"Oh," Emmett answered, "I thought you were going to tell me something I didn't already know."

Jack was now undeterred by the noise and disturbance of his brothers and the parlance being slung about the funeral parlor. He thought of Furman and Aberdeen and Granite and DeSales, all the nearby streets and the old ghosts from there as he went off into a catalogue of woes about his father—his kidney being the size of a pumpkin, and yet with the elephantiasis of his limbs and organs, his little woodpecker went at their mother every nine months, producing another child in the family. When the new child was born he or she invariably looked like the children already alive. The Coole mug they called it. What a poor excuse for a community of interests the family was.

"But if you needed muscle," he said. "If you wanted survivors. If the job was going to be messy and long and dangerous. If you wanted a fighter to go the distance, deep into the late rounds. . . ."

The funeral played havoc with the senses.

Jackie heard things that were not spoken; he saw things (mostly brothers) that were not there; he smelled things from a lifetime ago that no longer were part of the knowable universe; he touched the wood and linoleum and stones of this parish, but they only played tricks on him.

The whiskey neared the bottom of the bottles. Even the beer was soaked up. Terry was selected to go out into the mean streets and sent around the corner to a bodega where he purchased several more six-packs of beer, not Rheingold or Piels, the brew of their youth on Macdougal Street that their grandmother and aunts slugged down from quart bottles in the heat of summer, but the bargain varieties of their own time, the Black Label and Schmidt's and Old Ringness and garbage brands from Saint Paul and Philadelphia, none of the breweries in Brooklyn

operating any longer except for this upscale, yuppie swill that
bore the name of the borough on it.

"Be careful," Paddy shouted at his younger brother.

"Why?" Terry asked.

"It's a jungle out there," said Emmett, his eyes buggy with
mischief and foolishness.

When Terence got back, a comradeship of despair entered
into all of them.

They cried. They weeped. One caterwauled. A few grunted
out measly tears. Mickey had a case of the heebie-jeebies and
then the sniffles. Jackie pulled out a humongous snot rag and
blew his nose—the sound of Canadian geese passing overhead—several times. Upon realizing what he had done, Jack
thought what great clowns at the circus they would have made.
Emmett blew his own nose on his sleeve.

That's when Paddy ran at the coffin, hurling wild punches,
and Jackie and Emmett restrained him, getting him to walk
around the funeral parlor's rooms until he calmed down.

When Paddy came back inside, he mumbled things under
his breath—"You old bastard! You old turd!"—but his general
attitude was much calmer than before he went for the stroll. The
blueness in his face returned along with the red veins in his
nose, the jowls that each of them seemed to develop overnight,
along with pattern baldness—"Don't blame this one on your
father," Emmett shouted, "this is from your goddamn mother's
father"—the feminine breasts, the soggy beer bellies. All this
matter cohered once again upon the brother's body.

Here's to the Coole family, Jack the Wack thought. We'll dig
your ditches, drive your buses, police your streets, put out your
fires, run as corrupt underlings to even corrupter—and richer—
politicians. In better times we probably filled up the rectories
with priests and the convents with nuns. But these days few
of us were in the service industries. Instead we seemed to be
habitués of skid row, AA, detoxes, rehabs (drugs and alcohol),

criminal courts, insane asylums or whatever they call them now. But I wasn't going to make a scene about any of this, Jack thought. I'd have my say when the time was right or when it came around to me. Then I'd be done with it, and so recede back into my primeval calms.

Brother Emmett punched Paddy's arm, just like the old days.

"A penny for your thoughts," he said.

"Oh, nothing," Pat said, dreamy and out of the present tense, drifting in other worlds from the past or imagining what it would be like days from now, then months, and even years. Anything not to think of the present situation.

What he wanted to say to Emmett was that he couldn't imagine life without them and this dead father. I am a man now, he wanted to say, and I've paid my dues, I know what it is like to inhabit the loneliness of crowded, noisy bickering rooms, to eat slop nightly, to break my knees at the bedside in prayer. Bless me father for I have sinned. It was a great life with dear old Dad.

Jackie was speaking.

"No, Wolfe told me, that can't be true. He's going to outlive every one of us. He's that kind of person. He's spiteful that way. No, he's not gone yet. He's maybe a little drunk or maybe tired. He's not dead."

"Look for yourself," Paddy said.

"You told Jackie to look for himself?" Emmett asked, flabbergasted.

"I did," Pat said. "I told him. . . ."

"But I can't seem to remember what I told him. Can't seem to remember how many of us were there that night. Only the boys."

Jack paused to consider what he was saying.

"The old man, a few sons. I told them to go into the other room if they didn't believe me," Jackie said.

"Huh?"

"Put a mirror under his nose," says Jack.

"Put it close to his nostrils," Terry responded.

"Nothing," says the Great One.

It was as though the brothers had expected the slightest breath to relieve their anxiety, that perhaps the pensioner before them—their father, in other words—was only conked out on the floor from too much booze. But he was gone, Jack wanted to tell them. This time he went and died. Why do you think they're here back in Brooklyn? Or is this just another hallucination of a different kind?

"Nothing," Jack said. "The old boy wasn't breathing."

"Of course he wasn't breathing," Emmett shot back. "The asshole was dead."

"Now wait a minute," Terry said, standing belligerently, then backing down when Emmett eyeballed him.

"Get an ambulance, I called," Jack said.

"What good would that do?" one of them asked.

But Jack wasn't talking about right now. Right now it would be worthless to get an ambulance. What he referred to was that fateful night, as they say, that day that is only a bit shorter than all the others in our life. Jack meant that he told one of them to get an ambulance that last night. Either that or he was repeating what one of his brothers told him to do. Which was possible. Sometimes the brothers not only looked alike but often sounded alike too, and this was complicated further by the fact that they plagiarized each other's stories. For instance it might have been Wolfe, the youngest brother, who suggested getting the ambulance. But since Wolfe was not yet present, it was easy for fat Jack to co-opt his tale.

The old mick needed a hearse.

First his sons had to finish eating their orts and slops.

Jack went on: "He ain't breathing, I say, I tell him, because he ain't with us anymore. He's dead."

"Lord have mercy on his soul," Paddy said.

That got a rise out of them.

"What soul?" Emmett asked. "The last time he went to church was at my confirmation and I'm ready for the last rites myself."

He was right, Jack realized. If the old man had a soul, he lost it long ago and the question of it being lost in transit from this kitchen floor to the morgue was moot. He'd have to make his own deals from now on, or from that moment forward when he stopped breathing. Of course, Jackie recognized that there was a whole other school of thought than his own clan's, and that notion went that when he breathed his last breath, he breathed his last breath. There was nothing more to be written or said. He was dead. He was gone. The hereafter was nothing more than some heretofore blather made contemporary by their circumstance but remaining primitive nonetheless. Life after death was another one of those hocus-pocus stories the good priests told them as boys. And he was sure that no small number of his brothers figured that there was nothing more to it than shoving the old man in his grave and being done with him.

Jack's own thoughts were addled in this regard; he couldn't figure out what he believed, maybe because he hadn't believed anything in so long; he just had to presume he was right despite the miracles and exorcisms all around him. But within the family Jackie was sort of seen as the doubting Thomas. Still, the moment he stepped into this funeral parlor he had a presentiment, this funny feeling about everything, this crazy sense that the old man wasn't done with them or life, that somehow their father hovered about the room and would hover about their lives long into their own old ages and maybe even after they died. At least Jack the Wack didn't think he was done with the old man with this rite.

"Quiet!" brother Jackie shouted.

They all looked to the oldest brother as though he were an oracle. Or maybe it was that he was an apparition.

"Sorry," Terry said.

"Be quiet," Jack told him.

"Would someone please tell me what the fuck he's talking about?" Emmett asked, making a Brooklyn duckmouth that all the wise guys used to make to look tough on a street corner as they lounged in the doorways or on stoops, affecting their hard-assed attitudes.

Late the night before, Patrick had driven the empty streets of East New York, feeling like an undercover cop. He watched drug deals go down in vestibules of run-down two-story buildings. Saw more drug deals at the projects. People on the street walked with dogs: Dobermans, Rottweilers, pit bulls, all the meanest kinds, each breed more macho than the last. But in the dawning hours, the air so cold it formed crystals on the windshield of the car, he saw an old man wearing only a flimsy poly-cotton guayabera shirt; pointy, shiny black loafers, polyester slacks. His mustache was neat and trim; he had a slick-smooth shuffle; his hair was pomaded, probably with walnut paste, it was so black and iridescent, and instead of walking a vicious dog, he promenaded a scrawny Chihuahua that shook with palsy or just frozen by the weather.

It was like seeing Aunt Eileen's husband Jorge from thirty years ago; he was the one thing in this bleak scape that had energy and life, was familiar and real, not threatening and spectral. The man was alive and out walking his dog, underdressed for such a cold day. Yet, without question, he belonged; he was part of the landscape, and he wasn't a threat, wasn't a menace, was just another citizen, not a deep-throated bullying death-stalking pit bull owner, but a man with his skinny Chihuahua.

That's what the Cooles knew about the statistics in East New York; they lied. This was not simply the most dangerous neighborhood in the city, as the papers said, but an assortment of people who knew that being poor, technically speaking, was not a crime, though it was often punishable by death or worse.

There were lives to be lived, just like that man on the street with his Chihuahua, individual and distinct, not merely statistics. Not everyone was a drug addict, hoodlum, or thief. Every once in a while, a block looked good, the brownstones in repair, appearing neat and functional, and, if you came from Brooklyn, even lovely. As dangerous as East New York was, it was still beautiful at times, or maybe because it was dangerous it was beautiful, and, as Patrick and all his family knew, as far away as they had come from it, it was still part of them. But the man and his dog reminded Paddy of other matters, too.

Seeing that feminine dog in this macho place also reminded Patrick that his sisters would be there the next night, and even if East New York were macho-dangerous, the feminine side of the Coole family would counterbalance all that with their own notion of charm and civility.

Yet the minute the car moved and he turned the corner, the old rhythm out of the 75th Precinct set in. He heard other voices immediately. They said: Try to kill me. I dare you to try. You chickenshit. I knew you didn't have it in you to kill me. That's because you're a punk. You oughta move out to Long Island or New Jersey you're such a punk. Jesus, aren't you the guy we sent out to buy the beer when there was any action? And then we sent you home once the shit went down. Man, you're so doofus, such a shmuck, a lowlife, just a shlemiel. East New York talked to him, and those were some of the things it said, and even if Paddy were to survey people on the street about whether he belonged in this neighborhood or not—and they probably would say he was in the wrong place at the wrong time—his emotional history started and ended here. This was the place that really gave him chills like no other; this was the place where his own juju was at its peak, where the highest energy flowed through him. If he could roll back time and become the Patrick of his youth—not this marginalized bohemian adult he became, but the man he wanted most to be when he was a boy—

it was to be like Willie Pep, the small and wiry fighter whom Patrick was in fact built like, and then to become the boxing champion of the world, and if he had become that person, he knew he would fight best in some shady, sleazy arena underneath the el in East New York, because this is where his energy went through the rooftops. This is where he was most alive.

Of course, it all might be a false nostalgia for the city because years ago Paddy had been forced out of town to do his parole, once he left art school, upstate and working with wolves, all good stuff. But he missed the city, and the hunger for the city started in this part of the place, in this backwater ghetto where he used to live, the baby of the family when his mother only had five children, and before they had to give up the house on Marion Street to move out to Long Island to find bigger digs; in those years before double-digit children, when blond-haired and blue-eyed Paddy was his mother's heart's desire, and he was the toast of his brothers and sister, and then he would come back, as the Cooles always did, to East New York, to stay with Grandma Coole, little Paddy became a tough guy overnight when the street kids wanted to mess with the only white kid on the block.

Mickey Mack and Samantha got dark in the summer sun and looked like the Italians, but Paddy had that pale Irish skin that burned badly, and so he never stayed out in it unless he had on a long-sleeved shirt and a hat. When he fought on the street, his face turned apple red, and he looked like he might burst a blood vessel from the exertion. Still, it impressed the street kids, and they respected him after a while.

During his drive through the streets at the hour of the wolf, the bars had closed and the after-hours and bootlegger joints opened, while the crack houses and drug dens stayed open twenty-four/seven. When he stopped at a traffic light, a cop pulled him over.

"What the hell do you think you're doin?"

He was a red-faced Irish kid; his name tag said his name was Sheehan. Behind him, on the passenger side of the rental car, Paddy saw the cop's partner creep up, then flash the beam of her light into the car through the window.

"I'm stopped for the light," Paddy Coole said, hoping his breath didn't reek too much of stale beer.

Maybe in his grief he had become distracted; or maybe he was just tired. He didn't know which. Probably he should not have indulged himself like this, driving up and down the empty streets all night, reminiscing, and instead driven back to the Island to his sister's place and spent the night with family. He had been driving aimlessly down Broadway to Gates Avenue where the old movie theatre used to be, and was now a pile of rubble, and over to Ralph Avenue (Ed Norton screaming, "Hey, Ralphie, baby!"), then back to Eastern Parkway; up to Bushwick, then over to Stone, to Rockaway, and even beyond.

Sheehan's partner was back on the driver's side once they determined that Patrick wasn't a buyer or seller (a good thing they didn't know him in the old days), wasn't a Mafia kingpin on the lam, and wasn't dangerous; the partner said: "Didn't anyone ever tell you that you don't stop for red lights in this *fuckn* neighborhood at night?"

East New York was a bit like Pleasure Island in the Pinocchio tale. It always seemed to be contrary to the rules for the rest of the world. No one had ever told Paddy that he wasn't supposed to stop for the red lights in this neighborhood at night. He guessed it was just novel enough to confront a white man, not a drug addict, not a gangster, not an off-duty cop, not a member of the Medellin or Cale drug cartels—now that's a ten-dollar word! he thought—prowling these streets.

Patrick wore dungarees and sneakers, a corduroy jacket and a work shirt; he had a full beard that was closely trimmed to his face, and like his brothers, now that he was balding, had chosen to get rid of the long hair on the sides, and wore his hair short and trim. The mourning suit, as he called his dark suit, was tucked away in the trunk of the car with a clean dress shirt and a tie, a pair of shiny black loafers, dress socks, and changes of underwear, his toothbrush and other gear. Less from vanity than to protect his head from the cold where he lived in the northern part of the state, he wore a Donegal tweed cap.

He explained about his father's funeral, about coming from Marion Street as a kid and coming back all the time to his grandmother's house on Macdougal.

Patrick was tired and slightly hung over and a little doped out, so that he promised himself to get cleaned up when he got back to the farm upstate. He was getting too old to behave this way anymore.

The cops' radio blared about a robbery in progress on Sumpter. They went back to the squad car.

This might be Beirut, but it was Brooklyn.

They drove away into the urban auroras, their bubble lights flicking over the darkness as the first light was just beginning to scar the horizon. The siren crackled, screeched, whined, and belched, running out into a long skirl.

After the cops drove away, Patrick approached the red lights at a crawl, hoping they would change; but when they didn't change automatically, he looked both ways and then accelerated through the intersection, speeding on to the next corner a block away. His head was so bleary, he couldn't be sure if he was dreaming this. Later, sitting in an all-night diner on Atlantic Avenue, he found himself sketching his father on paper napkins, that ghostly, shrunken mask, that afterlife of this familial legend, the wacky Inspector Coole, who went out of the world, not with a bang or whimper, but in a demented aria, wearing Pampers and paper slippers, wandering the halls of a nursing home for dementia, his friends Alzheimer patients and other sports, though Jackie Ducks was something else, a wet brain, the old

Keltic curse, drinking his brain into a shrunken pealike state to where it was soaked with alcohol, and therefore pickled, and so did not work anymore, and as it dysfunctioned, Paddy remembered from the last time he visited him, his father slowly receding from life, the names of his sons and daughters evaporating as his brain became more pealike, until there were no more names, not of sons, not of daughters, no more Cooles, before or after, no sun, no moon, no cornflakes on the table, no pints of porter, no Mets games, no *Daily News*, no nothing, another one of life's bad jokes.

The biggest, baddest joke, though, was the codicil to the will, in which the old man informed his children, before he slipped off the planet, if not in body, then in his mind, that he was not to be cremated in Florida and have a marker placed next to that of his wife Rose Moody Coole. Instead, they were to bring him back to the city, up north, back to New York City, and when he passed away, when he *croaked*, as he so eloquently put it in his will, then they were to engage the funeral parlor across from Our Lady of Lourdes, have a wake, then a simple funeral, interring him with his father and stepmother and his stepsister Augusta, the Brooklyn contingency of the family.

Toward that end, Paddy had flown to Florida, taking his father, in his Pampers, gurgling at the mouth, big head flopped over onto his chest, and his body shrunken to almost nothing, back on a flight to New York, where he deposited the old man, with the indifferent consent of various brothers and sisters, into a run-down nursing home in south Queens.

The next time he saw him, Jackie had taken the old man out of the nursing home for the day, brought him to his own house where a bunch of the boys came for the holidays, intending to go visit their father, and were surprised when Jackie walked in the door with him. But it was only a short time later that the old man seized up in the kitchen, his bowl of chili spattering the checkered linoleum floor.

Paddy knew it didn't have to end like that; his father had chosen that end, because he refused to ever stop drinking, and so he
drank until the moment his brain seized up and malfunctioned,
got wetter and wetter, less and less effective as an organ, as a
cogitating muscle, the Big Cauliflower, and turned into a pickled cabbage.

The dirty Irish bastard. Poor old dead bastard. Poor Dad.

CURSED PROGENITORS (1)

1

THE COOLES HAD GROWN UP IN A HOUSEHOLD BEREFT of technology—no irons, no dishwasher, no radios, even no television set through most of the fifties. They were taught that there were only two reasons for using the telephone—if someone was born or someone died. Weddings you could hear about through a mailed announcement. Now they had telephones, radios, televisions, even stereos, but rarely used any of them. Like their father, they read newspapers. But every household like theirs—and there were plenty of households in Wilson Park exactly like the Cooles'—had its house intellectual, a boy or girl who did well in school, and might even go off to college. Mickey Mack was such a house cat. Not only did he read newspapers, but he subscribed to magazines, and he used his library card. So did Emmett, the family gangster, the only one of the boys to get a college degree, which he earned while doing time upstate.

But times had been rough on Emmett. For years he either could not find work or found work that was beneath contempt in his mind. Now he drove a cab. His gangster days were pretty much over. He was not a killer, not even genuine muscle, but a brawler, a wreaker of havoc. Today the wise guys preferred gunpower to physical chaos in the form of setting Mad Dog Emmett Coole loose in your bar or restaurant for lack of payment on the monthly installment of protection. A bullet in the femur was quicker, more efficient, its level of intimidation far superior to the old bullying ways. Instead of working under contract to some Irish hoodlum from Hell's Kitchen, Emmett drove his cab, grousing about making ends meet, long separated from his Italian princess and their children. He had become—or had become determined to become—the oldest crack addict in New York City.

Emmett never had much meat on his bones; it was his will-power that propelled him into mischief. Still, he had a little heft in the old days. Now he was little more than a bag of bones with a bad attitude. He lived in Queens, in Jamaica, not the Jamaica of palatial estates and stately mansions, but on the other side of Hillside Avenue, deep into the heart of drugs and black soul, the mean streets of South Queens. His black neighbors thought the neighborhood was going to hell, not because of drugs, which had always been there, but because of Emmett Coole. If the landlord rented to that crazy son-of-bitching pig, he'd rent to anyone.

So after work in the city, driving his cab eighteen and twenty hours a day, wired out of his mind on drugs and alcohol and a generally bad disposition to nearly all of humanity, Emmett took the subway home to South Jamaica, the reggae in the streets as evil a backbeat as any drummer ever conjured. In one pocket he carried a fistful of pepper; the other pocket contained dirt. Both were there to fend off attackers, some real, some imagined. Emmett had bad debts, bad connections, and had bad-mouthed anyone who tried to exert a force against his own instinct for self-destruction. He had a philosophy, though. You fuck with me, I'll fuck you up good. You fuck with me, I'll fuck with you. Sometimes the philosophy became even more minimal than that. Fuck it; fuck you.

After Mickey Mack had called Emmett and told him of their father's death, Emmett went back to listening to the radio, a blues show on one of those nonprofit stations, something he listened to every week. He sat in the one nice piece of furniture—a La-Z-Boy recliner chair—in his one-room apartment. He took out the glass pipe, smoked some crack, and immediately forgot why Mickey Mack called.

Fucking Mickey Mack, Emmett thought, he had all the advantages. Not like me. I had to suffer through everything. Fuck it. The crack went cold, and he lit the ice one more time. His head went into orbit, and he felt the top of it break through the ceiling. He cracked open a can of beer, the six-pack at his feet in a bucket of ice since he had no refrigerator after selling it the week before for some crack, no matter if the refrigerator belonged to the landlord and not to Emmett. Fuck him, he thought. No one had it as bad as Emmett Coole, so fuck you if you thought you were going to get over on him. He'd get over on you a lot faster. He was no dope; after all, he had a B.A. in anthropology from Saint Jude's College in upstate New York, and who was Saint Jude, if not the patron saint of the hopeless. Fuck 'em all, Emmett thought or maybe said, he didn't know which, since there was no seam between his mind and the external world.

If there was a rodent in the kitchen, it could just as easily be in his mind. If roaches came out of the woodwork, they invariably crawled into his ears and went right to the center of his brain.

He slugged on the beer to come down from the crack. Then he quickly opened another beer, and a third one, just to bring him down a little. He was too high right now, out of his gourd, floating over Howard Beach, making like Swamp Thing in the wetlands of Jamaica Bay.

It would not register until the next morning, hands shaky, groping for a Salem to smoke, that Emmett recalled the telephone call from Mickey Mack, though he couldn't immediately remember what the gist of the conversation was. Someone had died. Was it Jack the Wack, Paddy, Oona, Sam, who? Then he got his bearings, sipping his first cup of Lipton's tea. There was something about Brooklyn in his will, how they were all to gather in the old neighborhood—hey, it's a good place to score dope, he thought—and lay him out for a good old-time wake, let everyone see him, and bury his bones up in Highland Park or whatever they called those cemeteries between Queens and Brooklyn, Calvary or whatever. Then Emmett remembered he had tickets to a Knicks game that night. He'd have to sell those tickets because they were good seats at midcourt, gotten from a dope dealer for doing a couple of favors.

Instead of tea, Emmett opted for another can of beer to get his head cranked on right. He'd smoke from the glass pipe, too, only there were no more rocks left, and he'd already combed through the dirty cotton rug the night before, smoking seeds, moldy bread crumbs, and city grime, trying to find a high.

2

Quickly enough Emmett found himself thinking about that funeral room out in Brooklyn, which after all was the same place where Grandma Coole and Aunt Augusta had been buried when he was still a teenager. The family's pettifogging eulogizing and jackfoolery stayed in his mind forever. Then that slow wending in the broken-down jalopies they assembled for a cortege to meander and stutter its way through Bushwick and up through Highland Park and into the Evergreens, finally to the Catholic paupers' cemetery where Grandma Coole and then Aunt Augusta lay next to Jems, their husband and stepfather, respectively, and beside his first wife, Annie Wilde, Emmett's father's real mother. When he looked up, the Golgotha of the Manhattan skyline was in the hazy distance, almost like an apparition—like a mirage. Headstones, mausoleums, gravemarkers, memorial tablets: this went on for miles in every direction.

Emmett Coole would have preferred to think about anything other than his dead father, especially a dead father whom Emmett had not spoken to or seen but for a few brief moments since he was a teenager, and here he was a grown man, fast approaching his own oblivion.

What do I care about a dead father? he wanted to ask, he did ask himself, but it gave him no solace, only brought out that age-old family trait of shame and low self-esteem. By late morning he made plans to take the el from Queens into Brooklyn.

Instead of thinking about his father and going to the funeral parlor, Emmett thought of his brother Mickey Mack, the house scholar, and how his brother would get to Brooklyn from way uptown in Washington Heights, a long subway ride from uptown Manhattan, downtown, and then crosstown, out of town, across the East River, from one Broadway in Manhattan (neon lights and theatrical enterprise) to that other Broadway, a world away, in Brooklyn (chiaroscuro and violence, empty lots, stray dogs, glassine bags, dirty needles, crack vial lids, broken glass, salsa, posses, guns, crime, and death). Jesus, he thought.

Jesus, Mary, and Joseph, he thought.

The old man would play his tricks until the end.

He'd exact his pound of flesh, his homage.

But Emmett went.

First he needed to get a taste of something, stop by a bar near the el, get a few beers, maybe a couple shots of Irish whiskey, and pick up some cocaine, the only way he'd get through the day. But he'd have to do it on credit, since his taxi-driving job wasn't bringing in enough money to sustain the crack habit. Still, he felt edgy, out of it, ill-at-ease, and he needed a taste if he was going over to Broadway in Brooklyn and attend a funeral with his family.

As Emmett sat in a bar called the Green Rose of Shannon he thought of that telephone call from Mickey Mack. They ought to have the funeral in Brownsville, he thought, what with a brother like Mickey Mack, the Jew in the family, not just because he was studious, the house scholar and all, but he just looked and acted that way, like he was sheenie, not mick. What did Jesse Jackson call it, yeah, Hymietown, that's it. Have the funeral in Hymietown and get the Reverend Jesse Jackson to deliver the eulogy. That would be a gas. Because the old man and Mickey Mack could definitely pass for yids. "Am I right?" he asked, but there was no one in the bar but the bartender, who didn't have a clue who Emmett was talking to or what it was in reference to.

"Hello, are you there, Earth to fuckn bartender?"

The bartender looked as if he might reach under the bar and whack Emmett on the head with a baseball bat, knocking a little sense into the city's oldest crack addict.

"What you want, partner?"

"Another drink," Emmett barked.

"All you got to do is ask."

"I'm asking," Emmett said.

The bartender poured another shot of Irish and opened a bottle of beer, placing them in front of Emmett.

Emmett laid down his last bit of cash, hoping his girlfriend, Sally Winters, a hooker and addict herself, showed up soon, so that he could mooch some money off her. If she didn't show, he wasn't going anywhere.

After the bartender went back to the end of the bar to read his copy of the *Post*, Emmett went back to his old resentments with the Coole family. Since Mickey Mack was the last Coole to speak with him, he decided to dwell upon that brother to rile him. Emmett used to tease Mickey Mack that he was adopted, and when Aunt Augusta took them to the dress shop where she worked in Brownsville—it was called Shane's—Shane the Jewish owner liked to say that Mickey wasn't part of the Cooles; he was a Shane.

"Look at that nose," he said. "Look at those eyes. No Irish have eyes and a nose like that. This is no goy. This boy has a sad

Jewish face, he has no Irish-eyes-are-smiling, let-a-smile-be-your-umbrella to him, shake-hands-with-your-uncle-Mike-me-boy-who-kissed-the-garden-gate. None of that. This is an eastern Mediterranean face, not an Irish face. Augusta, where did you find this one? We'll take him home to dinner with us and raise him ourselves."

But Shane should have known that you didn't engage the redheaded terror of East New York so casually, especially if you were talking about her godson, whom she loved ferociously, at least if she were sober, and she was sober when she worked in the dress shop on Pitkin Avenue.

"Mr. Shane," she said, never one to mince words, "the kid is uncut."

"Wha?"

"You know," Aunt Augusta said.

But the Jew did not understand.

"You know," she repeated.

"Wha?" he said again, more terrified.

She went into the genealogy of her nephew's dick, embarrassing Mickey Mack right down to his root and stem. First she told the old Jew about how all the Coole children were born at Saint Mary's Hospital in Bedford-Stuyvesant, even after they moved out to Long Island. "I don't know why," Augusta said, "it's Rose, their mother, she's got a thing about that hospital, only one of them got borned down in Washington, D.C., on account my brother Jackie Ducks was stationed in the navy during the war, and the kid was born in a naval hospital where they don't cut the meat, ya know, they don't slice it up when the kid's born, but they leave it uncut."

"Wha?" Mr. Shane whirred.

"His pecker," she said, pointing to her own crotch.

"His pecker?"

She nodded toward the kid's zipper.

"His putz," she said, nodding.

Shane looked horrified now. So did Mickey Mack Coole.

"His shmuck," she said, hoping to mollify her boss and soften her hard tongue.

"His wha?"

"He's uncut," she repeated, "you know, he ain't, what you call it, circumscribed."

"Circumcised."

"That's it, Mr. Shane," she said. "The kid was born in a naval hospital in D.C. when his old man Jackie, my brother, you know, my stepbrother Jack the Wack?"

"Oh, Jack the Wack," he said. "How is Jackie Wackie?"

"He's fine," she said. "But like I was saying to youse, Mickey Mack can't be no Jew 'cause his meat's uncut, he ain't circumferenced, or whatever you call it, you know, no brisket, like you guys say, no brisket."

"Wha's that?"

"Ah, forget it, Mr. Shane," Aunt Augusta said, going back to folding sweaters in the dress shop.

Emmett decided that an addiction was not a bad thing because his own addictions permitted him not to become overly preoccupied with his dead father. He had to worry about getting toot for his nose and a few more drinks in his runty body, not think those lugubrious thoughts about his father. Instead of a dead, shriveled old man, he saw something dynamic and alive, his father in his youth, that broad-shouldered little terror, that black pig of Broadway, the Playboy of East New York, furious, indulgent, spiteful, vicious, sentimental, drunk, hard-working, brutal, full of his denial and Christian wrath. Dear old Dad, in other words. The terror of Wilson Park. Jackie Ducks himself.

He tried to think about the old days, recalling a time when he was married to the Italian dancer, and not a down-and-out cabbie but rather an associate of various organized crime figures in the Irish Mafia in Hell's Kitchen. These colleagues liked Emmett enormously, and so as a reward for his loyalty to them—he was the protégé of Harry Fitzgerald, the only mick gangster to grab a piece of the garbage collection, traditionally a guinea thing, out on Long Island—a stagehand job was conferred on Emmett at the newly opened Metropolitan Opera House. He lived in a nice, neat apartment on Avenue A, down in Alphabetland, and he used to run into Mickey Mack, probably the last time he regularly saw his brother, who worked at the new library at Lincoln Center, and they often got together at the Century Bar on Amsterdam Avenue after his younger brother's work ended and Emmett's only just beginning, though the stagehands regularly drank during business hours at the Century, where the great Thelonious Sphere Monk, pianist genius, held court, either at the bar when he was in the owner's graces or outside on Amsterdam when he was persona non grata.

Mickey Mack supplemented his income by selling opiated Nepalese hashish on Avenues B and C, and sometimes Emmett met his younger brother at one of the bars on Avenue B, drinking in the Old Stanley, Stanley's, Old Reliable, or the Annex, his brother a holy terror too, Mickey Mack's nickname back then Machine Gun, skinny and dark, bearded and grubby, more Digger than hippie, disaffected, stoned-out, angry, drugged and drunk, all around what they now called Loisaida, where Emmett would rather be going than back into East New York, a place no good, upstanding, righteous cab driver would ever take a fare, not in a million years.

Mickey Mack at least had his pretensions about being a literary person. Emmett did not have a career presently, not even a life-style, but rather a predicament.

Emmett thought of Aunt Augusta and her funeral in the same parlor that he headed toward, and how the younger boys were just little children then, and he was a wizened sixteen-year-old, already drunk and drugged up more times than he could remember. He used to think that Grandma Coole and Aunt Augusta's funerals were bizarre until he read this book about how in the old country they played games at the wake, hurling potatoes at each other's head, music awhirl, they jigged and reeled, horn-danced and ducked, just like Emmett's own brothers and sisters did, full of mischief, bored and cooped up in Brooklyn on a lovely day, the young ones had water guns, the older ones a Wiffle ball and then a Frisbee, and Brian put a whoopee cushion under an old uncle's butt that raised a commotion when the old fellow let out this humongous fart. Their father, Jackie Ducks, came over and cracked Terry first (always it was Terry first, no matter what was done or who did it), then all the others got socked around, their ears boxed, etc.

Outside, a passing car blared a song by Little Anthony and the Imperials.

Emmett contained this ancient hum of what he thought was an ancestral image: an old king enters, slouch-backed, furry-fingered, long slack jaw, grunt upon his tongue, right at home in Our Lady of Lourdes parish. He thought of how Mickey Mack used to tell him that they were related to Jack Coole the Fenian and Sean Cumhal the poet, and how the lineage went back to King Cormorant in the Land of Tantrum, but he knew that was a lot of bunk, nothing more than Mickey Mack's penchant for bullshit. Yet, thinking about his father, Emmett could not help but think that a long line of vile old men had come to a termination, that a lineage of sorts had reached its end.

Once, years ago, staying at Mickey Mack's then apartment on East 10th Street, he went out with his brother to a used bookstore on East 7th Street, looking for a book of poems by Sean Cumhal. Instead, Mickey Mack went off with a lady friend, and Emmett, on the lam and hiding out from the law at his brother's empty tenement, drifted over to McSorley's, the alehouse near the Bowery. A man had asked to sit at his table, and Emmett said okay, it was cool, but he didn't look up from reading a newspaper when the man asked.

Shortly after that the man offered to buy him two beers, since McSorley's sold its mugs in twos. Again, Emmett did not raise his head, but said fine, buy me a couple beers.

"Can't you say hello to your own father?" the man asked.

Emmett looked up; there was the old man, four ale mugs in his hands, a waiter behind him waiting to put down a tableful of cheese and onions for them.

"Dad," he said. "What are you doing here?"

"You never call home," he said.

"It's only been a couple of years."

"You left when you were fifteen," his father said, "and how old are you now?"

Emmett had just turned twenty-one.

"Your mother is worried sick."

So they got drunk, wound up in a Ukrainian bar on St. Mark's Place, from which they were thrown out, then to the Mafia bar on First Avenue near 10th Street, then back to the apartment Mickey Mack rented on 10th, to drink six-pack after six-pack, while Jules Potok, Mickey Mack's roommate, a Marxist anarchist from Chicago, lectured the old man about the working people on the docks, and each time Jules mentioned Marx, the old man said that he preferred Buster Keaton, but you never could be sure if the old man was being witty or ironical or plain dumb, until, four in the morning, his arms loaded down with wilting fruits and vegetables he bought at the open-air green-grocer's around the corner, he bid his sons good night, and waddled off into the night, drunk as a skunk, but with a built-in navigational device that would get him either to the piers, where he would sleep it off on a boat, or to Penn Station to take the Long Island Railroad out to Wilson Park. Mickey Mack guessed it was to the piers since the trains had stopped running, and the old man was too drunk to make that long trip in his condition. That was the last time Emmett and his father had talked,

though it wasn't really a heart-to-heart, but rather one drunk
buzzing away to the other, those sad-happy monologues behind
the mugs of ale and the plates of cheddar and onions, and the
final drunken argument in the kitchen of Mickey Mack's apartment, one light bulb in the ceiling, bathtub next to the stove,
a large poster of Albert Einstein on the wall, green and battle-
ship gray paint-chip walls and ceilings, almost like a reprise of
East New York.

Emmett imagined his brother Mickey Mack stopping off on the
Lower East Side before crossing into Brooklyn, and he wasn't
too far wrong about this. Mickool had transferred from an A
train at 14th Street, only to have the Canarsie Line train break
down on First Avenue, so that he had to get off and walk
through his old stomping grounds, through the East Village and
down into the Lower East Side below Houston Street, where he
picked up a subway train at Delancey Street, one that crossed
over the Williamsburg Bridge into Brooklyn, and traveled out
Broadway to the familiar destination in East New York.
  Once Mickey Mack crossed Houston Street, leaving that territory bounded by 14th Street to the north and Houston to the
south, his own old memories grew weaker, then faded. He got
a knish at a Jewish bakery, then headed down to Delancey to
get another train that navigated over the East River, pounding
through the rookeries of Brooklyn off Broadway, Myrtle, Kos-
ciusko, Gates, Halsey, Chauncey, the names totems more than
place-names, sounds to evoke the myth of geography and forebears, though as a boy the train rattled more, rocking and rolling almost as if it might tip off the elevated tracks, rattan-seated
cars as colorful as boxcars. There were times that Mickey Mack
was so estranged from his childhood here that he thought of
Brooklyn as a foreign country, and whenever he found himself
using the Battery Tunnel, Brooklyn, Willie B, or Manhattan
bridges, he'd get chills. It was almost as if he needed a passport

to enter Brooklyn, this foreign country of his childhood, where Grandma Coole spoke Yiddish and the Jews used Irish words and the Italians sometimes spoke of rabbis and donnybrooks; the mildew on the walls trapped the *cuchifrito* smells of his Spanish neighbors, and the Sunday suits on the Church of God black boys on Macdougal, their faces African black, their shirts whiter than any white boy's like Emmett Coole with blond hair and blue eyes.

Emmett wore a pair of black cross-training Nike shoes, dungarees, a black turtleneck, a dark sport coat, over which he wore a long black leather coat and a black leather taxicab driver's hat to cover his bald head, the leather hat slouched over one eye like a tough Irish hood. The look was effective camouflage in South Jamaica, and so he presumed also in East New York. Instead of getting off the elevated subway train at Chauncey Street, he exited later at the Gates Avenue stop, because this used to be the outermost universe of his childhood world when the family lived on Marion Street several blocks away.

The buildings had progressed further in their disrepair, but they were still recognizable. Malignant, decrepit, neglected, he still knew this place. Even though everything had changed, it was not unfamiliar; that is because, like everyone else in the Coole family, he had dreamed of this place all his life, and so the real East New York seemed to appear like the East New York he'd invented in his persistent dreams about it. Like inventing a dance to the devil, there was something beautiful about the dangerous, evil patterns. The most malignant of these berserked cells was the Gates, an old vaudeville house where, his parents used to tell him, Jackie Gleason got his start in show business, but for Emmett the movie theatre where his aunts took him to see horror flicks—characters in basement cells with no eyeballs and shaven heads—and afterward going with the aunts to some gin mill on Broadway, where they spent the night regaling the bartender and the customers with their Brooklyn Irish charm and beauty, their incredible poor-girl seductiveness, and the ten-cent allure of their perfume mixing with the noxious fumes outside and the backed-up beer taps in the saloon.

The Gates was a heap of rubble, though still vaguely looking like a theatre. Gargoyles floated above the ruins. Dust and shadows, piles of brick and plaster, chained doorways, bolted and posted no trespassing.

Immediately this decayed old facade, which resembled the aftereffects of a B-52 raid, brought back images and smells, old feelings and new emotions, that gave even Emmett Coole vertigo, not to mention that he was the only white face anywhere on Broadway, and already a few people stared at him in a way that seemed to say, "What's this ofay motherfuck doin on our turf?"

He took out a pair of black-rimmed sunglasses and put them on. They were prescription, so he actually saw better with them, but it was also further camouflage. He walked along Broadway, every step bringing back a new remembrance. Coole and the gang, he thought. Yeah. Jackie Ducks's kids. Just like the smokes. Kool. They cool. The crazy white people. Crazy sons of bitches. Crazy. Got himself sixteen, count 'em, children, mostly them ugly white boys, but a couple of them red-haired and dark-haired foxes in the bunch. Yeah. Coole and the gang. Jackie Wackie. Jackie Ducks.

Most of the stores on Broadway were boarded up. He had read in the papers over the years how nothing had been repaired or reopened after the '77 riots devastated this main thoroughfare. The only operations under the el were after-hours social clubs, shooting galleries for drugs, crack dens and the like, an occasional fleabag hotel, a storefront church, and the even rarer bodega or Korean or West Indian grocery. Where old tenements stood, there were projects or empty lots.

In the middle of the day, the street was nearly empty, a few clots of men in doorways, lazily eyeing Emmett, the outsider, the stranger, the white man, the Mad Dog of the Coole family.

Emmett went back to thinking about Mickey Mack Coole, the brother closest to him in age. Except for when Mickey Mack had called him to say their father was dead, the last time they had spoken with each other was a brief telephone conversation a few years ago. Mickey Mack was trying to write a piece about the Westies, the Irish gangsters in Hell's Kitchen. Nine of the Westies were on trial for murder, extortion, and forming a criminal enterprise in Clinton, that area just west of Times Square. In his infinite naïveté, Mickey Mack thought that Emmett and the old man would help out with his research. Emmett had explained that he only knew these guys, but he had no influence. Apparently someone had tried to muscle Mickey Mack at the federal trial in Foley Square, and now Mickool was freaked out about being whacked or something, so he wanted some name to use, someone to fling back at the hoodlums' friends in the gallery, in order for them not to bother him while he collected information for his piece about the Westies.

The old man spent most of his life working on 49th Street on the midtown docks, Piers 90 and 91 his and their headquarters.

Mickey Mack had spent five months attending the trial, listening to whacks and hits and body chops and men like Jimmy Coonan, the stone-cold leader of the Irish Mafia from Hell's Kitchen, saying that if there was no corpus, there was no habeas, so let's get Eddie the Butcher and hack these mothers into pieces; and shy, murderous Mickey Featherstone, Coonan's right-hand man, a Vietnam vet become neighborhood thug and murderer, testifying, a snitch, the cops had turned him, and now he was an informant, the feds' main man, looking more like a poet in his tan corduroy jacket and shirt and tie and his loppy mustache and quiet voice.

It was Mickey Mack who informed Emmett: "One of the attorneys came up to me during a break in the proceedings and wanted to know what I was writing every day, and I told him that it was a long letter to my mother. The next day one of the Irish goons in the peanut gallery—the Westies on trial were these tiny little men with hugely murderous hearts, but their fans and neighbors, cohorts and hangers-on and admirers came in all different sizes—who sat next to me was huge. This would never happen at a Mafia trial, I thought, because the Mafia was too classy to intimidate this way, and besides, I had a certain amount of sympathy for some of these gangsters, having seen them for years in the West Side theatrical bars in which I drank and because the old man was from there and worked all his life *down the piers*, like they said, where 49th Street met the Hudson River and the gang and their parents at least knew Dad because he drank in their sleazy bars in his—in those days at least— black customs uniform with a white shirt and a black tie, and they called him Little Jackie Ducks, just as they called his father Big Jackie, but not Ducks, just Big Jackie, though he wasn't a big man, only taller than Little Jackie Ducks, and not a Ducks, but a renegade drunk west coast of Ireland rabble-rouser, an original Westie, though no revolutionary, too drunk for that, and, any- how, it was hard to care about anything when your best thought every day was your first one; *Fuck it*, Big Jackie would say, and go and have himself a beer at a nearby saloon. Fuck it, he'd say. Grandpa Coole had no meat on his bones, all ears and smooshed nose and big scared eyes, a man from the bogs, not a cabbie from Hell's Kitchen, which is what he had become, and a runner for the Irish gangs that preceded the Westies, back in the days when Frank Costello was mistaken for an Irishman and Frankie Carbo controlled the Irish fighters working out of the Garden except for Billy Graham and his crowd headed up by Whitey Bimstein at Stillman's gym on Eighth Avenue up the block. . . ."

Emmett whacked Mickey Mack across the chest to shut him up.

"What's the point, man?"

"The point?"

"What is it you're trying to tell me?"

But Mickey Mack, as was often the case, could not remember what the point of all this was.

Emmett suggested that he not call the old man in Florida because, as Emmett put it, "He's going to take all his secrets to the grave." But when his brother persisted in his paranoia about being bumped off by the gangsters for writing about them, Emmett said, "Go ahead, give the old man a call, but he's not going to tell you anything I haven't told you already."

"Sorry, pal," the old man said, "I don't know nothn."

"Come on, Dad," Mickey Mack frantically screamed into the telephone. "Just a name. These guys could kill me."

"Sorry, pal," he repeated, as if he didn't know his son's name, which probably by that point he didn't.

"I could write the Keltic version of *The Godfather* with this information and retire a rich man."

"Sorry, pal," he said—not son, not Mickey Mack, but pal, chief, buddy, mister, ya lousy bum, the names he used to refer to his children.

Emmett thought: What the hell did he expect? The old man would take all his secrets to the grave.

3

The subway roared overhead every couple of minutes. Light on Broadway—what there was of it—filtered through the elevated tracks and the railroad pilings.

The stores along Broadway were boarded up, but for one or two bootleggers and crack houses; in the groceries, cash register and clerk protected by bulletproof Plexiglas.

Already Emmett noticed those looks, sidelong, checking him

out, wondering what he was, what type of white man: landlord, gangster, drug dealer, cop. The Man. Man's a Man, man. Take your pick. There were no other kinds of white men in East New York. The Man. All the others had left in the late fifties; then the rest vacated after the riots in '77.

One storefront was called Saint Michael, and had an eye inside a six-pointed Star of David, and under that said: Botanica. Under the word *Botanica* it read—Fresh Herbs, Card Readings, and Cigarettes.

Emmett rattled on the door to get a pack of cigarettes, but no one answered, even though he saw people moving around inside. So he walked a few doors down to a Korean grocery.

At Pak-Si Greengrocers, Emmett bought chewing gum, aspirin, potato chips.

To the scared-looking Korean behind the Plexiglas, he said: "Kool tambae han gap jusaeyo hana copi . . ."—Korean words he had picked up living in Flushing, working with Korean taxi drivers, and going to Korean restaurants in midtown. He wondered if Mickey Mack, who was married to a Korean, spoke any of their language. But then he faltered. He said: "With milk, no sugar."

A pack of Kool cigarettes and a cup of coffee with . . .

The Korean did not blink an eye but gave him what he wanted, not asking where he learned to speak Korean, or even if he spoke it well, which did not matter to Emmett because at least the man got him what he asked for.

"Komupsomnida," Emmett said, his speech thick with the borough in which he stood, saying thank you in Korean, the latest language of New York.

"Chunmanio," the merchant answered, it's nothing, don't mention it, and went back to reading his *Daily News*, the headline, advice to Princess Di about Charles: THROW THE BUM OUT!

A man came skittering out of an abandoned building; he

raised a revolver in Emmett's direction, aimed, then lowered the gun and squinted at the white man dressed in black. Emmett loved guns because one pointed his way allowed him to raise the ante. Now he was allowed to do anything he wanted to the man, though Emmett preferred—like his father—the fist to a revolver, and a baseball bat was his weapon of choice. The man took aim again, lowered his weapon. Then he turned, slipped through a fence, and skedaddled across an abandoned lot, through another fence, and disappeared. When Emmett turned onto Marion Street, the street was empty, maybe because of the time of the day and year, the gray skies, but also had the slightest edge of bitterness to it, the air biting and cold, so that the street was unreal, but again, like the Gates, not unfamiliar, so that maybe he didn't mean it was unreal but rather hyperreal, superreal, realer than real, with the luminous edges of dream, because it resembled a movie set, almost like one for Spike Lee's remake of *Do the Right Thing,* but instead of the pizza parlor, it was Hymie's candy store, and Marion Street could be a stand-in for the rest of that mythic street in the movie.

The place where the Italian gangsters ran one of their operations out of a taxi company was now an abandoned, boarded-up factory. All that remained was a candy store on the corner, looking just like it had when he was a child, only now it was closed, the shades drawn in the middle of the day, but its wooden trim around the windows, painted green and neat, as if someone had been enterprising with it quite recently. HYMIE's had been painted over to read ABDULLAH.

He stopped in front of the old brownstone, but it was no longer a brownstone, and instead had a false facade of fireproof stucco and pastel shingles, colorful and tacky. From a first-floor window, what used to be their living room, Emmett saw a blind bend up and a pair of eyes shoot out at him.

4

It was Mickey Mack's birthday, his cousins and aunts and uncles there. The kids were raucous, running around the house, up the stairs, into the bedrooms, back down and through the living room and dining room and into the kitchen where the Dalmatian bitch Midgie barked at them. His cousins from Flatbush and Ridgewood were there, and even a couple of cousins from Long Island. His aunts from around the corner were there and his parents and his mother's sisters and the girl next door who played with Leland and Emmett.

Mickey's godmother Aunt Augusta had given him the silver Hopalong Cassidy guns he wanted, but she also bought him a Hoppy hat, black shirt and black pants, and she even took out a pair of Hoppy black and white leather cowboy boots, the most beautiful things he had ever seen.

Before he attended to anything else, Mickey Mack went up to the boys' bedroom to change, then came back down in his black cowboy suit, moving slowly down the narrow stairway in his cowboy boots.

He did not know it but the grown-ups had been drinking throughout the party, and drunk now, though not yet unruly, they drifted away in their attentions to the younger children. That's when Mickey Mack mounted the chair backwards, and as a 78 Victrola played the heavy Uncle Remus records—"Zippity-doo-da, zippity-aye"—and the cousins and his siblings raced around the house full of sugar and cake and soda, Mickey rocked and rocked on his chair backwards. Rocked and rocked. Yippee aye taye yo. Git along little doggie.

Uncle Remus sang, "What a wonderful day!"

He heard his mother's father singing that silly song he sang to the children.

Mares eat oats and does eat oats and little lambs eat ivy. A kid'll eat ivy too, wouldn't you?

Rock and rocking and rock and rocking.

The chair tilted backward and Mickey Mack went flying off it, splitting the side of his head on the radiator behind him. His scream was piercing, and the music stopped and the adults got quickly sober.

Blood spilled everywhere.

His mother's sister, Gerty, another nurse like his mother, shaved his head on the side and put alcohol on it and then she stitched it shut right there on the spot.

"A butterfly stitch," his mother's sister said. "There won't be any scar."

Mickey Mack cried, then whimpered, then simpered, then shut up. Emmett called him a crybaby, which he was, so, so what? Leland complained when the party ended abruptly because the birthday boy was hurt.

"Plenty of sunshine heading my way," Uncle Remus sang, and through the veil of sorrow and tears, he imagined Brer Rabbit and even Brer Fox listening to the soothing black voice.

His aunt tried to convince him that the split in his skull was less painful than the rusty nail he stepped on the year before when he had to go to the hospital to get the tetanus shot. But she was wrong. When he stepped on the rusty nail, Mickey didn't feel a thing, only a little dizzy when he saw his shoe fill up with blood. She was right that the day after the shot, it hurt. Not the hole from the nail, but his backside where he got the shot.

"Zippity-doo-da, zippity-aye!"

After everyone went home and all the children but Emmett and Jackie went to bed, the two oldest boys sat in the kitchen, waiting for some rolls to be heated and then eaten.

Jackie had a murderous look on his face, maybe because it wasn't his own birthday, and so he had no presents, no cowboy hat, no boots, no gun and holster, no scarf.

Emmett was sick of hearing the Uncle Remus record and wanted to break the thick 78 recording over Jackie's head.

Instead, he asked his oldest brother if the stove was hot.

"What?" Jackie growled back.

"Is the stove hot?" Emmett asked.

"Hot?" Jack asked.

"Play nicely," they heard their mother call from the living room, where she was still straightening up after the birthday party.

Jackie grabbed Emmett's hand and put it on the hot surface of the oven door.

The oven was an old porcelain-coated one with four gas jets on top and an oven door with a thick round glass to see what was inside.

The oldest of the Coole children kept his brother's hand planted to the door, even as the smell of burning flesh became evident, even to the adults inside.

Emmett was so hurt and shocked and mortified, so bullied and overcome, he didn't know what to say, and it wasn't until Mother Rosy ran in and pulled Emmett's hand off the stove that Jackie let go.

"Why?" she screamed at Jackie, clutching Emmett into her breasts.

"Why?" Jackie said laconically, his buck teeth making him look like an evil Bugs Bunny. "He wanted to know if the stove was hot," and got up, left the room, went upstairs, and put on his Dr. Denton pajamas.

Emmett looked down at the scar on his hand that was still there forty-five years later, and his resentment for Jackie was so complete, he could bring it up every day of those forty-five years, and instead of diminishing, it grew. Which is why Emmett always called Jackie a sadist. And as soon as he told you about Jackie burning his hand on the stove in the kitchen at Marion Street, he'd tell you the other Brooklyn tale, years later, when they were ten and eleven years old, and staying the summer at Uncle Mackey's in Flatbush, and how Jackie pushed

Emmett off the top of the billboard on Flatlands Avenue.

To no one on the street, Emmett said aloud: "The kind of guy he was."

5

An old round black woman, wearing beat-up tennis sneakers without socks, a thin cotton housedress, an overcoat and a Bulls cap, hummed and pushed a supermarket cart filled with empty cans and bottles. She muttered to herself, and her big frame reminded Emmett of Mamie in the Moon Mullins comic strip, which in turn reminded him of Macdougal Street and his grandmother. Grandma Coole really looked like Mamie Mullins, minus a star tattoo on her bicep, and Emmett liked to think of Leland as Moon to his own Kayo Mullins, their father always a kind of useless Uncle Willie. (The Cooles always seemed to be from the Moon Mullins strip while the Moodys were more of the Lord and Lady Plushbottom order.) If only, like Kayo, Emmett thought, I could lay down in a drawer for a nap, puffing on a big cigar, everything would be all right, all would be fine. Or was he mixing up Kayo Mullins with Swee'pea?

Emmett stood in front of the old brownstone now, and decided that if it once reminded him of the Moon Mullins comic strip, he wasn't sure what it reminded him of now, maybe Frank Miller's futuristic comic book *Ronin*, the desolate urbanscape filled with violence and crime, the only justice the kind that was administered at the end of a samurai sword.

If he closed his eyes, he heard the family yatter, could smell the two houses, one their own, the other his grandmother's, mildew and old oil, rotten cabbage, coal, burnt meat, stale beer, old ice in the icebox.

He'd sleep the night away, listening to Aunt Augusta screwing her transit-worker boyfriend on the couch or Aunt Eileen screwing her passionate Cuban and Puerto Rican boyfriends in the bedroom closest to the living room, for Emmett's red-haired aunts were his first introduction to sex, and crazy Aunt Nora even wanted to pull his pecker and get it on with him, always asking that he sleep in the same bed with her; and she was warm, had tits and an ass, but a face on her that was a hopeless wacky immigrant stereotype, so it was not a good idea to get too attached to Aunt Nora because everyone knew she was crazy.

Besides, each of them had a favorite aunt. Aunt Augusta was Mickey Mack's godmother, and she spoiled him and Samantha with presents. Aunt Nora liked Paddy, and Grandma liked Jackie. Aunt Eileen adopted Emmett as her pet, giving him cigarettes and sips of beer whenever he wanted. The other kids in the family never got into the old man's family, and so by the time they were growing up, Aunt Augusta was too far gone to form an attachment to her, Eileen was involved with Jorge, and since Nora never went out and the younger Cooles never came to East New York, none of them knew her, though they had heard of her, and sometimes did come to Brooklyn to visit Grandma.

On Rockaway Avenue, two black children duked it out, flailing away at each other with lethal punches to the head. A tall, muscled man in a dark gray nylon warm-up suit came over, collared them, and bonked their heads together, then dragged them inside into a decrepit building that looked as if no one should inhabit it. The concussiveness of the man's blows could be heard across the street, almost like banging two coconuts together, and Emmett—the toughest, most vicious one of all the Cooles—winced, not just because of the immediate pain the boys must have felt, but also those residual pains, the remembered ones, the scar tissue from that time long ago, so that he was not so much feeling their pain as their pain made him re-experience his own pain in East New York. But the pain could be mixed with some other powerful feelings, and just because

Jackie bullied Emmett, it didn't mean that anyone else, in or out-side the household, was going to push him around.

It was summer in East New York, the backyards in the neigh-borhood blossoming with roses and ailanthus trees, sycamores and privet, the tiny landscapes a complete contradiction of the naked streets outside the homes, the wide Brooklyn byways without any trees on them. Their own backyard even had a grape arbor, but the deep purple grape was too sour to eat.

"Out in the yard," their father said, ordering his sons out of the kitchen door into the backyard.

He flung a pair of authentic fourteen-ounce leather boxing gloves at Leland's head.

"From my friend Bumpy," he said to his wife.

"Who, dear?" she asked.

(Rosy called everyone dear, just like her own mother.)

"Callahan, Callahan," he said irritably. "You know, that fighter I went to Adams with, Bumpy. He detached his eyeball, getting hit, he couldn't fight no more."

"You mean Billy Callahan?" she asked.

"Of course I mean Billy Callahan, Bumpy," he said, "Bumpy Callahan, the ex-welterweight."

While their father stayed behind in the kitchen, drinking his first beer of the evening and Rosy made him dinner, the boys laced on the gloves in the backyard. They had no hand wraps, and the gloves were too big.

Leland placed the gloves on Mickey Mack Coole's hands, then the boys took turns whacking the third child around with the other pair, their younger brother a human punching bag, even better than that inflatable Joe Palooka doll that one of the aunts got them every Christmas though it had a puncture hole in it even before they were served breakfast.

The two older boys punched Mickey Mack until he went un-conscious, then Emmett sauntered back into the kitchen.

"Mickey is sleepy outside, Mommy," he said.

"Well, wake him up," their mother said, "it's not time to go to bed yet."

Leland kneeled over his kid brother, slapping his face.

Mickey Mack dreamed of a white room of white walls and white floor, organ music playing, myrrh and frankincense in the air, a soft breeze rippling the curtains. Or so he once told Emmett as they got drunk, years later, on the Lower East Side.

Emmett came outside with a bucket of water and splashed his brother awake.

When Mickey Mack came to, he jumped up, unleashing punches left and right at his two brothers, but they slipped the punches easily, laughing as they stepped away.

"Sugar Ray Coole," Leland said, laughing.

"Mickey the Monkey," Emmett called, as he stepped out of his baby brother's way.

"Are you boys playing nicely out there?" their mother called, nursing Samantha in her arms.

"Mickey's crazy," Emmett said.

"He thinks he's Gene Tunney or somethn," Leland shouted back as Mickey Mack landed a punch on his thigh, giving him a slight charley horse.

As Emmett laughed, Mickey Mack landed a punch on his jaw, but instead of acting hurt, Emmett became furious and knocked down his kid brother again. But Mickey was not out like the first time, only woozy.

"That wasn't nice," their mother said.

"He asked for it," Emmett fumed, his fourteen-ounce leather boxing gloves resting on his hips.

This time Mickey Mack was not in dreamland, gossamer and pale white. This time he was only groggy. Instead of the softness and hush and peace of the white room, he smelled the sour grapes in the arbor, and he threw up on the ground.

Mickey Mack became Leland and Emmett's sparring partner. This simply meant that in a context of sport, the two older brothers were allowed to beat the crap out of him. The third Coole boy learned, if not to win, to slip punches, to bob and weave away from them. He learned the beauty and necessity of footwork, of moving side to side. At the local bar, when the grown men watched the Friday-night fights, all of them studied the footwork of the fighters; Emmett studied how they held their hands and watched how they set everything up with the jab, how they punched in combinations, doubled up when an opponent was hurt. Mickey Mack made a vow then that he would revenge this hurt that Leland and Emmett had put on him; he would get even. Neither of them were easy to live with, and were much harder than that to fight. So he thought it out carefully. If he was not going to be able to beat either of them just yet—and he knew it would be many years before he could take either one—he decided that he would learn the art of defense, and so when either of them laced up the leather gloves, Mickey Mack learned to move his head side to side, bending at the waist, slipping under and around their punches; he learned to move his head away from an oncoming punch, lessening its impact. All of this made Jackie and Emmett better fighters because they had a talented sparring partner who challenged them to greater heights. Emmett let Mickey Mack believe that all he needed was a little more training to beat them, but every time they fought, Emmett always ultimately got the better of him. Still, Mickool learned to get on his bicycle and backpedal the feet out of harm's way. Living with these young men was a dangerous activity, Mickey knew, and he was determined, early on, to survive their onslaughts; was determined to survive and eventually win. But he never did win. Emmett or Jackie always beat him. Even though Mickey Mack knew how to fight an awful lot of people, including professional boxers, he still hadn't a clue how to beat Emmett or Leland in a fight. Especially

Emmett, who seemed to invent new ways to win fights daily. Jack and Emmett had all the cards, psychologically speaking; they knew all the routines that would burn a sense of shame and humiliation into their younger brother and turn him into a wooden drugstore Indian incapable of counterpunch and retaliation; they were past masters of the head games fighters play on each other, and Mickey'd be a long time in hell before he figured out how to beat Emmy or Jack the Wack. He wasn't even able to beat the old man until he was in his late teens.

The recollection made Emmett smile. Instead of proving to be a dangerous place, East New York was proving to be an empowering ground. Still, Emmett's stomach—his Achilles' heel, he liked to call it—churned and boiled and made him nauseous. It was both good and terrible to be back—how shall he say it—to be back *home*. It was like pouring oil over burning waters, but also like spilling honey over an acidic ache.

6

The vertigo was back. Maybe it was time to leave this street and go meet the family around the corner at the funeral parlor up on Broadway. But he couldn't leave, was even tempted to walk up to the door, knock, and ask to come inside, make himself a cup of tea, go upstairs to look at his old room. He heard Leland, boyish, mischievous, wild, uncontrollable, ill-mannered, uncivil, shouting, calling, teasing, wheedling, cajoling; he heard his other brothers call him inside, beckoning him upstairs into one of the tiny, narrow bedrooms.

The house was long and narrow, the ceilings high, and the building probably once was the elegant abode of some upstart Irish immigrant at the turn of the century. But not in postwar America. When the Cooles moved in, the old place was in disrepair, a bargain, and the only thing the old man could afford with his salary in the U.S. Customs, himself just released from intelligence duties in the navy.

An even older feeling invaded Emmett Coole now; instead of being like a homecoming, he remembered now, no matter how he sentimentalized it in his dreams, that all he ever wanted to do in East New York was get out. By the time the fifth child arrived, Emmett didn't feel himself abandoned so much as crowded out—neglected, one of the forgotten older boys.

A water balloon broke across the back of his leather coat, and the cold splash rode up his neck and down his back, chilling him. *Motherfucker,* he said. The bad attitude was never far underneath the surface, either his or theirs. Emmett turned to see where the water balloon had come from, but he saw no one on the street, and no one appeared to be inside any of the brownstones and row houses. He took out a handkerchief and dabbed it on his neck, wiped his hair.

Always a secret optimist, Emmett said aloud, "At least it wasn't an egg," and went back to remembering because remembering was what homecoming was all about, and, besides, East New York never scared him. There was really nothing these new ghetto kids could say or do that he and his brothers hadn't done to them or done to themselves. This was a brain-stem operation, not a thought in the world was necessary to walk here; it came from instinct. If he did not win a fight, at least he would draw blood, gouge out an eye, leave some scar tissue so they'd never forget him. This was not the law of the jungle; it was the rules of engagement in an urban backwater. It was how their father had instructed all his sons to fight.

He must have been four years old the first time he thought of running away. He came into the kitchen at the back of the brownstone, the best-lit and the biggest room in the house, and announced his departure. He wasn't sure where he had learned these procedures, but he had fastened a supply of clothes and food into a handkerchief and slipped it over an old broom handle. He had always wanted to become a hobo from the first time he laid eyes on one of them near the Long Island Railroad tracks up the block. It was reinforced by the only other source of information in that childhood world, the funnies. There he would marvel at the bums, the hobos, the down-and-outs.

He would find a boxcar, climb aboard, and journey around the world, just like Uncle Willie, his mother's brother, who occasionally stayed with them when his ship hit port. He'd hop a trolley to Flatbush.

Jackie had bullied him for the last time, and he was tired of his mother having babies, ignoring him.

When he told his mother, "I'm leaving," she had said, "Close the door from the outside, dear."

Of course, she didn't believe him, maybe never believed him, or probably it was never a question of belief, but rather she did not hear him, never heard him if he thought about it, maybe was deaf for all Emmett knew.

"I'm leaving," he said again. "This time for good. I'm running away."

His immediate family wasn't impressed, but the other relatives liked to say that little Emmy, so cute and blue-eyed and blond-headed, had a gift for language.

"See you in a bit, dear."

He walked around the block, past the pickle factory, the numbers parlor, the taxicab shop, past Hymie's candy store, past the backyards and the brownstones, the tenements towards Rockaway Avenue, past everything that was his little world, around and around the block he walked, and then daringly, crossed Rockaway and went up the block and entered the schoolyard from the opposite way he usually did, which was on his grandmother's block and down an alley between two buildings. This time Emmett crisscrossed from the main entrance of P.S. 73, and then up the alley and over to his grandmother's, and there onto

Macdougal Street, where he saw his grandmother, her big tits hanging out the window, arguing with the banana man who sat at the reins of his horse-drawn cart, yelling that word over and over.

"Bananas! Bananas!"

"Get ya foockn fingers off the scales and give me the foockn bananas."

"Aye, Grandma," he said, "you drive me crazy!"

"And bring them up to the stoop where me daughter can get them from ya, I have no legs for walkn."

Grandma Coole had legs, but they were swollen and discolored, a blotchy blue-green and pink and malformed. Her foot was missing from her right leg, and she either hobbled about the railroad apartment or used one crutch. Usually she had a cigarette or a glass or bottle of beer in her crutchless hand. Still, this was no handicapped woman, and you had better not get on her poor side because she was a terror, verbally and physically, wielding her words as charmingly as any person Emmy ever heard or thrashing the air with her crutch, as if it were a scimitar.

"Emmett of the Uprising," she shouted. "Be the love of Jaysus, what are ya doin in me quarters."

"I'm running away from home, Grandma," he said.

"Well, come in and have a cookie and a cigarette before you go," she said, and shouted to Aunt Nora to open the door for that little divil Emmett Coole.

7

Another balloon of water crashed down on him, freezing his scalp, and sending a chill down his back, and his first moment of fear since arriving back home. *Motherfuck*, Emmett said, jerking around. There never was a place, situation, or person that

Emmett ran from. He liked to fight, maybe liked it better than anything else in life, so that if these punks from East New York wanted to mix it up with him, he'd oblige them. Just come out of the woodwork, you little cockroaches, stop playing this Vietcong guerrilla bullshit and fight like a man, you cocksuckers. I'll show you what a little one-on-one is like. I'll give you a taste of a knuckle sandwich served up by Emmett Coole. You won't be the first nose I bloodied in East New York, and it won't be the last because Emmett Coole was one of the few taxicab drivers in New York City who didn't have a protective plastic shield between himself and the passengers and who actually took fares into the heart of Brooklyn, the deeper and darker the region, the better he felt.

His fellow cabbies, who didn't pick up black passengers and never went into the heart of Brooklyn at night, called them safari rides into darkest Africa. Emmett called it stopping back in the old neighborhood.

Emmett looked around, but no one was on the street; he heard childish laughter but couldn't locate the source. He could have his memories of East New York, but his actual presence was not encouraged. By now he had drifted off of Marion Street and was headed toward his grandmother's house on Macdougal, and after he assayed her old two-story building, he would walk up the two blocks to the funeral parlor to meet the rest of his family and attend his father's funeral.

He went through the schoolyard at P.S. 73, school out, and the playground empty except for two young boys, wearing hooded sweatshirts, dungarees, and hightop basketball shoes, who shared a glass pipe for crack. They could not have been more than twelve or thirteen years old, and upon seeing Emmett, thinking him The Man, they scattered out of there, one going one way, the other in the opposite direction, a trick Emmett had showed Mickey Mack in this same schoolyard. He stopped where they had been, hoping that some of their rock had spilled out, but there was nothing littering the playground but a pile of broken matches.

Emmett couldn't find his grandmother's house because he forgot the number. Now it was either more decrepit—if that were possible—than when he lived there as a kid, or it was simply a pile of charred beams and bricks, burnt to the ground. This would appear to be the case. When Augusta died, she was the last white person, not on Macdougal, but in the whole area, and while everyone knew her, and some even liked her, one or two might even miss her when she died, the newcomers didn't give two shits about Augusta Morgan, Eileen Panaqua, Nora and Grandma Coole, their brother Jackie Ducks, or Mr. Ducks's myriad children, Emmett just one-sixteenth of that familial baggage his father carried around with him when he lived; so maybe they torched the joint back then, or maybe they burnt it to the ground during the '77 riots, or maybe it was a recent arson.

Even before the '77 riots, that notion of getting out pervaded anyone who was in here.

Each sister and brother would walk down this street thinking the same thought, how she or he was not like the others, was special, different, unique, and would get out, strike out on her or his own, make a name in fashion or baseball or, like Jackie Gleason and John Garfield, on the stage and in films; how she or he was smart but didn't have advantage. The others were fuck-ups. In a sense, it was the only monologue any of them knew. If there was a theme, it was to get out as soon as you could, to run for the hills, to make a break, not to look back until you got 1800 miles away, and then turn around slowly, never trusting that maybe one of them might be right on your heels, ready to pull you by the ear back home.

8

Mother and Emmett fought. They were always fighting. They never got along. And he told her that he was leaving again. He was leaving home again. The streets were wide as big rivers, and they were empty of trees, like the tops of high mountains. There was a book his mother talked about called *A Tree Grows in Brooklyn,* but there were no trees out on the street, only in the backyards, and he never saw her read anything.

The names of the streets in Brooklyn—Sumpter, Ralph, Chauncey, Stone, Rockaway, Macdougal, Marion—sounded like the names of minor devils in hell, and the supermarket (Einhorns) and movie theatre (Gates) sounded like semidemihemidemons, henchmen to Lucifer.

Perhaps he would visit his grandmother and his wacky aunts around the corner on Macdougal Street. Maybe he would go there. They were always good for a laugh. Emmy walked out the door, about to give her one last chance.

Mother made peanut butter and jelly sandwiches for the other children, the ones she really loved and who were not there but up the block at Our Lady of Lourdes, seeing the Tom Mix serial feature. Emmett had had an earache, and so had not gone to the weekly movie on Saturday afternoon.

"I'm leaving," Emmett said.

"Where're ya gonna go?"

"I'm leaving home," he said seriously.

His mother laughed.

Her second boy seemed to go through this same scenario every Saturday.

He remembered a time long ago, far away now, when he was the baby of the family, and he could come into her upstairs bedroom early in the morning, Jackie already outside playing, and his mother, dressing, still naked, smiled at him, and she was the most beautiful woman on earth, and her breasts were the finest on earth, too, and once upon a time he still could remember sucking on those breasts, and he was momma's boy.

But now she laughed, not the nurturing mothering woman from that time ages ago, but already a woman who chose to neglect and abandon him to the dangerous world of his oldest brother Jackie.

"I'm running away," he announced.

"Well, you know where the door is," she said, calling his bluff.

"I'm running away for good," he told her, "because I hate everyone in this house."

"Close the door softly," she said, smiling.

His black and white Dalmatian Midgie barked at him as though he were a stranger. Up until that moment he had planned to take the dog with him for protection, but now that the dog barked at him, he decided that the dog deserved a life with this family.

Outside, Emmett walked slowly, hoping his mother would run out and beg his forgiveness and ask him please please to reconsider and come back home. What would the house be like without him?, and so he backtracked, in order to give his poor mother a chance at making retribution for her offenses.

Once he circled the block, he came back and circled it again. He stole up to the window, and instead of hearing his mother weeping for the loss of her son, he heard her singing in her awful soprano.

"It's a great day for the Irish, it's a great day for us all!"

Her voice was terrible, and her food was not much better.

Emmett stomped off into the rain puddles. That woman's love was a rotten kind. She didn't fool him one bit. He had more love from Grandma Coole, and she didn't even have that much love in her heart for anyone, being already old and infirm prematurely, and even though she never told him this, Leland had told Emmett that she was not related to them, was their father's stepmother, just like in the fairy tales, except instead of being mean and making them scrub floors night and day, she made them Irish pancakes and told dirty jokes.

"They opened a whorehouse," she told Aunt Nora, "right up the block next to Our Lady of Lourdes."

"No they didn't," Nora said.

"They opened it and Pastor Hare was upset."

"There's no Pastor Hare at Lourdes," Nora corrected her.

"Pastor Hare went over to the whorehouse to complain to the madam about the noise and disruption," Grandma Coole told Augusta and Eileen. "While he was inside the house, arguing with the madam, the police raided the place and carted every-one off to jail."

"I heard this one already," says Augusta, toking on her ciga-rette and reading the *Daily News.*

"Let her finish," Eileen said. "I never heard it."

"When they were booking the pastor, he told the arresting sergeant, 'You can't arrest me, I'm Pastor Hare.' "

"It's a good one," Aunt Augusta nodded, pushing the strands of curly red hair out of her face.

Grandma Coole went on to tell her daughters and grandson: " 'I don't care if you're halfway up her ass,' the cop says to Pas-tor Hare, 'you're still under arrest.' "

"I don't get it," Nora said.

"You wouldn't," says Augusta, stubbing out her smoke and going into the other room.

His grandmother spoke Irish, smoked Pall Malls, Chesterfields, and Raleighs for the coupons, and drank cheap red wine from gallon jugs, and beer by the quart. Aunt Noreen never left their apartment on the first floor of a two-story building around the corner. His Aunt Eileen worked in a factory off Eastern Parkway and had boyfriends who spoke Spanish. If Aunt Augusta took Jackie, Emmett, and her godson Mickey Mack into Grim's Bar and Grill on Broadway, Mr. Grim told her to leave immediately, although if Teddy or Paddy, the bartenders, were on alone without the owner, they served her enough to drink so that she walked like a man on a ship in a great storm and her words got loud and harsh and full of fuckn this and fuckn that.

If he decided to live with his grandmother and aunts, he would hide in the dumbwaiter or even take the dumbwaiter down into the basement and hide in the coal bin should his parents or brothers show.

When he rang his grandmother's bell no one answered, which they often did not, depending upon how much beer they had drunk and how many bills were outstanding with creditors, because Emmett knew that Nora was never out and his grandmother only went out into the backyard to curse at the people in the tenement on her rear fence when they threw garbage onto her grape arbor. Nora did not even venture into the garden out back.

He walked up the street to Broadway, sneaking past Mike the Barber's so that Mike would not see him this far from home without his parents or his older brother. The el rattled past overhead, sparks leaping down into the street. Broadway was always nighttime dark because of the el.

Emmett went into Our Lady of Lourdes, not into the auditorium where his brothers watched the Tom Mix serial, but into the church proper and then to the rear where the blue grotto was. He sat in a pew and took his belongings from his slicker pockets: toy soldiers, metal variety; two Snickers candy bars; his little soft blanket that he slept with between his legs and made his pee-thing cozy; rosary beads; picture of Saint Francis of Assisi; two unmatched socks and one clean pair of underwear. He forgot his toothbrush, but Emmy did not like to brush his teeth.

The rain poured down on the domed roof and the only time he could not hear the rain was when the el went past and made everyone a victim to its sound. His clothes were hand-me-downs, his look hangdog. If it got rough out on the street, Emmett planned to pawn his slicker and flannel shirt and denim pants and his Keds sneakers.

There was enough fat on his bones to stow away on a tramp steamer heading to the South Seas and survive until he got there. If he could not make it as far as the South Seas, he planned on going to Oklahoma or France. Italy was okay too, but he did not want to meet the pope. Ireland was out because he had relatives there and he didn't want to see any relatives ever again. All relatives were squirts, Emmy decided as he walked in the rain over to the church. He did not want to be Irish and from Brooklyn; he planned to become a Norwegian sailor, and live on the other side of Brooklyn near the docks where his father worked, though he would make sure not to run into his father anytime soon. He didn't want to head across Fulton Street and into Brownsville where Aunt Augusta worked because they never treated him well. That's the territory he would bequeath to his brother Mickey Mack. His brother Mickey planned to become Jewish and Italian because he liked the way the guineas looked and behaved, and the Jews always treated him well when he went to Pitkin Avenue with Aunt Augusta, the women pinching his cheeks and talking about "what lovely eyes this boy has," or admiring his big nose, saying "he isn't your boy" to Augusta, "you stole him from a yeshiva. . . ."

Even Aunt Augusta was too much, because once she got drunk, she pinched Mickey's cheeks hard (not sweetly like the onion-breathed Jewish ladies who, when they leaned over, revealed big brown bosoms, and once in a while even dark brown nipples).

Emmett hated when Aunt Augusta did that and kept repeating herself. He decided that he might miss his puppets and his neighbor's cat and he'd miss poking the broom into that little kid down the block or into Mickey Mack. Emmett knew a lot of dirty tricks from Jackie and he decided that all of them would come in handy if he was to see the world.

Suddenly, Emmett saw Mamie, the crazy lady who lived above his grandmother. Mamie came to church, they said, to steal the poor-box money. She wore many dresses at once and several hats on her head, was dirty and skinny and talked to herself all the time. Emmett told his brother Mickey that if he ever touched Mamie he would get warts all over his fingers. Now he believed what he said, looking at her. You'd get warts and some things worse than warts.

He imagined Mary the Mother of God speaking to him.

She said, "Go back home."

"They have no manners," he answered.

"Give them a chance," she said.

"Okay," he answered, and left.

9

The water balloons from earlier were replaced by zinging objects, first pebbles and gravel, pinging off his neck and head, then rocks, one hitting him squarely in the small of his back.

"You little shits!" he shouted.

More giggles, but from where he couldn't tell.

Then it was no longer giggles, more like a low growl, maybe a pitbull on a leash.

He found himself at the train tracks near Eastern Parkway, the zigzag of various subway lines crossing, making it resemble the Cyclone at Coney Island. Instead of the bocci courts, Old World Italians arguing the various ball placements, it was a bald lot, humanless, treeless, even without rubble like the other empty lots. It was almost as if the Italians had never lived here, just like it was almost as if the Jews had never lived here either, nor the Irish.

It was time to get over to the funeral and get inside with his brothers; at least there were numbers at the parlor.

A group of teenage boys stood in his way, and one of them, their leader, a dark Hispanic kid, bumped into Emmett.

"What you doing in the hood, chump?"

They all laughed.

"Chump?" Emmett asked. He loved this shit. They didn't have a clue, he thought, and they weren't prepared for how relentless and merciless Emmett could be in a fight.

Ask Oona, he thought. She had a boyfriend who was ranked as the Number Five welterweight in the world, and after Emmett found out that he was beating Oona and her son, Emmett got into a fight with the guy, Joselito Borinqueño, a made-up name if ever Emmett heard one, and though he lost the first couple of minutes to the guy, the ranked fighter went into shock when Emmett, his own face pounded to a bloody pulp, made a comeback after biting off the guy's left ear.

Emmett smiled at the punks from East New York. He was glad to meet them.

When he got tired, there was a meanness in Emmett that always surprised him, and he was tired now.

"You heard me," the kid said, poking a finger into Emmett's chest. "I axed you a question."

"I'll tell you what I'm doin," Emmett shouted, moving quickly towards the kid, who then backed off, stepping to the side. There was something about Emmett, skinny and unhealthy looking as he was, that could put fear into a person when they looked into his crazy eyes.

Gotcha!

Now the kid stammered.

"No problema," he said. "Me and my posse take care of this turf. No harm, no problem, no sweat."

Fuckn punks, he thought, then moved off. He saw this ringleader once again, trailing him a half-block back with his posse, maybe six more kids now, and as they walked in and out of the shadows and light of the elevated tracks' pilings, they moved closer and closer toward Emmett Coole, who now dreamed of tearing their hearts out.

This wasn't his turf, though. Grandma's house was gone; he didn't recognize his own house. What mattered was no longer there: the butcher shop on Chauncey, the pickle factory on Rockaway, Hymie's candy store on the corner of Marion, but it was shut to the public. Eileen and Nora were gone, as was Aunt Augusta, the crazy redheaded goddesses of Brooklyn, the city spirits. So was that demigoddess of Irish hospitality and Yiddish profanity, his grandmother, old Mrs. Coole. Louie Panaqua, stovepipe pants with yellow pinstripe on the leg, silky shirts opened to the midsection, was gone, too, OD'ed long before it was fashionable to do such things in Williamsburg. Gene the Bean, too shaky to open his cans of beer, paying the kids money to do it, so he could get drunk, was gone. No one remained. Even Jackie Ducks was dead. Fuck these punks, he thought.

"Fuck you, you fuckn punks," he said aloud, but not loud enough for them to hear, though they got closer and closer now, and the funeral parlor was only a block away.

Mike the Barber's was gone, even Our Lady of Lourdes shrine church was gone, probably another neighborhood arson, one more artifact of the '77 rampage that torched and tore down the old place.

The wailing of the Hasidim was at an end, or too far down Eastern Parkway to be heard. They were gone, but Emmett could still hear the voices of Nevo and Henley over the back fence of Grandma Coole's house, their Jamaican lilts, and their scrubbed shiny jet-black faces, Church of God children, sons of a minister and man of the cloth, upstanding and righteous as Muslims. Mickey Mack and Sam and Paddy's friends. The banana man in his horse-drawn cart, Mr. Bacigalupi, and the iceman in his horse-drawn cart, telling little Jackie to shut up, "I'll crack ya across the lips," he said, when the oldest son announced, "The iceman cometh," whatever the hell that meant, Emmett thought, though it sounded wise-guy funny at the time Jackie said it.

The old *guaguanco* of East New York turned Emmett into guava jelly, but the footsteps behind him made Emmett travel on, bereft of nostalgia. Let him get inside and think about black beans and yellow rice, medianoche sandwiches, and a plate of *tostones* with red-hot sauce, or oxtail soup in some all-night restaurant in Brownsville. That little prick and his posse was only a few feet behind him now, and Emmett was almost in front of the funeral parlor, could even hear his brothers' voices through the opened stained-glass windows.

He remembered that time they moved from Marion Street out to Wilson Park, Uncle Harry in front of the house in his new four-door Packard.

Harry Miller was a gruff newspaperman, married to their mother's oldest sister Lizzie, and obviously disdainful of being in Brooklyn, even though he grew up not too far from here and went to Brooklyn College and now worked for the *Herald Tribune* as an advertising salesman. He chain-smoked strong, unfiltered cigarettes as he waited for the truck to be loaded, the house cleared out, and everyone to get into the car. Emmett could see him now almost as if it only just happened: beige camel hair coat, fedora cocked to one side, cigarette in the side of mouth; dark brown suit, thick silk tie, shiny light brown shoes. His hose were dark blue and slightly transparent.

Like Rosey O'Coole, Lizzie Miller, the oldest of the Moody girls, was a baby-making factory, and was two children ahead of her productive younger sister Rose.

Uncle Harry puffed his cigarette, waiting impatiently for these chaotic Cooles to be ready and get the hell out of this godforsaken place, the nuns of Lourdes forgive him for saying that.

All Emmett's life he would suffer from a dream in which his Uncle Harry loaded the Packard with everyone in the family but him, and soon they drove off, Broadway to Atlantic Avenue, and then eastward, outward, onto the Island. Not everyone was unaware of his absence either. Always, Jackie smudged a pugged nose up against the inside of the rear window of the Packard, sticking out a tongue, giving his younger brother the bird, waving good-bye.

"See you, sucker."

So they moved away from the old parish, and postwar, full of false hope, they set up house in Wilson Park at the city limits in Nassau County, parvenu, ersatz bourgeoisie, the House of Coole come to Long Island, the bride and bridegroom of the boomers of Bedlam, excised from East New York, but the ghetto smell still in their clothes, their hair, their manners.

Now he had come back full circle to East New York and his father's funeral, a great eternal loop, and just to keep it at the level of the brain stem and not the upper reaches of the mind on fire with imaginative facts, there was the matter of that posse behind him, breathing down Emmett's neck.

The teenage boys surrounded him before he got inside the door, some of their faces pitch black, others chocolate or light brown, come out of the el's shadows like a wolf pack, one with a knife, one with a baseball bat, all of them a half-foot shorter than skinny but dangerous Emmett Coole. They had more expensive clothing than you might expect ghetto kids to wear, warm-up jackets, Georgetown and Syracuse sweatshirts with hoods, hightop Nike sneakers, baseball caps, colorful jeans.

"Chill," the ringleader said.

"Yo!" he heard from inside the parlor. "Hey, the fuckn black pigs got Emmett surrounded outside."

The brothers did not necessarily love Emmett, but he was blood, and even if he wasn't, a fight was a fight, and what better way to pay homage to their dead father than to kick some ass on his old turf, so they lunged for the legs of chairs, grabbed broom handles, pocketknifes, and maybe even, who knows, some of them had guns, and came outside just as the posse scattered, the roar of the rattle-clank-clatter train overhead shaking them down to their bones. After the posse vanished down a side street on the other side of the elevated train tracks, the brothers shook hands and wacked backs and generally let their gonads swell with testosterone and grief. Then the objects came flying again. Water balloons at first. Then eggs zinging in. Rocks. Even gun shots.

"Get the fuck out of the hood!" someone shouted from the other side of the el.

Emmett stepped inside, his heart beating tachycardia, no longer that sensual clave beat that had possessed him earlier, one-two, one-two-three, hips gyrating, East New York style, like Louie Panaqua had taught them thirty-five summers ago.

Emmett Coole thought: Oh, Pop! Dear Pop. Dear old Dad. Shalom. Salaam. Slainte.

SISTERS

SAMANTHA WALKED INTO THE FUNERAL PARLOR WITH Oona and Deirdre, followed by Elizabeth Ann and Mary Grace and Eileen. The sisters gave a lot more solace and comfort, put the old man in focus, if you will, better than any brothers did.

The old man used to say, "Give me girls any day, they're so much nicer than boys."

The sisters were small, tough, and pretty. Leland used to say they had convent smiles of Irish schoolgirls, drop-dead Hail Mary eyes with a touch of wantonness, and the go-go dancer's wiggle. Some of them were dark and fierce; others were pale and blonde; and two, Eileen and Elizabeth Ann, had red hair like their Coole aunts.

Sam and Deirdre now lived in Florida, while Oona lived out on the Island. Mary Grace, the most saintly and innocent-seeming of them, was the gun moll of a mafioso in Bensonhurt. Eileen lived in the Bronx in some undefined—ill-defined—world, and Elizabeth Ann was a nun in a convent in Philadelphia, of a liberal order that allowed her to wear civilian clothes, not the nun's habit, and she was the least nunly of all of them.

Four of the sons had left in search of a pizza parlor, leaving only Patrick.

He was of the impression—proved wrong by their arrival— that some of his sisters hated their father so much that they

would never come to his funeral. He expected the rest of the
angry sons to appear, some of them begrudgingly, but instead
all the sisters arrived, and none of them anywhere as bitter as
some of his brothers, and, after all, five brothers did not make a
quorum in this family, and was not even a majority vote, some
of them lost in this very borough, maybe, or wearing cement
sneakers off Gravesend or South Brooklyn, or maybe dead in
some cocaine jungles in South America or in the Witness Protection Program, or maybe they simply didn't want to show, were
aware of these familial events and decided to stay home, watching a basketball game on television or the Tuesday-night fights
on the cable or too tired from work to bother to come by. Who
knew? Who cared?

He was surprised that Wolfe hadn't shown because Wolfe
had always seemed close to his father. Was Pat Coole the only
one in the family to notice the absent brothers? the only one
to find it disturbing? But probably he was wrong, he decided.
He couldn't read their minds. They could be off bowling away
their grief; they might be off howling with grief, and he did not
know it.

Once the old man retired and he and Rosy moved to Florida,
and lacking a center on Long Island to visit, failing to have a
house where they might show up at Christmas and Easter,
Paddy lost contact with some of his siblings, not to mention the
fact that for five years he was not allowed in the city because of
the conditions of his parole after the drug bust at the art school,
and so he was thankful not to be doing heavy time, but then the
country, at first, grew weary and lonely and thin experience for
a city kid. Eventually Paddy came to like and then love the iso-
lation upstate, but the trade-off was that, even though he invited
members of his family to visit the place in the Adirondacks, a
large contingent of them only came maybe once, and never
again. As a result, he lost contact with most of the family and
the geography of the city except for his antique deals in SoHo

and the Village at the flea markets. As for his family, he forgot to call, did not visit, and when he got the urge, they were almost all gone.

In the case of his sisters, maybe guilt or remorse overcame hatred, because all six of them did show this evening.

Ah, but the Coole women were stunning creatures. If their Coole aunts were the ghetto goddesses of East New York, they were the goddesses of the lumpen suburbs, blue-collar queens, working-class furies.

Patrick used to imagine his mother and her sisters like a pack of Barbara Stanwycks, a bunch of tough broads from Brooklyn, you might say. The daughters of Rose Moody were something else, though. He remembered that the sisters were small like their mother, not broad like their father. Visually they bore no resemblance to Bette Midler, but they sounded a bit like her, only more nasal, more Brooklyn, less Honolulu if you will. They all had big knockers like the old lady, were short and small-footed, their feet no bigger than cucumber seeds. Their hands were as dainty as demitasse cups; their hair was mostly wild and curly. They were stunning creatures because, unlike their father and their brothers, they had magnificent teeth. They had teeth, magnificent or not, and none of the boys did. Their hawk noses were like little sparrow beaks, hooked but so daintily, as one might hook a black gossamer stocking to a garter.

But the imagination was deceptive. Some of the sisters were as flat-chested as high-fashion models. All of them, unlike the high-fashion models, were small, just like their mother. Like all Cooles, they had bad teeth, or at least problems with their teeth. Patrick was correct about the sparrow beaks, and their hands were indeed as dainty as demitasse cups, but instead of not looking like their mother, they were each one of them her stand-in, spitting image.

Rose Moody's images of spit, Paddy thought, looking around the parlor at them now. And just as each one of the Coole girls looked alike and also looked like their mother, their mother and her sisters all looked alike, too, and, in turn, looked like Grandma Moody. In that sense, except for the small hawk noses, the girls were all Moody, with only a touch of Coole, just like some of the brothers were more Moody than Coole, too, though Patrick J. Coole, as everyone said, looked exactly like Grandpa Moody, his look-alike image of spit, and how many times had Patrick spit, thinking of that image? And as the Coole girls looked like the Moody girls of another era and like their mother Gertrude Mojo McGillicutty, this face, these countenances, had been a part of the Brooklyn landscape for as long as there had been a Brooklyn. And in the sense that Patrick looked more like a Moody than a Coole, his own countenance had been around an equally long time, first with his mother, then his grandfather and his great-grandfather and so on, back to the Moody clan in Albany, and, Patrick imagined from living upstate now, back to the Mohawk and the Irish of Belfast, the Irish of Dublin, the two mother-country cities of the Moody clan.

Seeing the sisters, Patrick could think only of their mother, and thinking of his mother, he could only cry, though everyone thought, then, that it was out of a profound compassion for the old man.

"Paddy Joe is really something," Oona said. She went on to say that the old man hated and abused him as bad as any of the boys, and yet Paddy still has compassion to mourn his father.

"A bunch of them will be here," Paddy said, defending the five of them who hadn't yet shown for the wake.

"Where are they?" Oona asked.

"Busy," he lied. "But they'll show. Don't worry about that. They'll be here."

"Right," answered Oona.

"See that scar?" Sam asked. "Paddy gave me that."

"Paddy Waddy Cooley-Wooley?" a few of them said on cue.

Even though they had heard this story hundreds of times, they had to respond this way or it wasn't worth Samantha's telling or their listening.

All still referred to her as Samantha Coole, her maiden name, even though Sam had married Arnold Blitzer and had taken his name. But then they got divorced, and though her son was called Dylan Blitzer, Sam had gone to a numerologist who had explained that all her problems originated with the fact that her name did not have the appropriate number of letters to insure her success in life. That's when she changed her first name to Sky, and instead of returning to Coole, a name she always felt cursed by, she took her mother's maiden name, Moody, and so was now, legally speaking, Sky Moody, though the only time any of her siblings called her Sky was when they wanted to be sarcastic. No one had yet pointed out to her that Sam—no one called her Samantha—had the same number of letters as Sky, Moody the same number as Coole. So much for numerology.

The sisters had arrived at the funeral parlor, almost like a sea change. The sisters, all present and accounted for: Samantha/ Sky, Oona, Deirdre, Mary Grace, Eileen, Elizabeth Ann.

Samantha, the oldest of the Coole sisters, was the only one who really had any memories of East New York, and her busted kneecap was one of her favorite stories to tell the younger sisters, all of whom had grown up—no matter how bad it seemed —in the relatively more gentrified world of Nassau County out on the Island. Brooklyn, to the younger sisters, was only a story their mother and sister and older brothers and father told, not a real place, more of a phantasmagoria, the collective nightmare of a clan, not a geography, but a locus of feelings (shame, guilt, inadequacy, low self-esteem), and yet oddly enough, the place where each one of them had been born, so that if there was a curse of being born—and most Cooles would tell you that there was—it was Brooklyn, even if the burden of a life occurred in a more easterly place out on Long Island.

That being the case, the younger sisters gathered together in a fearful knot, scared to death at the sight of where they stood, and dependent upon their brother Paddy to provide muscle if anything untoward should occur while they had gathered there.

"He pushed me on the stoop," Sam went on, "I fell on the concrete, right in front of Grandma Coole's house down the block on Macdougal, and I had to get forty stitches, and we never made it to Coney Island."

"This is not how it happened at all," Paddy interrupted his sister. "It didn't happen like that."

"Let her finish," Eileen said, looking a touch like her namesake, Aunt Eileen.

"Yeah," said Mary Grace, "I haven't heard this one in a long time."

"But it's not true," Paddy protested again.

"And instead of feeling sorry for me as I bled all over, Paddy screamed, 'Shit, now we can't go to Coney Island. . . .' "

"Baloney," Patrick said, defending his name and reputation. But he didn't really have to worry; all his sisters, unlike his fighting brothers, loved him dearly, including Sky Moody, the narrator of this horrible tale.

"After all, I was the brother least likely to push and shove," he said.

"Yeah, yeah," Sam answered, punching his arm.

Their father was laid out across the room, and the assembly of sisters avoided his snarling countenance for a few beats longer. But Inspector Coole was a hard man to ignore, especially if he was your father, so one by one the sisters stepped up to the coffin to see their dead father, kneel in front of him and say a prayer.

"Dear God, be kind to this mean old fart," Eileen prayed aloud.

"Lord have mercy on his sorry ass," Oona said.

"Praise the Lord and pass the gravy," Mary Grace said, laughing. "Remember that short version of Grace?"

"Fuck him," Elizabeth Ann said at first, but then kneeled down to say a prayer for her father. "Oh, Lord," she prayed, "give him enough praise and encouragement in his afterlife to make him worthy of your love, and since his life here was often hell on earth. . . ."

"Hell on wheels is more like it," Samantha said.

"Grant him a touch of salvation because he was a rotten old bastard but he doesn't deserve to burn in hell forever just because of his character flaws, about which he was helpless to do anything. Amen."

She stood to face her family.

"Nicely said," Patrick told her, always impressed by a well-turned phrase.

"Thank you," she said, then abiding by the innate hierarchy in the family, she slipped to the back of the room with her younger sisters, Mary Grace and Eileen, leaving Samantha, Deirdre and Oona nearest their father, where they talked with their brother Paddy.

This gesture by Elizabeth Ann—not the prayer, but that receding into the background, to be present, not as an equal to her older sisters but as a shadow, a supernumerary, even at her own father's funeral—reminded Pat of the crazy order in the family, and how it was easier being someone like himself, a painter, who could create a canvas in which the focal point was these three older Graces (Samantha, Oona, and Deirdre), while the three younger Graces (Mary Grace, Eileen, and Elizabeth Ann) were their shadows, more like faceless creatures in a de Chirico painting, especially in the light and shadows of the elevated train on Broadway, than Degas-like or Renoir-like or Gauguin-like creatures—probably he meant like feminine spirits invented out of the warped mind of a demented Rembrandt because this property was once a Dutch settlement that prospered in the shadow of Manhattan island.

Paddy Coole would know how to find the balance and

shades, the right coloration for this group portrait, this study
in black. To evoke his family was always a juggling feat, finally
an impossible balancing act because some of these sisters—just
as some of his many brothers—would never be fully developed
on the canvas because they were never fully developed in life,
were minor players among these other minor players; because
they were less and less important to the nature and purpose of
things, being damned to marginality in all respects, a family living at the edge at best, and over in the abyss as the years went
by, so that calling them "a family" was just a convention, not
a real point of distinction or fact; really they were a loose-knit
fellowship that happened to share the same parents and last
name, but other than catastrophic events—like their father's or
mother's deaths—which brought them together, they rarely
ever saw each other, and nearly all of them preferred not to have
children, being fully aware of the consequences, and those that
did have children (Emmett, Mickey Mack, Sam, Oona, Mary
Grace, Eileen) had only one child.

"I had a lot of compassion for your hurt," Patrick said to
Samantha about her wounded knee and her perpetual soft
grudge about it.

"No better than Leland or Emmett," she said, echoing an old
hurt that had become numb and joky.

"Those guys thought I was a wimp," he said. "Wimps don't
push girls on stoops."

"Yeah, right," Oona answered him, joining the goof.

"You slipped and fell and probably imagined that I pushed
you. . . ."

"Oh, you pushed me all right," she said.

"And I never said, 'Shit, we can't go to Coney Island.' Once
again you felt this and imagined it, Sky."

"Why would I lie about it?"

"You're not lying," he said. "You're just imagining it instead
of recalling it as it really was."

But already there were other matters to occupy them. Sam went to the back of the room, either to talk to the young ones there about drinking and doping in the funeral parlor, or maybe to partake of their goods herself.

As she went to the back of the room, followed by Oona and Deirdre, Patrick, the lone wolf male, stared at his other sisters Mary Grace and Eileen and Elizabeth Ann, and then thought of the other women in this world. There was his mother, Rosy O'Coole, née Moody, of course, but her mother, Grandma Moody, and then Grandma Coole, not two of a kind, these grandmothers, two of the oddest-matched people you could imagine. Neither of them had ever been in a room together, even though their lives, as they unfolded here, were only stones' throws away from each other. Patrick thought of them because it was the women in the family who had allowed him to flourish as an artist, starting with those demented—but lovingly remembered—teenage days spent in the attic of the house, sniffing glue and making car and airplane plastic models, later painting them, and how those tiny bottles of metallic paint and small cans of spray paint intrigued him—of course, the marijuana and acid helped too—and solidified his feelings about going to art school instead of regular college, not that he could get into regular college with his grades. It was the women in the family who said it was okay to paint the day away instead of going to the basketball courts or trying out for football—besides which, he was well-built but too small—or even wrestling (which he was good at), instead drawing and painting and getting high. The getting high blended into getting into painting, until they became indistinguishable, and so therefore one. But it would not have been possible without his mother's laissez-faire attitude (some would call it indifference), and his maternal grandmother, old Grandma Moody, telling him that they were related to the Hudson River landscape painter Wilfred Smith Moody, whose paintings Patrick had seen at the Metropolitan Museum, and had admired since he was a young boy, believing that cock-amamie story his grandmother fed him.

It reminded Patrick that this old neighborhood of theirs had a gender, too, and it was not womanly, rather this bullying male's, with what the hoods on Rockaway called big *cojones*. There was nothing delicate and feminine about this neighbor-hood.

2

Sam reminded Patrick of how irritated she could make her father, especially in her choice of boyfriends, particularly this hood known as Johnny Stiletto, the quintessential greaseball from New Hyde Park, Long Island. Johnny was a car mechanic, and so had perpetual grit and dirt under his fingernails, and his passion was motorcycles, which he rebuilt and then raced fur-ther out on the Island in backwaters like Commack. He wore what amounted to a uniform, too, not from the Mobil station where he worked, but an off-duty uniform, which consisted of engineer boots, dungarees, a garrison belt with the buckle on the side of his pants, and a T-shirt with the sleeves rolled up, where he kept his pack of Luckies. (Say what you want about Johnny Stiletto, he was generous with his Luckies, Pat thought.) His forearms were covered with matching dragon tattoos, and on his right bicep he had a cartoon devil, and on his left a naked woman. Johnny wore his hair in a greased-back duck's-ass hairdo with a flattop and sideburns, and he had that requisite fidget in his leg. He was all attitude. In that respect, he was nearly a half-pint-sized version of Jorge Panaqua (Aunt Eileen's husband), and he seemed to evoke the same feelings in the old man that Panaqua did.

"That dirty guinea bastard," Inspector Coole said of Johnny Stiletto.

"He's Yugoslavian," said Leland.

"That Slovakian bastard," he said, not losing a beat. "If he puts his foot, if he steps one foot in the door, I'll chop his arms off, I'll sever his spine."

But then came Sam's prom, and when Johnny showed up in a Cadillac Fleetwood (later reported to be stolen), he was dressed in a tuxedo, and even his grimy fingers were clean. Samantha wore flowing white chenille, strapless, so that her tiny rose tattoo on the wing of her left shoulder was exposed.

Pat, the kid brother, sat by, admiringly, both of his sister's chutzpah and her boyfriend's degree of rebelliousness and unrespectability, all qualities which Patrick aspired to.

Yet no one matched Oona for creating *agita* in her father's chest cavity. After Sky Moody graduated from high school and disappeared, Oona appeared another full-blown nightmare for her father. Smoking dope and drinking beer in the back of shopping centers out on Long Island, she discovered the Beatles and became a swooning, screechy girl, but nearly as quickly, dropping acid, undid these bonds, and so became the first member of the Coole tribe to join Krishna Consciousness, moving to the temple they owned on Henry Street in downtown Brooklyn, the old borough always reclaiming Moodys and Cooles as if they had never left, no matter that instead of a convent and the True Faith, Oona Coole returned to the land of happy dreams a devotee of a swami in India, a follower of Krishna, whose chant was heard in bus depots and airports, and right alongside the shaved heads of the chanting men stood Oona Coole, begging alms like Saint Clare herself, heaven help us.

Before too long, Oona became the wife of a high-up Krishna official, a demigod of American ancestry, and together, his wife impregnated, they traveled to India and the Ganges. The robe was pale orange and she had a yellow line running down her nose, and she wore a nose ring for all occasions just the way she used to wear a favorite scarf. Oh, how her father yelled—the exact response Oona wanted from him—when his sweet little Oona became a Krishna nun, and departed from his beloved Christianity.

All these accoutrements of the past had been banished to memory and even forgetfulness. Tonight the sisters dressed conservatively, wearing skirts and dresses and dress suits, stockings and high heels; very out of place in East New York, they looked like matrons from Park Avenue out doing charitable work in the old ghetto.

Patrick sat in the front row, staring at his dead father, but he heard his sister Sky in the back of the room, talking to relatives from Ozone Park and up by Yankee Stadium. She had her skirt yanked up and was showing them the scar.

"It was my birthday," she said, "the Fourth of July, and we were supposed to go to Coney Island with Aunt Augusta—you remember her, don'tcha?—and Paddy pushed me off the stoop and my kneecap broke on the curb, splattering over the concrete, and instead of Coney Island, I wound up in Saint Mary's hospital getting forty stitches."

If Brooklyn was not about facts, as brothers Leland and Mickey Mack liked to say, but about the imagination, then it did not mean that it should lack its truths. The truth was that Patrick had never pushed Samantha off the stoop; she fell, and he stood at the bottom of the stoop on the concrete, watching her fall, and instead of saying that they couldn't go to Coney Island that day, he got so scared that his heart dropped into his stomach, seeing all those guts from her knee hanging out on the stoop like that, and as he looked on helplessly at his older sister, he remembered the other neighborhood kids standing by, all of them black now, like Neville and Henry next door to Grandma Coole, and then Charleston from across the street, all of them watched, too, as her guts from the knee hung out and she screamed like a bloody banshee and let out a honk of pain like a broken bagpipe.

"I never said that," Patrick whispered in the front of the

parlor away from the clutch of sisters and the bevy of relatives. He shut his eyes and said, "I did not say it."

"He said, 'We can't go to Coney Island,' " Sam told the distant relatives in the back of the room.

"He's just like his father," the relative said bitterly. The man was one of those Ozone Park Irish, a man who had seen the specter of hell already, the skull showing through the mask of his face, his blue veins jutting out from his workingman's hands that shook with alcohol palsy: "He may look like a Moody, but he's a Coole all right, I can tell. And his father was just like his own father, a bloody bunch of savages, if you ask me, I don't understand for the life of me what Rose Moody saw in any of it. She should have married one of the Kennedys, the kind of family she came from."

Yet it was the nature of being a Coole that other Coole relatives said things like this; and it was the nature of being a Coole that Patrick had never laid eyes on this relative, and yet the man spoke as if he knew everything there was to know about Paddy Coole. Inspector Coole had a mixture of shame and governmental secrecy in everything he did—that deadly combination of Catholicism and intelligence work—making him the great repository of all familial secrets that he would, as Leland, his son, told Paddy and Terry years earlier—"He'll take all these secrets to the grave with him, so don't try to pry them out of him, because he's not going to open up like an old oyster. . . ."

The bitter relative, probably a cousin on the old man's mother's side who detested the Cooles, went on ranting to Samantha at the back of the parlor.

"The Cooles are an awful bunch!"

"I'm a Coole," Sam said.

"So am I," Eileen told him.

"And me, too," Elizabeth Ann said, now surrounding him.

"Don't get me wrong, girls," he said, "because I can see your mother—God bless her—in each of your faces, whereas a little shite like that Paddy Coole up there, I can only see the devil in a face like that. Why, look at him, he don't even look one whit Irish, he's like one of them Germans from the old beer-hall days on Bushwick Avenue, one of them Aryan Nation fellows, or he could be like the guy who sold me a used Volvo, this creature from the north country, those Scandinavians and what-have-you. That's the trouble with the Cooles. What are they? Who are they? And the truth is, I never liked one of them as far as I was concerned, and never trusted any of them beyond my own sight. But you girls, you're all Moodys, I can see it in your eyes. You're your mother's little helpers, Lord have mercy on ya."

"The fact is," Mary Grace said, "you're talking about my brother like that, ya veiny stump."

"What?"

"Paddy's my brother."

"Her favorite brother," Elizabeth Ann said, "and mine, too, he's a great painter."

"And mine, too, he's my favorite," Eileen tooted up. "So watch your step, fella."

"I don't have any hard feelings with your brother Paddy," the relative said, backing off from his previous stance.

"I heard you say these awful things about him," Mary Grace went on, chewing gum and letting it pop in the man's face.

Besides which, her near-husband Nicky Roma was Italian, and she didn't like what this potatohead from Ozone Park was saying about Italians earlier . . .

"He did say something bad about Italians, didn't he?" she asked.

"Probably," a sister said.

. . . and Mary Grace was joined by Samantha, who after all had converted to Judaism when she married Arnold Blitzer and her son little Dylan was confirmed, no, what did they call it, bar mitzvahed out in Jersey only just a couple of years ago.

"He say somethin bad about Jews?" Sky asked.

"Yeah, yeah," another sister said, not sure, but what the hell.

"I got nothin against Paddy boy," the relative repeated. "It's his father that always made me mad. I don't even know why I bothered to come by here tonight," and so he went outside and down the block and disappeared into the pitch of night.

When he was gone, the girls felt closer together just as Paddy, paranoid from having been picked on, felt further apart.

His relative's spleen toward the Cooles was something he never understood, something that always discombobulated him.

But then his sisters came around him and formed a circle of family, bringing him back, like a prodigal son, to the fold.

"I never liked that guy," Sam said.

"Who is he?" Oona asked. "I never saw him in my life."

"One of the old man's relatives."

"And who knows how he's related to those bogmen," Deirdre said.

"Who knows," Elizabeth Ann agreed.

3

Big families have a tendency to read each other's minds, or maybe because they each think so much alike, one progression blends into the other. At any rate, Paddy had been thinking of Charleston, the black kid who was the bully of Macdougal Street when his sister Samantha informed the other sisters that "It was his first great fight." He beat this bully, as was the case with so many of his early fights, by luck, his sister said.

"It wasn't luck," Patrick protested.

To see him now, a man, even aging already, though not prematurely but right on schedule, small of height, thick in his shoulders and arms, well-built and solid, it was hard to imagine that Paddy would have trouble fighting anyone, even that innocent, quiet boy who lived in fear of his older brothers.

"You couldn't fight your way out of a paper bag in those days, bro."

"I wasn't as tough as Leland or Emmett," he said, "but I could handle myself okay."

"He was lucky," Sam went on, "believe me, I was there, I should know, I'm his sister." She returned to her narrative: "When Charleston slipped on mango peels in the schoolyard, Paddy was able to get him into a headlock and then bash his face into the fence, and next thing Pat knew, the fight was over, the bully was crying. Next day he became Pat's best friend, and was outside on the stoop every morning waiting for us to come out."

"What were you two doin there?" Mary Grace asked.

"There were too many of us," Paddy said, by way of explanation. "Every summer and every winter vacation, the older kids got shipped out. Leland and Emmett and Mickey Mack went to Flatbush and Uncle Mackey's house. Sam and I, though sometimes Sam and Mickey, or even me and Mickey Mack, were sent to East New York."

"Not just holidays," Sam said, "but any time there was a crisis in the house, Mom sick, the old man freaked out, finances bad, whatever, we got shipped to Grandma Coole's."

"This place seems horrible," Eileen said, getting chills at the thought of spending any time there.

"It was bad," Patrick agreed.

"It was okay," his sister corrected him.

"Not so good," said Paddy.

"Better than that," his sister answered back.

Though Samantha/Sky now lived in her planned community of Coral Slip in the town of Ocean Sights, Florida, East New York was still her place. Even when she crossed the bridges over the East River, when she still lived in the city and worked as an organizational planner, starting her own agency called Friday, and into neighborhoods for which she had no memory, Brooklyn Heights, say, after walking over the Brooklyn Bridge, she knew she was home again, back in Brooklyn, and a combination of thrill and chill, fear and tear, woe and begone, clutched at her consciousness, forcing her to acknowledge this place, even when she didn't want to recognize it at all.

Samantha's two realest, bestest childhood friends were the boys who lived next door to Grandma Coole, Neville and Henry. It was years ago—not just years ago, it was a lifetime away when the Coole children were poor and dirty little kids living at their grandmother's house in East New York, that dirtiest part of Brooklyn. Nowadays Samantha/Sky owned a one-bedroom condo in Coral Slip, a place that, like East New York, had seen better days and now was a laundering depot for Medellin drug money before it went down the road to Miami and out of the country, down to Panama, and back to Colombia. She was little curly haired Sam, daughter of Jackie Ducks and Rose Moody, granddaughter to Mrs. Coole of Macdougal Street, sister of the Coole horde, the oldest girl, a devilish little thing with dimples and eyes that sparkled like Shirley Temple's, her uncles said, though why she always wanted to play with those black boys next door, her aunts and Grandma Coole never understood. Sam called them Nevo and Henley, these Jamaican boys whose father was a minister in a storefront on Atlantic Avenue. But to Sam and Mickey Mack, their Jamaican speech was like poetry, so lilting, especially when Sam heard it over the backyard picket fence that divided their yard and her grandmother's because then their speech mixed with the gutsy profanity of her aunts talking that bad Brooklynese they had, full of fuck you this and that, bullshit and cocksuckers and cunts, just the foulest speech Sam or any of the kids ever heard, and it became downright symphonic after Grandma Coole had a few quarts of Piels or Rheingold in her empty stomach, and this one-legged creature stumbled around the apartment, her County

Mayo speech fouling up the airwaves, foockn this and foockn that, and foock the banana man for his high prices and foock the watermelon man, may he die of heart spasms.

Foock everyone for that matter, Grandma Coole said.

Technically, Grandma Coole wasn't even the Coole's relation, not Sam's grandmother even. She was the old man's stepmother. But Sam and Mickey Mack especially got along with her like bloods whenever they stayed at her apartment on Macdougal Street. The old man had several stories about his real mother. He used to say that she died when their apartment on the Upper West Side of Manhattan burned to the ground on Christmas Eve. Later he said she died in her thirties from stomach cancer, and out in Brooklyn, just a few blocks from here. Sam suspected that Grandpa Coole, who was long gone boozing himself to death before she was born, had killed her: either outright killed her, with a gun or knife or his bare hands in a fit of drunken, reeling fury, or wore her out with his behavior. The first Mrs. Coole—the old man's real mother—was said to be cultured, a hedgerow teacher from west-coast County Mayo, so how was she to tolerate Jems Coole and East New York? One of them maybe, but not this neighborhood and that man. That was impossible. So she died, Sam figured.

Nothing was ever said about the old man's father to the Coole children, and he didn't have too many words for this woman the kids called Grandma Coole, either. A little cocaine would be nice right now, she thought, relieve the tension in her neck, uncork the feelings that had become balled up in her chest. She closed her eyes, erasing the funeral parlor, and first thought of her home in Coral Slip, the palms and greeny blue surf, but then found the image she really wanted, that of the woman she called her grandmother, old lady Coole, not her father's mother, but his stepmother, that crazy one-legged fury whom she loved, cherished, and suddenly missed for the first time, just as she missed Aunt Augusta, a good, generous, fallen woman. Then

Grandma Coole took hold in her mind.

Imagine mackerel stink and poteen, potatoes and the salmon-gorged rivers as Grandma Coole's girlhood. But as a grown woman, she never got beyond this apartment in Brooklyn. She called little Jackie's curly-headed girl Katy, Samantha didn't know why, and hobbled about the flat on her one good leg, the other amputated from gangrene. This one-legged old gal drank her beer by the quart, and after a few in the morning, her head out the window to the produce man in his horse-drawn cart, she shouted, "Ye gobshite foockn bastard banana boat refugee, if I had two legs I'd bash your face good, Guido, ye snipe, ye shite, ye evil foocker, I'll collar ye yet, and break your bones, I'll mash you into peet, and rip off your eyeballs to boot and cook 'em like taters," and then taking a breath, she said, "Now give me me produce before I git angry," and the banana man was so intimidated by her that he gave her what she asked for and more, and all of it at discount, maybe even half the price, and he undercharged her every day of her life in Brooklyn for the fear inside of him about the old one-legged gal with her tits like watermelons leaning out the first-story window.

Even though Sam loved Grandma Coole for her foul tongue and her wicked humor, she liked the two black boys next door for reasons that were quite contrary to why she loved her grandmother. Neville and Henry would never speak like that; they were gentlemen, future ministers themselves no doubt, the pride of their clan, A students at the local public school, where they wore starched white shirts, winter or summer, and black pants, and shiny clean black shoes, and always unadorned bow ties. Seeing the movie about Malcolm X's life reminded Sam/Sky of those two boys from Macdougal Street because the Black Muslims also wore starched white shirts and bow ties. But Neville and Henry were no fruits of Islam; they were apples of Christianity. If Samantha thought about them next door to Grandma Coole's, she saw it was her grandmother's sense of humor and generosity, her crazy attitude and how tender she was to herself and Mickey Mack, her two favorites, but what Sam admired about Grandma Coole's neighbors was their righteousness, almost like those biblical prophets of Pitkin Avenue (and as energetic as the Old Testament men making their pushcart profits), for unlike the Catholics who knew the New Testament and only snippets and phrases from the Old Testament (an eye for an eye, etc.), the boys were versed in both ends of the Bible, their father being a man of the cloth, God-fearing and full of a sense of the evil that lurked, not so much in the world, as it did in East New York, right here on Macdougal Street, between Rockaway and Stone, white evil, black evil, Italian and Jewish evil, Irish evil, even Jamaican evil (the spliff smokers even back then, the gamblers and whore-meisters, the numbers runners and bag ladies, the cheaters and procrastinators, the judgers and the unjudging, the people without an ounce of judgment or justice or righteous glory). Hallelujah!

Still, Neville and Henry were only background noise now. They weren't large enough to replace that hobbling one-legged creature next door.

Other blacks in the neighborhood were the wretched of the earth, the Cooles being East New York's salt. In that respect, these boys didn't belong here, were in fact too cultured to be part of the atmosphere of Macdougal Street. Everything about these boys had to do with heaven above and hell below; East New York and Brooklyn were merely stopping places on the road to these edge-of-life resorts. The Cooles were another story. This was their home. East New York was where they did belong. Let those boys—nothing like Reverend Al or Reverend Ike—let these pontifical, ecclesiastical, and sacral boys, squeaky clean and vivacious disappear out of Samantha/Sky's recollections because they were intruders now, no longer friends, not even fond memories if they crowded out Sam's remembrance of Grandma Coole.

Yet every night, in front of her grandmother's mirror in the dining room, Sky Moody née Samantha Coole tried to speak like those two young gentlemen with what she thought was their British accents, but she was a hopeless failure. She'd never be able to quote chapter and verse from the Bible as they did, enunciating every word, their pearly smiles and their clear-as-heavenly-pool eyes and their blue-black skin. She was a little foul-mouthed white girl from next door. She would never speak like either those boys or her grandmother, one of them speaking English more perfectly than the English and the other speaking English as if it were a bloody curse. It reminded Sam that she was the only one in the clan not to speak with a Brooklyn accent.

But her accent was indeed from Kings County, i.e., Brooklyn, as thick as mushroom-barley soup at a deli underneath the el at Brighton Beach and as identifiable as if she had a tattoo on her forehead that said, Hey, I'm from Brooklyn.

Then she thought of Grandma Coole again.

Grandma did not have a Brooklyn accent either.

She had a brogue, and maybe the brogue was as cool as those boys next door with their Jamaican accents. Sam, though, would have preferred an old Louisiana accent—why, she didn't know, but she liked how it almost sounded like Brooklyn but wasn't—the *earl* in the car engine, the peeled, *burled* potatoes from the hot water. Only in Brooklyn could something ending in *-ing* come out *-een* as it did with the ubiquitous Spaldeen high bouncer, the only ball you played with in the playground, not only because it was cheap, but because it had the best bounce, ya know.

When she would speak to her grandmother about this, because sometimes Samantha came running in the door crying when the Jews in their pushcarts or the Italian banana man in his horse-drawn cart told her that she was either Jewish or Italian, and that those crazy Cooles had stolen her out of a baby carriage, because in the summer Samantha got good and dark like a Gypsy, like Ladinos in Brownsville or the Eyetalian bocci players on Eastern Parkway; she got dark, even sometimes like the Cubans and the Puerto Ricans, so that everyone liked Samantha in this neighborhood, and yet she still cried when one of them teased her about not being Irish but Jewish or Italian or Puerto Rican.

"You'll make your own music, Katy," Grandma Coole said, whatever the hell that meant, and she patted her granddaughter's head and told her to play in the backyard with Neville and Henry, and forget about playing outside with the bullies, the riffraff, and the teasers.

Until Grandma Coole called her Katy, no one had ever called her anything but her real name. They called her Samantha or Sam, but never Kate or Katy Coole. But that one summer after Grandma Coole called her Katy, that is what she became, to Charleston in the playground, to Neville and Henry next door.

The sewers smell like they are backing up. The buildings smell of garbage and mildew, dampness and sweat, even in the dead of winter. Hallways are filled with the hieroglyphics of graffiti artists, the artless kind who write only their names and streets—their tags, as they call them—up and down the hallways and vestibules, and on the sides of buildings. The streets are no longer cobbled. This is a neighborhood defined by wars. Some of the earliest streets toward Brownsville have Revolutionary War names. Then in the immediate neighborhood it is filled with Civil War names. The latest additions do not come from the Great War or World War II; Korea and Vietnam are noticeably absent, their histories not East New York's. Instead, the last war was that crazy war that somebody or another invented called the War on Poverty. The War on Drugs. The War on Disadvantage. The War on Despair. Which always translated: the war against the poor. Always for their own good. Drive them out of everywhere else, then drive them crazy in their own honeycomb of wretchedness. Mind you, Sam's not bitter, she kind of liked the new names for the old places, Stone Avenue no longer Stone Avenue, but Mother Gaston Boulevard. Too bad they hadn't changed Macdougal Street to Grandma Coole Alley. Even the homeboys could get behind that name.

Samantha/Sky got out of here, had her suburban education, even married well and got the hell out of the city entirely, moved out west, got divorced, moved back east, lived in the country, in other cities, and now lived all right—comfortably, okay—in Florida. The Cooles have nothing to do with any of this anymore. They are survivors of East New York, but not East New Yorkers anymore—in a technical sense. Only the slightest kernel of this ghetto remains lodged under her skin, and though not cancerous, it is a malignancy, and aches inside. It's all about attitude, and Sam still had ghetto attitude, that ability to go from tranquillity, not into anger, but full-blown rage, in a heart-beat. Sam could tell you that she transcended this place, and it is only her father's bad sense of humor, his sense of absurdity and his old idea of practical jokes that brings her back. That and family obligations. That and a recognition that once they be-longed here like anyone else; once they belonged here, and now they almost still did.

Even Sky Moody.

This is the territory of the losing side. Poverty won big. So did ignorance and self-loathing, crime and rage. So did human deg-radation. So did drugs. Despair. Unreasonableness. Illiteracy. Lack of education. Lack of opportunity. So did big shots off in Manhattan, guys and gals like me, only with bank accounts, careers, and prestige. People whose fathers did not have to play practical jokes on them at the terminal moment, so that they could go off, laughing drunkenly into eternity.

The old buildings are still around, making it seem not that long ago that she lived here. But the new buildings assure her that she is now an outsider, not just an unwanted white girl, but a kind of cultural trespasser, a woman with enough sense to flee this place—so why did she come back? Why did she return? She used to be the darling of the Jews and Italians and later the Puerto Ricans and Cubans, but the black faces that see her here think she's some kind of nasty married-to-the-mob gun moll coming to collect her blood money from the drug trade or looking for her Carlo or Gino or Tony who's playing around with another woman, and when I get my hands on her. . . .

Blame her father.

Blame his dying and death. Blame his last will and testament. He wanted it this way.

Because she never honored a thing her father requested, Sam/Sky thought that she ought at least to bury him back in the old neighborhood, if that was his last request. Let his body decompose in peace in the shadow of Cypress Hills. But, sitting in the funeral parlor with her family now, she thought that maybe her father didn't really want to be waked and buried in East New York but Florida. Yet because they never honored their father, maybe he figured he would get his request by asking to be buried in East New York, when he really wanted to be buried in Florida along with his wife, their mother. But it was too late to act upon this perception because now he would be interred in Brooklyn.

Aunt Eileen's husband's Jorge Panaqua had OD'd on heroin, not in East New York, but heading toward "the city," westward on Broadway to Williamsburg and a river view. Their daughter Consuela drowned playing near the East River. Then Jorge escalated his drug and alcohol intake and finally overdosed, and died. A social worker assigned to their case first took Eileen and Nora (Quif and Quim, the kids called them) to Bellevue for psychiatric evaluation—Kings County being oversubscribed that week—and talked them into getting the inheritance from

Jorge's death, and moving them to California. Once they got to
Ojai, the social worker absconded with their money, leaving the
twin sisters to vegetate on their own. Helpless and desperate—
Nora had survived a fire in the basement of their house on Macdougal Street that left most of her body ravaged by burns—the
ladies were taken up by the welfare state and wound up in a
nursing home at the ripe old age of thirty-eight, and lived out
there in Ojai, with intermittent jaunts to break out and get laid
and drunk or laid or drunk, depending if you were talking
about Eileen (laid and drunk) or Nora (drunk but not laid), until
Eileen died a few years ago of lung cancer, leaving Nora the soul
survivor of her generation of Cooles, bless her carrot-headed
heart; her bonny bonny bony arse.

Not a bad deal, Sammy thought.

"He looks terrible," one of his distant relatives said, looking
down upon him in his casket.

Her name was Maeve Pugh, and her boozy red nose was lit
up like a candle.

"He's dead," Sam reminded her. "What the hell do you expect? Wait until they put you in one of those boxes, Maeve, you
won't look so sweet yourself."

"Aren't we the uppity ones tonight," the cousin said, un-
steady on her feet.

"He's my father," Sam continued. "That's who you're talking
about, my father, so watch what you say, or if you can't do that,
watch how you say it in front of me, okay."

"That whole family of yours had airs," Maeve shot back. "The
way you left this place and moved out to the Island. I told my
cousin, Jackie, I said, don't marry that highfalutin Rose Moody,
her family is a bunch of lace-curtain bastards if there ever was
ones."

"Just fuck off," Sam said.

"The same to you, sissy," Maeve said, then drifted into the

shadows at the back of the room. As she was leaving, Maeve kept saying, "So he is, so he is," and within seconds had departed out the door with a phalange of other distant relatives.

"It's the best I ever saw old Jackie," his cousin Siobhan said. "Poor old sot."

"A beautiful coffin," his cousin Christy from Ozone Park said, reeking of booze and cabbage.

Christy and his father Leo once had a cow farm in Ozone Park, the last of its kind in Brooklyn, or really at the Brooklyn–Queens border, and his shoes were muddy and he smelled of cow flops. Now he only smelled of liquor, but also with a touch of old Brooklyn, and now old age. He lived nowadays, he said, in Inwood, the last Irish neighborhood in Manhattan, though, he said, "Even Inwood is becoming full of something else indeed."

"God," Christy said, "they're worse than the Irish, if that's possible."

He talked about the new immigrants, the Hispanics, and up in his place, the Dominicans, all of them Catholic like himself, and like the Irish, big believers in having lots of children.

"We procreated like rabbits. They're more like single-cell organisms, one of them in front of you one day, two the next, four the third day, eight the fourth, and by the end of the week there are sixty-four of them."

Besides being the son of an Ozone Park farmer, he was also a retired high-school math teacher.

He reiterated his remark about the coffin, making it into a refrain. "What a beautiful coffin."

Toward the rear of the room Patrick noticed some of the younger cousins and children of the old man's friends either from East New York or Hell's Kitchen—Patrick noticed them drinking from a bottle of cheap Irish whiskey, and even a few of the younger ones among them snorting coke by the back windows. Sam once again went to the rear of the room, either to scold them and tell them to put the drugs away, or maybe to partake of it with them, and she was joined by Oona and Deirdre, while the other sisters were already ensconced back there, and the gaggle of relatives and friends, and together they gathered around, either to get rid of the drugs or partake of them, again, Patrick was not sure, and so he sat again, staring at the coffin, but not really looking at his father. He'd seen enough of him already and would have to deal with him again for the rest of the night; better not to be looking at him every moment he stood or sat in this funeral parlor.

4

Seeing the sisters reminded Lizzie of all the women who peopled her life, not in Brooklyn, which was just some kind of ancestral land, but out on the Island mostly; and even though it was a household of men—more brothers than you could shake a stick at—it was not the brothers Lizzie thought of when, in her Philadelphia convent, she thought of home. It was the sisters, the mother, the grandmothers, not the brothers, not the father, not the grandfathers. To be a Coole was to be part of that great gynecocracy that was at the center of this male-engendered madness. Both her parents were drunks, Lizzie thought, but her father was a mean one and her mother was a dreamy one. After all, it was Grandma Moody, on her last legs in Flatbush, who pulled the young Lizzie aside and said that the young girl had a calling, she must go into the convent, and Lizzie obliged her, anything to get away from home. She packed up and left.

Being a nun wasn't all that bad either; she got a free education, earned a master's in psychology, and might even get to do a Ph.D. Most of the time she wasn't even near a convent, teaching at colleges and working in hospitals, living with two other nuns in an apartment in Philadelphia. One of the other nuns had a regular boyfriend, a Jesuit priest, and they talked about leaving their orders. The other nun was indifferent to anyone else's activities as long as she had time for her own pursuits, which included a love of music and painting. Lizzie had broken her vows, too, once with a fellow student—an older man going back to school—and once with another nun. Oh, if her mother only knew; if her grandmothers; even if her sisters only knew.

If Grandma Coole was the essence of Brooklyn's funkorama and shantiness, Grandma Moody was the essence of lace-curtainness. The daughter of an affluent, well-educated mick newspaperman and lawyer and a continental (French!) mother, she was born in Brooklyn, but raised in boarding schools in Connecticut, and married well into the family of William Moody, of Albany and Brooklyn, raising her eleven children on Madison Street in a twenty-six-room house.

Lizzie's first memory of Grandma Moody: she was gray-haired and always wore black, she had a pillbox hat, which she stuffed on the top of her head, and in winter she wore a long black wool coat that reached almost to her swollen ankles, and always she wore black shoes (sensible ones) with a small heel. She was four feet eight and had the largest bosom of any woman Lizzie had ever seen, then or now, and a swelling to her joints everywhere. Her hands were like a porcelain doll's. She did not curse, she prayed. She prayed for all of them, living and dead, and she scolded the children when they misbehaved. Her smell was 47-11 (from Europe), her eyes dark, her skin pale white, her lips handsome and her nose hawkish. Her hair was tied into a bun, which she let down to comb at the beginning and end of each day, and when it unraveled, her hair reached to the floor. She told Lizzie once that it had never been cut in her life, and after combing it out and putting it back into a bun, they went out to church—not up the block to Our Lady of Lourdes, but to Saint Aidan's out on Long Island in the little community of Wilson Park at the city limits. Lizzie could never imagine Grandma Moody in East New York, though technically she once had her household and family in Bed-Stuy. Still, she saw her only in Wilson Park, or in Rock-ville Center at another aunt's house, or back in Brooklyn at an uncle's house in Flatbush, where she finally died.

Every morning in Wilson Park, Grandma Moody went out the door, Lizzie remembered, and she stood next to the old, vital woman, offering her support because the old one was slightly crippled by arthritis, though she remained an active, even vigorous woman until she died. They went, grandmother and her granddaughter, to the seven o'clock mass, the one Monsignor Lowe said, first thing every morning. After church, Grandma told Lizzie that she had a calling, a calling, she said, and Lizzie should become a Maryknoll missionary or at least a Franciscan like Saint Clare, but Elizabeth Ann interrupted her by saying that it was a school day and she had to get home for breakfast or she would be late. In the late afternoon Grandma Moody and her daughter Rosy tooted on the red wine, and Grandma Moody said, "We live so long in my family because we have a glass of wine every day and take an aspirin." When she died, she was ninety-eight. Broken hip. Flatbush. At her funeral, Lizzie saw her bone white face, still wrinkleless—"the Noxzema," she once told her granddaughter—and the nun who had accompanied Lizzie from Philadelphia asked how could an old woman like her have no wrinkles?

"Noxzema."

"What?"

"A family secret."

"It's strange."

By contrast, Grandma Coole came to America without a pot to piss in, married poorly, and lived in Brooklyn, out here, right down the block on Halsey, with her husband, a sickly man, and her daughter Augusta. Her husband was Teddy Morgan, a stevedore, whose lung collapsed after being stabbed in a bar brawl, and he died. After Grandpa Coole's wife died, he and old lady Morgan got married and moved to the old house on Mac- dougal, which she never left again until she died, raising Lizzie's father and two more daughters, and became the woman that all the Coole children called their paternal grandmother.

Grandma Coole: Came to America without a pot to piss in; left this world, not of America, but Brooklyn, with not only a pot, Lizzie thought, but a bathroom, and a four-room railroad flat which they owned from Grandpa Coole's insurance money when he died—what a difficult man he was!—from his swollen liver.

Not that Lizzie had ever been there, or if she had, she didn't remember it. She knew this because everyone in the family—her parents and older siblings—talked about it constantly, and she had formed an impression in her mind about it. Oddly, when she finally got to East New York, it was not so much that it looked unreal as it resembled the East New York of her dreams about Grandma Coole, and in that sense, it was not foreign.

But it wasn't just Grandma Coole and Grandma Moody Lizzie thought of; being here also reminded her of her aunts, Augusta, Nora, and her sister's namesake Eileen (the sister closest to her in age and temperament), the last two the redheads of the family the same way that Lizzie and Eileen were. And she also thought of her mother's sisters: Vanessa, Virginia, Hattie, Genevieve, Samantha, Gertrude, and Pamela, real ladies of Brooklyn with their Victorian names in the early twentieth century, and hardly the pure products of East New York. The maternal side was a whole different ball of wax. They lived in Richmond Hill, over across the cemeteries, the reservoir, and the parks. Or they lived in Flatbush. Or out on the Island in Nassau, others in the boon- docks of Suffolk County, complaining of their tainted well water and raccoons with rabies and neighbors with BB guns and psycho dreams. Lizzie preferred the redheaded Coole aunts, who were more her speed, closer to the real madness that stirred in her family's blood.

The Moodys were more grandiose, with their lineage going back to the founding of Brooklyn, with relatives on the *Brooklyn Eagle,* or her mother's great-grandfather, a contractor, building Prospect Park and Eastern Parkway, Oliver McGillicutty by name. The Coole family, by contrast, was considered crazy, even by East New York standards, or so Samantha had told her. The Irish called them the crazy people; the blacks and Spanish called them the crazy Irish. Whatever the different ethnic strains of the place, these pockets of humanity always referred to them as crazy. Even in grade school the other kids called her Crazy Lizzie, and in high school, with her demented, pretty look, they called her Lizzie Borden, the ax maiden. Crazy Rosy, Crazy Jackie Ducks, Crazy Leland. And they never disappointed anyone who labeled them that way, Lizzie thought. We *were* crazy, completely insane and berserk, fueled by alcohol and religion, and later drugs.

I am not imagining this madness, Lizzie thought, for all she had to do was look to the front of the room and see her dead father. Even in repose, he had this mischievous cast to his mouth, a kind of smirk, both playful and wild and, yes, crazy. It was almost as if at any moment he would arise and go out and take himself a good stiff drink of beer, burp, and then get angry at them. What the hell are you looking at, Crazy Liz? he might ask, for even her father called her that. But the one good thing about East New York was that she didn't have to feel out of place and uncomfortable about herself; she might have to feel out of place and uncomfortable about the environment itself, but she didn't hold it against her own character. The Cooles belonged here, even if a few dissident voices wanted them to finish up their funeral and get the hell out of town, back to the city or out to the Island or across the bridge into Staten Island. This was, after all, not quite home for her, but maybe the ancestral home. And Lizzie was a Coole; and if you were a Coole, this was really the only place that was home to the

Cooles, Lizzie thought, even though she had no actual memory of ever having been "home" to East New York. This was still home to them.

Some bowed to Mecca several times a day; others made pilgrimages to Jerusalem, climbing to the Mount of Olives. Others read the cobblestones on Eastern Parkway, seeing an oracle there. The Cooles turned west from their vantage in Nassau County or north from their digs in Florida, shouting Hosannah in the direction of East New York, or if not Hosannah, Praise the Lord, they shouted epithets, they cursed and fumed, grew resentful, and barked in the direction of East New York, goddamned shithole that it was, she thought, hellhole of their youth, wellspring of their hearts, worm in their apples, scourge upon their cattle.

Although none of them spoke often with each other now, they were all oddly aligned in agreement about their feelings and thoughts at that moment. In another vein Patrick thought about home, too, and instead of the violent men with their psychotic dreams, he also thought of mothering dreams, if not of relations, then women hanging over back fences in East New York with names like Consuela and Maria, Angela and Ann-Marie, Ruth and Flo and Mona and Ellen and Ella and Stella. They weren't the smiling, clean-faced Irish girls that Paddy was related to, but busty creatures with real complexions, in paper-thin cotton housedresses, leaning, leaning over back fences, their Jewish, Italian, black and Puerto Rican·breasts full of milk and love, full of little veins and networks, nearly all of their breasts bared when they bent over the back fences.

When Patrick thought of drawing and painting naked women, that is what he saw; he saw dark nipples, nipples that invited—even at that early age when he saw them—nipples that seemed to say, Suck me good, oh Paddy boy! With these breasts he nearly always saw trees, not in spring flower, but summery bloom, weighted down with fruit (apples, pears, plums, even peaches or cherries), or if not fruit trees, then grape arbors, the vines interlaced— like the strings on their black toreador pants —with the latticework, and each of these fruits glistening (the only time I ever really saw that word, he thought) and gleaming, sweating with humidity and heat, and bursting with an aroma that promised to go sour in a day or two.

This is what Patrick really thought about when he thought about Brooklyn, even as a child, living here. Brooklyn was the only place on earth where he didn't dream about escaping when he was there; the present, though poor and abusive and funked up with rottenness, was not anything he wished to escape from, but rather wanted to embrace. Of course, this was not a transcendent dream of embracing the tenements and sewers, the bocci and handball and stickball courts, but only those olive-skinned women whose forebears came from Jerusalem, Abruzzi, San Juan, and the belles of the cotton fields of sun-steamy Alabama, and especially those breasts hanging over back fences, their voices full of Brooklyn, "I'll break your fuckn neck, Ant-a-nee!!!"

Once, sitting in their backyard on Marion Street, Patrick looked over the fences to the tenements on Sumpter Street, and, in the heat of summer, one of these Maries showered at an open window. As she dried herself in her tub, staring out the window, humming "Tennessee Waltz," she saw him, this tiny boy, a toddler, and rather than cover her vagina, so dark and mysteriously beautiful to his baby eyes, she held it up to the window and jerked her crotch in his direction, and when he turned confused in the face, she let out the heartiest laugh he ever heard, and blew him a kiss, went on toweling off, whistling her song. Wasn't this a better memory than the knifings, the shootings, the brutalizations, the miseries?

Patrick could as easily return to his aunts, and recall how Aunt Nora never left the house on Macdougal Street, not from the time she was burnt in the basement fire, which was years later, but after high school, even though she had never been robbed or raped or hassled by anyone. She just decided enough was enough, that it wasn't safe out there and was going to stay indoors with her mother. Let Augusta and Eileen work in their dress shop and sweater factory; Nora would sweep the floor—not cook—but stoke the coal fires in the basement, wash the dishes and make the beds, and anything she needed to know about the outside, she'd find out later in the day when one of her sisters brought home the *Daily News,* whose pages were proof enough that Nora had made a wise decision.

Nora made Patrick sleep in her bed, fondling him to sleep, while Emmett would tease him about it when they left there to go home to the Island.

Better to think about Marie over the fence, in the bathroom window, her dark bush, her brown dugs, her big dark nipples, singing "Tennessee Waltz."

5

Mary Grace sat in her chair, drinking champagne, not sipping it but slugging it down as you would a beer, while her sisters prayed upon their beads for deliverance of their father. When they rolled the last crystal bead in their tapered fingers, Oona asked Patrick to make some kind of eulogy. He told her there had been quite enough of that kind of stuff already; there was no need for him to add to the babble, explaining to her about the tales of King Cormorant, the Moodys versus the Cooles, and so on, that he would just as soon sit in respectful silence for the remainder of his tenure in this twilit parlor.

"We're really descended from Francisco de Cuellar, that lone survivor of the Spanish Armada when it wrecked off the coast of Ireland in 1858," Sam said.

"Fifteen-eighty-eight," Mary Grace said.

"What?"

"The date of the Armada," Oona told her.

"What about it?"

"It wasn't 1858, but 1588," Eileen said.

"What's she talking about?"

"Forget it," said Deirdre.

The girls waited for Patrick to make some kind of parting shot about their father. So he brooded and thought, and tried to come up with something cogent, pithy, and maybe even wise; he tried to stanch his bitterness, and even his rage, for this family, particularly, but also this borough, and especially this neighborhood. Pat realized that he felt the same way about his family as he felt about East New York. Sometimes he was proud, but mostly he stewed in more negative emotions. The only pride he really had was that he had survived. This pride and anger were mixed in a salsa of fugitive memories, some true, or at least factual, others part of the family legends, not really facts, but resonating with truths about the Coole family like no hard fact ever could.

"If I associate the red wagon with my Aunt Augusta and Aunt Eileen," he told his sister, "prowling the bars on Broadway as they pulled us in it when we were tykes, I associate a pink racing bike with my father and my brother Leland, Jackie Wackie."

These words would not mean anything to anyone not a Coole, yet to the assembly, it was like uttering a truth before mere meaning; this was a kind of Song of Songs. The red wagon and the pink racing bike were not simply objects from their past; they were icons of memory, emotional tablets in the family's history by which to mark time. If you said Aunt Augusta, you might see her before you, but then again you might see instead that beautiful red wooden and metal wagon she bought for Paddy's birthday. If you said Leland, Senior or Junior, you might see the old man or an oldest brother, but then you might also see the pink racing bike.

Even a younger sister like Mary Grace knew what Patrick was talking about, even if she hadn't been born when the incidents referred to had occurred. She had heard everyone in her family talk about them so often that the red wagon and the pink racing bike were a part of her own experience too. Mary Grace wanted to set that bicycle in a time in the late fifties or early sixties, when their attachments to East New York were coming to an end. Grandma Coole would die; Aunt August would die a year later. Then Eileen and Nora would disappear into the welfare system, winding up in California. Her father would eventually retire from Long Island and move to Florida with the rest of his cadre of civil service friends, those without strokes and heart attacks, to succumb to the heat and sunlight in other ways, like skin cancer. But I am losing myself already, thought Mary Grace, looking around the funeral parlor at her siblings, and then to the front of the room at her inanimate father, his waxy complexion glistening from the light bulb in the ceiling over his head.

The pink racing bike, Mary Grace thought, I want to place it in the yard, not here in the city, but just beyond the city line where our striving after respectability—finally an impossible notion—had taken us. There was a party in the backyard between the dilapidated yellow stucco house with hollyhock out front and lilac out here—and the rundown garage that had been struck by lightning during a hurricane in the early fifties, and never repaired. All of this before she was born. Leland Jack was going in the army. The Brooklyn aunts were present, as were a couple of the Moody clan, her mother's sister Hattie from Flatbush and her husband Buzz Mackey, as well as relatives—again Moodys—from Ridgewood and even Long Island, for Leland was popular in high school, among his friends and his family. A Buddy Holly record played over and over, Jackie Wackie dancing with his cousins and his girlfriend, with his sisters, his mother, and his aunts. The party was for Jackie, but he was also *the life of the party.* Nobody was on anything like a wagon, and the pink racing bike leaned against the broken-down garage siding. Mary Grace realized that it had never been in anything but disrepair, but she had heard about, too, how it had come to that state of disuse. Like so many things in the family, once it broke, it was not fixed or discarded, but took up space, became a kind of homage to the family's inability to do anything right.

Aunt Eileen and Aunt Augusta sat in metal lounge chairs, also pink, but rusted, smiling idiotically at their suburban and ex-urban and bumpkin relatives. Jorge Panaqua suddenly took off Buddy Holly and put on a Cuban rumba album, sweeping my mother around the yard, Eileen remembered. It was only one of a handful of memories that she had about her namesake, the crazy redhead who had married this wild Cuban man.

"La Rosita," he called Rosy, Mother Rose, licking his lips and making lascivious noises.

"Knock it off, buddy," Inspector Coole warned him, but when their father was not in an alcoholic rage, they forgot what an ineffectual man he could become.

Jorge ignored their father, and so their father was silenced and cowed by him. Finally the old man had had enough of them all and stormed out, ostensibly to do more shopping for the outdoor barbecue.

Once a paper cup became soggy from the Irish whiskey, one of the redheaded Coole aunts drained it and got another cup and another fill-up of whiskey.

At the moment, the old man was supposed to be a few blocks away shopping for more burger buns and frank rolls, mustard and paper plates, and more charcoals for the grill. Instead, Eileen knew he sat in Fife & Drum saloon, knocking back shots and beers with his cronies, the retired jockeys, ex-caddies from the golf course, and disabled vets. He was dead drunk already.

"He was dead?" Oona asked.

"He is dead," corrected Sam.

"Dead?" Deirdre asked.

"Dead," Sam said.

"Dead *drunk*," Eileen said. "Not dead. Dead drunk."

"Oh," went Oona.

Though La Rosita would become as much a lush as anyone in the family in later years, in those halcyon days she was as dry as a Mormon, though the old man kept getting drunker and drunker as he drank shots and beers and nervously watched Jorge Panaqua produce a conga drum from the back of his souped-up Ford convertible, and now even the neighbors looked out their windows as he whacked the skin and sang "Babalu" or whatever it was, out-Desi-ing Desi. Both of these Cubans with redheaded comediennes, too: Desi with Lucy and Jorge with Aunt Eileen. Yeah, Eileen realized, almost as if it were a revelation, and the old man and Mom were like Fred and Ethel Mertz, wow!

Finally Eileen couldn't take the tension between her father and Jorge, and so she went inside the house, where Uncle Jack Moody watched a ball game and talked aloud about Corvettes and Thunderbirds, and what the essential difference was between a Ford sports car and one from Chevrolet.

Uncle Jack was the first person, either on the Moody or the Coole side, to join Alcoholics Anonymous, though he was not yet in the program. This was a dry run. He was not drinking; he white-knuckled it, boring in on the television and the baseball game, trying to avoid the sounds emanating from the backyard, those drunken laughs and shouts, the pawing and hoots.

"If you ask me, Eileen," he said, "I think the Edsel is the car of the future."

Jack Moody appreciated his nieces because he was the father of twelve children, only the first one a girl. Plus the family he grew up in was mostly women, too, and his own sisters had indulged him all his life, putting up with his binges and breakups and bust-em-up behavior. He liked to say that his own mother was a saint, but that his father—a man universally adored, even after he lost everything and sank into a self-induced senility—was a mean-spirited man who never understood Jack Moody. His sister Rose Moody had told her own children that Grandpa Moody, though a wonderful man, had been mean to her brother Jack from that time during the Depression when Jack dropped a bottle of bootleg gin on the stoop outside their tenement—the Moodys evicted from their mansion two years earlier—and the bottle broke over the sidewalk, and Grandpa Moody, never a man to hit his own children, hit Uncle Jack so hard that his sister Rose said, "Jack went flying across the street into Staten Island. . . ."

Uncle Jack handed his niece Eileen a stack of postcards with a photograph of the Edsel on it, as well as a stack of addresses and a pile of stamps. For a penny a card Eileen—or for that matter, any of the other children too—would label the postcards, stamp them, and mail them off. If she did five hundred or a thousand in an afternoon, Uncle Jack Moody, a used-car salesman recently upgraded to a new-car salesman, paid her five or ten dollars, which is how she made money in those days, if she wasn't cutting lawns or watering gardens, babysitting or housecleaning.

Her brothers, at least, could caddy at the golf course or sell local papers during the week—helping a friend with his route— or selling the *Tablet* in front of the church on Sunday. She made money by writing names and addresses on postcards for Uncle Jackie Moody, her mother's perpetually adolescent brother, the World War II combat hero, survivor of Pacific theatre death marches, shot up by the Japanese, heavily decorated for saving his unit in cross fire, this Moody known as Uncle Jack, the perpetual fuck-up, the good old boy, the family toy, who was practically a part of her own family because his wife threw him out so regularly, thought Eileen. But she liked Uncle Jack, and so did everyone else in the family. Every time his wife threw him out for being drunk, he slept on the couch in their living room, and lately it had become his permanent home, so that he was in the living room more often than not, working to get back into his wife's good graces after a bender two weeks ago.

After Uncle Jack stopped drinking for good, his wife divorced him, and he spent his days in the black section of Freeport on Long Island, living with a go-go dancer. When he died twenty years later from an auto accident, they had an Irish wake, full of booze for the drinkers and soft drinks for his program friends, half of whom were black. But he was extraordinary for other reasons. The girls used to joke that Jack Moody was the most Jewish gentile on earth, and he even said himself that his own father was successful in business because no one knew he was Irish; they thought his family were Jews from Belfast because they had businesses in clothing and linens, not to mention his haberdashery shop on Prince Street in the south Village in Manhattan.

Grandpa Moody's partner in the hat shop was Jake Blatsky, and the two of them made a fortune together, Moody drawing the Irish, Blatsky the Jews, and both friendly with the local Italians. Jack Moody was his father's son, only he acquired more the gestures, manners, and, most of all, voice of Blatsky than of Moody, so that everyone joked Blatsky had *shtooped* Grandma Moody. . . .

"Terrible," Mom said, getting angry at her for only the first and last time. "Wash out your mouth. That's my mother you're talking about."

"Well, she's our grandmother," Oona shouted back, "and I think it's funny to think that Grandma Moody got shtooped by Blatsky in the back room of the hat shop on Prince and Sullivan, and Uncle Jack was the result."

"Ha, ha, ha," Uncle Jack would laugh, not at that anecdote, which he never heard his nieces talk about, but at just about everything. That nervous laugh was his tag, and he placed it at the end of every sentence he uttered, chomping down on his big cigar as he chortled; and it was that laugh, Eileen thought, that was the most hymie thing about her uncle, and the only reason he sold used cars on Long Island, because his customers, all Jews (the Catholics couldn't afford his prices), thought Jack Moody a son of Moses and David, and when they asked, for instance, "You're Jewish, right, Jackie?" "What else, ha, ha, ha," he said. "What else do you take me for, a goddamn goy? *ha, ha, ha. . . .*"

"Ha, ha, ha," they would say, because his tag-laugh was infectious. "This Jackie Moody is a real Borscht-belt comedian."

And he was, Eileen thought. He was.

6

Mary Grace tried to catalogue the images, not the thoughts, that careened through her. All she could see was the red wagon, the pink bicycle, and now her Uncle Jack's Edsel, because these are the things all of them had been talking about, sending up a wall of words in order to fend off the idea of their dead father, that wordless wonder up front, stealing the show by his silence, by his dumbshow, once again ignoring all of them, collectively and individually. In life or death, he would never know their names; dead, he was no more insensitive to them than he was alive. Or so Mary Grace thought, so she felt and believed; there was no point in arguing this.

So from the red wagon she saw the pink bicycle, which in turn made her see Uncle Jackie selling Edsels. But when Mary Grace, the good-looking mistress of a Bensonhurst hoodlum who cared for her as much as he cared for any bimbo he fucked, looked around the funeral parlor at her own father's wake, she didn't necessarily think about any of this. She saw her sisters, and had a craving for the kosher pickles from the barrel, briny and delicious, odor of garlic and dill and pickled wood over on Chauncey Street, no, Bainbridge Street, right next to the butcher who always gave a slice of fresh baloney for free, she thought, not out of her own memory because these experiences had never been hers, though she had felt them because her family told about them over and over to the point where it almost felt like they had been her experiences, and now in this mythological place known as East New York, it was almost as if she could remember everything that happened to the family here, though that was impossible because she had not been born yet, though when she was born, it would be in Brooklyn, Saint Mary's Hospital, right down the block from where all of Mrs. Coole's children but for Mickey Mack were born, the pediatrician Dr. Antonio Lancellotti, their mother's doctor, and how Rosy used to say, you can take the Cooles and Moodys out of Brooklyn but you can't take Brooklyn out of them, nor can you allow any of them to be born, no matter where the family lived, outside of this fertile basin, because Saint Mary's had an aura about it, a sympathetic magic, that insured each birth was a good one, and each birth was easy for old Rosy. That's what she was really thinking about; she thought about how good the baloney tasted, even though she never tasted the baloney. How she never tasted a pickle again as tasty as those ones from the barrel of Rockaway Avenue just before it collided with Broadway.

It made Mary Grace think about a nature show she had been watching on cable right before the telephone call came about the old man dying. The show was about Galápagos turtles, and how each time one of them came to fruition with an egg, no matter where it was in the briny, big ocean, it managed to find its way back to the Galápagos Islands, where it deposited its egg on the beach, covering it up with sand to protect it from predators. Swimming away, the mother left its payload behind, and soon the egg broke, and the young turtle made its instinctive maneuver toward the shoreline and the ocean, and its life in the sea.

Rosy was like the Galápagos turtle, always needing to come back to Brooklyn to give birth, and once the child sprang from her, it would inch its way to the border, and into the safety of Nassau County, Wilson Park, and home.

Her mother was not like salmon, though, who after all died once they deposited the eggs in the ancestral creek bed, the eggs transforming into salmon which swam out of the creek or river into the saltwater and the sea. Brooklyn was more like the Galápagos Islands than a river or stream, and Mother Rose was more like a turtle than a fish.

Mary Grace also remembered her oldest sister Sam's stories about this place, and how she sometimes would experience food as good as this in Brownsville, the only place in childhood Brooklyn where she felt loved and wanted, sort of like that old Lenny Bruce line about how everyone in New York is Jewish until proven otherwise, and how the Jews of Brownsville had adopted Sam and Mickey Mack, not as token goyim, but as the real McCoys, who somehow wound up with this Irish *mishegoss* on Macdougal and Marion streets.

But it was not just the frankfurters and knishes of Brownsville that Mary Grace thought of now. She remembered how the older children recalled how Grandma Coole made pancakes whose taste was inimitable. They were dark and foreboding, Sam told her—"I mean quite ugly and heavy, but delicious"— and Grandma Coole called them *bubelehs*, what they thought meant pancakes in Irish until someone pointed out to Mary Grace in adulthood that probably she was using the Yiddish word for little grandma but also darling or sweetheart. So Grandma Coole's pancakes became an extension of her in the borrowed language of the neighborhood; they were little grandmas that she served her grandchildren. How like Grandma Coole! Mary Grace thought, even though she had never met the woman, or if they had met, she was too young to remember. Brooklyn did that to your senses, played tricks with time and all, turned the moment inside out, and drew the past into the future and the future back, while the present festered in the cankerous air and the shadows of the Broadway el, the harsh machine noises of the elevated subway, the sparks and screeches, with gunshots and shouts taking up the slack.

Uncle Jack Moody was dead, and his brother Willy died going overboard on a freighter off the coast of Korea during its war. That left Uncle Brian Moody, Father Moody, the Maryknoll, who now stood in front of the casket, saying a rosary.

Where he came from and when he appeared, Mary Grace just could not tell, but she knew he wasn't an apparition.

The Moodys were good for plenary send offs, so she shouldn't have been surprised by Uncle Brian's presence. Besides, the family needed a priest like Uncle Brian to negate the imprecations made by the various daughters earlier, including their own link to the Holy of Holies, Elizabeth Ann, the funky radical nun, who had cursed her father worse than any of his other daughters.

Now Oona sat in a front row chair talking with Uncle Brian, telling him about her days in India, where he had done missionary work. She related to him how the old man had come out to California to see her, just back from a long stay at an ashram on the Ganges, and to witness the birth of her firstborn. Of course, this was ancient Coole history, because Oona was a girl back then, and now she was fast approaching her own middle age.

Besides red wagons and pink bikes, Edsels and a Maryknoll priest, Mary Grace now saw bo trees. But she thought—as is often the case—I have it all wrong; I mean, I have Brooklyn wrong, the Coole family, my sisters, and this bo tree. Oona had become a Hindu, I believe, and the bo tree had to do with Buddha. But since I was stuck in Brooklyn with this family obligation, I couldn't readily get to the New York Public Library in Manhattan, or for that matter—the one at the foot of Eastern Parkway and the gateway to Prospect Park, where, if they

landed you from a flying saucer and you assayed the territory
—the verdure of the park, the colossus of the library, and the
grandeur of both Eastern Parkway and the Brooklyn Museum,
not to mention the Botanical Garden—you'd conclude that
Brooklyn was the most beautiful, civilized place on this earth.
Which it still was occasionally and had once been. But not here.
Not in East New York. Not underneath the el. Not on Broadway.
Not across from Our Lady of Lourdes. Not in this dive. Not
among these pigs known as the Coole family. Or among the pig-
lets tonight—myself included—since this was ladies' night out.
Maybe we'd all go to a go-go bar after they closed up the funeral
parlor, and watch naked men dance for us.

The highest form of culture in this part of the world was
Mike's Barbershop across the street, and that closed nearly forty
years ago.

Oona was a Hindu, had been one, and was probably now just a
lapsed Catholic like her sisters; she used to be called Ramesvari
devi Dasi, or something like that, and if you were not enlight-
ened—you were unenlightened!—you were in maya, especially
old Jack-in-the-Box across the room. He was the king of maya,
the father to all illusions, Mr. Maya himself.

Oona still appeared girlishly impish, a mere Puck. None of
the Coole sisters was a breath taller than five feet, just like La
Rosita Moody, their mother. The second daughter Oona still
had pretty tendril curls of strawberry blonde hair. But a sister
like Mary Grace, being younger, saw Oona Coole more than
Ramesvari devi Dasi or Una Einstein (her married name with
the first guru) or Una Dos Passos, her new name, or as the boys
liked to call her, Uno Dos Tres. Eileen remembered the older sister who screamed like a hellhound, threw tantrums—ah, King
Cormorant!—and was nearly as lunatic as her brothers or even
the other habitués of this borough and this neighborhood and
this block.

Oona was a quiet kid, and really no problem until she discovered the Beatles, marijuana, LSD, and meditation. She took the Beatles the hardest, falling for them at Yankee Stadium, swooning, fainting away, screaming upon being revived, Oh John, oh Paul, oh Ringo, oh George. . . .

While her family drank themselves into oblivion, Oona sought out the oblivions in the auroras, the auras of springtide, of springtime, in the spectral autumns, the bare suburban nightmares of winter—"Hey, let's get stoned at the Planting Fields"—and to think the old man moved them to Long Island to escape the traumas of this place only to learn that they, as their mother used to say, brought Brooklyn with them—and the whirling dance of summer around the empty beer cans in the living room.

7

"After high school," Deirdre said, "I took a job in a burger joint on the Jericho strip, and would come home nightly with Rosita bombed out in the living room and Inspector Coole geezered senseless at the dining room table, with assorted siblings lounging around the place in various states of drug-induced narcosis. That's the word, isn't it? Narcosis?"

A few of the sisters, along with Patrick, nodded their assent, okay, sure. But Deirdre did not pick up the slack in the conversation; she stopped eulogizing, either herself and her life or the old man. None of them could tell which.

"He's dead," she said.

"No fooling."

"He died a few nights ago."

"Amazing, isn't it?"

"It smells in here."

"Open a window."

"The rocks," Patrick explained. "If you open the window, the kids start hurling rocks into the room from outside."

"Oh," Deirdre said, and sat exhausted in her chair.

Sam did not pretend to be Aunt Augusta in her cups; Oona had not pulled an Aunt Eileen; and Deirdre clearly was no Aunt Nora. No one had ripped their dead father from the coffin, cursing and moaning as the aunts did in this same room when their mother finally died. Times had changed.

Sam once was the affluent wife of Arnold Blitzer, the founder and president of Huh? jeans, who made a few fistfuls of millions before he was twenty-five years old, and when they divorced, acrimoniously, without pomp or circumstance, and essentially leaving their sister bereft of any claim to his money or even child support for years, Arnold went on to bigger and greater things, like Uh-Oh leisure suits, Wowie dresses, and his ultimate masterpiece—So What? sneakers.

The jury was still out on Deirdre; either she was plain normal or the most secretive member of the Coole family. She sat there sober, neat, clean, dry and without chafing, saying hello, taking the visitors' commiserations like a trouper.

By contrast Eileen felt like a refugee from the Catholic orphanage over by Atlantic Avenue, which reminded her, when she drove past it earlier, of a scene in a movie remake of one of Dickens's tales. Even though it was the first time she had seen it, she remembered, seeing it, that it was the place the older children talked about, the place they were threatened with if they were bad, but it had seemed like another possibility when the Coole household became too much to take. They usually drove by it, Eileen was told, either coming into Brooklyn or going back to Wilson Park on Long Island. The old man slowed his car and shook his fist and whacked you over the head.

"You'll end up an orphan in that place," he said, pointing to the bleak building behind the dreary brick wall with the concertina wire and broken glass shards at the top. "One more crack outta ya and yer gone, my friend."

My friend, he said, not son or your name or wise guy or you little shit. Not my daughter. My friend. Yeah, right.

8

When Oona first came home a Krishna devotee, she told her mother, "The moon and stars are Krishna's eyes."

"Where's his toes?" Jack asked.

"His nose?" Emmett queried, for clearly none of them took this transformation, this conversion seriously.

The old man walked in the door after a week of toil and struggle on the docks. He was dead drunk. He said, "What's all this bullshit on her face?" pointing to the orange makeup, the caste dot on the forehead, the nose ring.

"She's a saint," Rosy Coole said.

"Have you been drinking again?" said the old man to his saintly, martyred wife. "If I find that bottle of wine, I'll break it in a thousand pieces."

"Maya," Oona answered.

"Maya?" Inspector Coole asked. "My mother came from Mayo and my father from Clare."

No one heard from Oona again until the year Sam married Arnold Blitzer, that crazy wedding of yarmulkes and Jameson's whiskey, of a *hoopah* and Irish relatives. The band was country and western, the photographer a black militant who apprenticed himself to Diane Arbus and who found the Coole family intriguing subject matter. He treated them with the fascination a scientist brings to bacteria recently discovered under the lens of the microscope.

After a night of bagels and lox, chicken liver and sweet Jewish wine, Inspector Coole announced that he was going to fly out to Los Angeles to visit his pregnant daughter "Rona Swanny Devious," he called her—or something to that effect.

Oona was out on Sunset Boulevard, belly out to here, selling Krishna literature, chanting *Hare Krishna, Hare Krishna, Hare Rama,* and her father always made it sound like a rug salesman.

"Harry Krishna," he called it.

The Vietnam war boomed murderously across the Pacific; the protesters flickered on the streets at home. Oona, husbandless, was pregnant; cute little Oona Coole. After a day at Disneyland, the inspector finally visited his daughter at her ashram, taking out a pair of brown wooden rosary beads he bought at the Franciscan church near Macy's in Herald Square; he ran off a few Hail Marys on the beads, all the time looking not at, but through, a Krishna statue, the room sickening with the smell of flowers, the food sickeningly sweet, and his daughter like a colorful orange-robed nun was the most sickening sight of all. What a shame! What a curse, an embarrassment, what a sin! Little Oona, lovely little Oona, a Krishna nun, one of those nuisances he and his friends joked about at the airport, those stinky scoundrels they cursed because they were as persistent as cockroaches and as annoying as flies, buzzing about your heels with their literature, and that goddamn drumbeat always, *Hare Rama Rama Rama. . . .*

Didn't he always want one of his daughters to become a nun?

"Jai!" Oona said, greeting them.

"Hi!" her father answered.

It was the Swing Festival, wreathes of carnations, wildflowers strewn on the floor, cultivated yellow buds, bright-bursting red pips with handsome greeny stalks. The Swing Festival was a colorful event here.

The festival food was pasty with honey, grainy with uncooked stalks, "in a word—disgusting," the inspector later said.

The parents removed their shoes and roamed on cat feet in

the festive room. Their gestures were governed by a past that made them treat this new religion with their old paraphernalia, and so they related to the temple as though it were a Hollywood version of Mother Church, the only way to get through this.

None of this changed Mother Rosy's sparrowlike composure. Plus she was three sheets to the wind, coming to the end of her own drinking career shortly.

The old man stood by her like a chophouse waiter, waddling back and forth on his tiny white-socked feet toward the purple-faced deity. He stood in front of Krishna, genuflected, and made the Sign of the Cross.

This was no stranger for Inspector Coole than the black funeral parlor in Harlem he went to for a fellow inspector's funeral. The man's name, in fact, was the same as his, Jack Coole, but instead of calling this huge black man Little Jackie or Jackie Wackie or Little Lee or whatever, the stevedores and inspectors called this other Mr. Coole Johnny B. Coole, and he was that. He was cool, the good inspector agreed at the funeral. As his son Paddy might say, Johnny B. Coole was a cool dude. A soulful man. A man who had God on his insides, sticking to his ribs like a good meal on one of the ocean liners. And on the outside, he drank with the Irishmen on the piers like he was one of them, shots and beers, one after the other after work, Johnny B. was okay.

Hell, that was a lot more colorful than this Harry Krishna place. There were more flowers at Johnny B.'s funeral on Amsterdam and 135th Street; more flowers and more people, whiskey flowed like water, and there was enough weeping and gospel music to make the devil a believer. There was enough gospel and moonshine, ribs and black-eyed peas to make Jackie Ducks, Mr. Coole himself, the real Little Lee, think it was an Irish wake, and Johnny B. often told Little Lee, "I'm one-quarter Irish, McCoole, it was your granddaddy that porked my grandma."

"My grandpa was back in County Whatchamacallit," he said, defensively.

"One of your relatives," old Johnny B. from Harlem said.

Rama Rama. . . .

9

"My philosophy in life," Elizabeth Ann heard the chief say, and so looked up, surprised, astonished—flabbergasted. After all, he was dead. Or she thought all along that he was dead, but now she heard him speak. Then she realized what had happened. All the Cooles loved to imitate the old man, and right now Deirdre did her imitation, throwing her voice toward the coffin. The effect was eerie, and humorous only as an afterthought.

After Paddy, Oona did the best imitations of the old man. But she was in a corner, brooding, and Paddy was being quiet. Lizzie asked Oona to imitate the old man's brogue, but she looked at her baby sister like she was crazy. Then from across the room, after Lizzie walked away from her, she heard the old man again, this time more distinctly, not an imitation but the real Jack the Wacker, her old man himself.

"Kids these days," the voice declared. "In my day, we respected our elders. We didn't talk back. Didn't think we knew it all. We were good kids, hard-working. All of you had it easy. We had to grow up during the Depression. Now that molded us, made men out of us. Then the war came. We had to defend our country against those cruddy Japs and no-good Krauts. We couldn't afford childhoods, couldn't waste our time reminiscing about the past, when food had to be put on the table, U-boats might be off the coast of Jersey any day, and the goddamn Japs were going to crush us the first chance they got, those dirty Jap bastards. . . ."

Deirdre's mouth was still, and Sam drank a beer, so it couldn't have been either of them, while the quieter, younger sisters in the back were busy yapping to each other, not paying attention to anything at the front of the parlor where the others were. Then Lizzie saw Oona smile, and saw her sister wave shyly, like Olive Oyl waving to Popeye.

"My philosophy . . ." the old man said. Then there was silence. Which is how he always did it. His philosophy—then silence. Either that was his philosophy or he forgot his philosophy or he didn't have one or it was one of silence or forgetfulness, was just a bubble of free-floating anger, a kernel of rage.

Oona went on imitating her father: "Kids today," she said. Paused, then, "In my day, back in the Depression, I worked hard, apples cost a small fortune, you kids don't know how good you have it. I always put food on the table, some clothes on your back. What the hell you complaining about? Think about the kids in India with none of this. Think about the Korean orphans who don't have a pot to piss in."

Like a refrain all of them said, "You should have lived during the Depression to know what it was like to go hungry and starve."

But they didn't all really say that.

It's just that Lizzie saw several of the girls moving their lips as if to say, just as she was doing, and a few of them said it aloud from the back of the room.

"You kids had it easy," he would say.

What they did grow up in was the affluence of postwar suburban America, surrounded by the rich, the would-be rich, the mediocre, the tiny pockets of the poor. Leland once characterized them as "upper lower-class as opposed to lower middle-class, equal parts shanty and lace, but economically a middling disgrace, misplaced parts, the whole worse off than the parts, the means that justified the end, that is, we all die and go to heaven because we're Irish Catholic, and live happily ever after, now pass the salt and shut the fuck up. . . ."

The Cooles were surrounded by other large families, Catholic by religion, vaguely Irish by surname, all of them immigrants of the Brooklyn diaspora. Yet these others fit in, they adjusted; they made do, and then made good. We languished, Lizzie wanted to say, we exploded across this frontier. She couldn't remember how often a town hall member visited their house, begging them to fix the broken-down garage from the hurricane early in the 1950s, which had never been repaired. She couldn't recall how often truant officers visited for Leland or Emmett, and later for Paddy and even Samantha, and later still for Terry and Wolfe, Rory, Brian, Parnell, and Frankie, and then they also came looking for Eileen and Mary Grace, though Lizzie did well in school, hardly ever caused much trouble. That was her role, her curse, to be good, to achieve, and then to have none of them, parents or siblings, ever acknowledge her accomplishments.

"Brownnose," Eileen said.

"Teacher's pet," Terry teased her.

"All is folly," Leland taught her, "so why bother to do well in school? You're a Coole. Nobody cares whether you do well or not."

And so instead of going to college the regular way, Lizzie became the one sacrifice to the church, became a nun, and found her education via that route, the penguin costume, and later simple dresses the order allowed her to wear, and eventually she would be allowed to teach at a small Catholic college in Philadelphia, all those letters after her name ameliorating this upbringing, this heritage, which she rarely if ever thought about, except now, right here, at her father's funeral when she had to confront it, and all it did, with her degrees and positions in life, was make her ache like the others. There was no escaping it, no getting away or around it.

Can't remember how many times the police pulled up to the

house, Lizzie thought, breaking up a brawl in progress in the backyard or one of the clan setting the house—or a neighbor's house—on fire, so can't remember either how many times the fire department arrived along with the police.

She did recall that blue-haired ladies in conservative dresses and shoes visited the house every Christmas, their arms laden with presents for these poor, unfortunate children, the blue-haired ladies' hearts pumping with that good feeling Christians get when they give generously to those less fortunate than themselves.

How she delighted in her brothers as they took care of these hags, throwing them into the snow with their presents, telling them to stay off their property, that if they returned, Leland would call the cops or Emmett would bash their brains out. Rory and Parnell might slit the tires on their cars. That's when she felt proud to be part of this big, unmanageable family.

Or the old man himself.

How he fought with the neighbors, with the grocer, the butcher, the laundromat owner, with off-duty police officers, with priests, executives on the Long Island Railroad at the East Wilson station. And Lizzie, like the others, was both fearful and proud. She was scared to death, she realized, but felt good to be part of the House of Coole.

10

"I can practically see the old man in front of the Calderon Theatre in Hempstead," Sky Moody said, "waiting to take us all home from a horror movie."

"We owned that big old Oldsmobile 98," Oona remembered.

The car already approached the decade mark, a gas-guzzling hog in deep snot green with four doors. It defined the family, this object, the way Emmett's pink '55 Ford convertible defined the rebelliousness of all the neighborhood kids of a certain time at the beginning of the 1960s, or how the old man's first car—which Uncle Jack Moody sold him, a '42 Ford sedan that got them through the first half of the fifties—defined the striving so unsuccessfully the Cooles did when they left Brooklyn to attempt living in the newly made suburbs after the war.

To the long list of Edsels, the red wagon, and the pink racing bike, the Maryknoll priest, and their lives, add the pinkness of Emmett's Ford convertible; but don't forget that snot green Oldsmobile 98, another Coole object.

For such a brawler his arms were not meaty, Lizzie thought; he had slivery forearms, spindly wrists, but bulgy in his upper arms, biceps on up. His arms were as long as a gorilla's, and reached practically to his kneecaps. That was what he used to make up for his height, and where he found the leverage in his knockout punches. But unlike classic fighters, his hands were delicate and small like a maestro's. He was pale and his hair was jet black, and as he worked into his furies, his skin turned fire-engine red.

His hair stayed black until he was an old man, Deirdre told them, as if they didn't already know, then it turned white overnight. Unlike his sons, cursed by early baldness (Fuck you, Grandpa Moody, you old senile geezer!), he had most of his hair past retirement. He was not a logical man, not a reasonable one; his register was toward the irrational and overly emotional. After his stroke in old age, none of them could tell the difference between his half-dead brain and his formerly active and alert one. He did not remember his children's names, but when did he ever remember any of their names? He got impatient within a few seconds of engaging you in a telephone conversation after his stroke, but when they were kids he used to rip the phone out of the wall and fling it across the room on the slightest provocation. So what was the big difference? Deirdre asked.

Her remarks got Eileen to thinking about her father now because it was unavoidable that she had to do that, what with him there in front of them, not staring, his gaze was inward and blank now, eyes closed, that smirk on his lips, so Mona Lisa-like, a clueless gesture, but the closest, she knew, that her father would be to happiness and contentment. How appropriate that the funeral parlor was permeated with the smell of roses, no doubt to commemorate his long, dissolute association with his Rosy.

Seeing the old man, you'd think him almost lethargic, that beer belly and his up-close jitteriness, all nerves, always on edge, ready to brawl at the slightest provocation instead of discussing it. His idea was to discuss it over beers after you had it out physically, in the backyard, out on the street, or inside the bar. Like a lot of great fighters, he was slope-shouldered, so that it was hard to figure out where his punches might land if you were only calculating their point of origin at his shoulders; they looped over defenses and crashed into the side of your head, on the ear, at the temple, or smack across the jaw.

All the brothers, if not the girls, knew about his punches. But that did not stop Mary Grace from talking about his punches. She might not be as knowledgeable as her brothers about fighting, she said, but who among them had avoided getting slammed by the old man? Maybe Mary Grace, because she did not get hurt as often as the others, simply knew how to slip a punch better, she suggested, knew how to roll with the hooks and crosses. She never wanted to hang around to feel the full impact of his crashing rights and slashing hooks to the body, his insulting jabs into your eye sockets and mouth.

And yet the inspector, unlike a lot of other violent men from the ghetto, rarely belted his daughters.

In front of the Calderon Theatre in Hempstead on Long Island, the old man waited out front for a bunch of his children to pile into the snot green, ten-year-old Olds 98 four-door. It wasn't falling apart; rather it was an elegant heap at the curbside, their fierce, dark, fat, brooding father at the steering wheel, his usual agitated and distracted and dyspeptic self.

He asked a man double-parked in front of them to move so that he could get this show on the road and back home, Samantha told them.

Again: "Would you move your car." Said it in his politest voice.

"Fuck you, fatso," the guy answered.

"What you say?"

"Up your ass, buddy," the galoot said.

Oona picked up where Sam had left off: "The old man opened the door, not getting out, but leaning his big oxlike head out of the car."

"I've got daughters in this car," he said.

But just as quickly Sam took back the narrative: "The other man lit a cigarette as though the old man were not there. You sensed what the other man was thinking: he was not moving for anyone, much less this tub of lard with his scraggly band of children stuffed everywhere like a pack of circus clowns in that green jalopy."

"Here it comes," Paddy whispered to a sister. Or so Oona related it to them now.

Crack, the old man smacked one of them good.

Then, he was out of the car.

"He went up to the double-parked car," Deirdre said.

"You weren't even born," Paddy said.

"Yes I was," she answered. "The other car was blue, looking like it was right out of the showroom."

"It's a Ford," one of the young ones said.

"It's not a Ford," another answered. "It's a Pontiac."

The older brothers were in the front seat with the old man, and the rest of the kids were crammed into the backseat, piggyback style, one on top of the other. Little pyramids of flesh and aggravation.

The show had been a horror movie, and they were hyped up and adrenalized, and the old man was pissed as hell at all of them for interrupting his day twice, once to drive there and once to pick them up.

He was the world's worst driver and all of them knew it, so they were careful not to talk to him or get him started because his temper behind the wheel was ballistic.

"Before engaging the double-parked lout in front of us," Mary Grace said, "the old man turned around to wallop me on the head and crack a brother in the teeth. Just for good measure. Not that we had transgressed or anything like that. It was a warning before the fact, a way of letting us know who was the boss and what would happen if we really misbehaved. He was feeling his oats, you might say. He meant business."

"You weren't even born," Sam shouted.

"Yes I was born," Mary Grace shouted right back. "I was in the backseat of the car, a little kid, but I was born all right, I was there, I should know."

"Any fight he was losing stand-up," Eileen said, ignoring them, "he turned into a street brawl, but always concluded by returning to a sort of stand-up fight routine, his fists raised properly, knees bent, and turned sideways to his opponent, like he was a professional boxer, not an amateur bar and street fighter. Like he was goddamn Mike Tyson or something. Right fist cocked next to right ear. Left fist extended in front of his face and raised up just below his eye. He bounced on his feet as though listening to ancient airs in his head, penny whistle stomps, bagpipe hoedowns, drumrolls, and deep tenors. He circled and circled the downed person, expecting at any moment that the fellow would rise from the dead and do battle with him again."

"Now let's get this straight," Oona interjected. "Are you claiming that you were in the backseat of the car, too?"

"Oh, I was there all right," Eileen said.

"You weren't even born!" Sky Moody shouted.

"Of course I was born," answered Eileen.

But then Lizzie interrupted this with: "The second oldest turned around from his privileged vantage in the front seat and said: 'It's a Chevy, now shut up!'"

"You definitely weren't there!"

"Of course I wasn't there," Lizzie said. "I wasn't even born."

"Then how would you know what any of the older boys said?" Sam asked.

"You told me."

"I told you?"

"A thousand times."

"A thousand times?"

"Maybe a million," Lizzie said, indulging in a family need to multiply all numbers out of any realistic proportion. "A zillion," she added.

"If you got on the wrong side of one of the older brothers, they could give you worse treatment than the old man, so all of us in the backseat shut the hell up."

Thus spake Deirdre.

"The guy in the late model Chevy was about to get out of his car and the old man slammed the door on him, cutting him at the kneecaps. Through the open window of the new car, the old man delivered a crashing solid right to the man's face.

"When the man got out of the car, he towered over our father, really immense, I mean, like a noseguard—they called them middle linebackers in those days—nearly as huge vertically as horizontally. First, the old man hit him one in the liver with one of his sneak left hooks and then hammered his right fist into the man's heart and worked on the guy's face. Second, he got the man into a headlock and pummeled the face with his left fist, but as quickly as that, the middle linebacker had the old man in a headlock, tit for tat, bashing the old man's ox-head into the side of the brand-new blue Chevy, making tiny dents into the steelwork."

"That is when all of us piled out of the Olds 98 and went to work ourselves," said proud Oona, "boys and girls alike, the older ones, the tiny ones, the ones like myself, in the middle, we clawed, scratched, bit, gouged, pulled, and jerked. The two oldest worked on the fellow's face."

It felt like hours, but like the old man said, it probably was no longer than a minute.

Then the police arrived.

"He was best to watch when he fought someone twice his height, some burly truck driver or pizza man or plumber who ripped him off for repairs paid for and never done," Lizzie told them. "Someone who forgot the onions and then said something nasty about the old man's ethnic background. Truck drivers who said mean things about his mother or wife or even his daughters. He was effortless in these brawls, and you saw the joy in his face as he fought. That joy was never there at any other time in his life, not with his wife, his children, his cohorts on the midtown docks, his bar friends, his Knights of Columbus pals, his relatives."

"If someone were getting the better of him in a fight," says Eileen, "he got downright dirty, and later he taught all of his sons to fight the same way. Once I saw him bite a man. Others he clawed as though he were a cat. He used sticks, brooms, baseball bats, but never guns. He was licensed to carry a gun, but even at his job he never used it, much less wore it around. Something about a gun he didn't like. Its bulk, its heft, or maybe how it annihilated the primitive joys of using one's fists against another human being, the primitive one-to-one relationship of a good honest fight."

He said (he used to say), he says: "A fight only lasts a few seconds, and the worst of them a minute or two, even if all of them seem like forever when you are engaged in them."

This was one of his lectures about how to beat up other people, which all of his sons did on occasion, some of them more frequently than others, and a few of them still doing it to this day.

Leland seemed the most savage in those rarefied days, coming home from school suspended for one fight or another. He detached retinas, broke jaws, cracked ribs, busted spleens at the slightest provocation, and he had a reputation, even among the wrestlers and football players in high school, as a person not to fool with lightly, not to kid or tease. While the daughters were livelier with their tongues, if put to the test, there was not one of them, including the holy Lizzie, who couldn't bash someone in the nose if need be, just like the brothers, or maybe even better than any of the boys, pound for pound, rage for rage.

"He never lost a fight in his life until his sons grew up," said Mary Grace, "were maybe fifteen or sixteen years old, and one by one, each of them went out into the yard to have it out, and if you returned to the dining room the victor, then you had just become a man. I left home before any of that nonsense happened with the daughters too," she went on, "and found myself back in Brooklyn, living with a guy who was no better and no worse than any of my brothers or my father, how you like that?"

Patrick added, "I left home for good right after my successful battle with him, not as traditionally was done in the yard in front of the lilac bush, but in the side yard where there was hardly room to maneuver, his fancy footwork worthless. It was like fighting each other in a telephone booth.

"Even after such victories, all of us knew them to be an illusion. He could just as easily the next week take you on and come away with another win. Which is why I left when I did, tired of this interfamilial messing. I saw him as this berserk immigrant orphan, and nothing more, not even as though he were my father, which he never acted like, but this old crazy relative whom I had endured for fifteen years and now was done with. Good riddance, I thought."

"Give that other guy a ticket for double-parking," Jackie Junior yelled at the cops and pointed toward the galoot.

"He assaulted my father," a sister shouted.

"All of you!" a police officer shouted back. "All of you—shaddup!"

Static arose from the patrol car radio, and after giving the man a ticket for double-parking and the old man a reprimand for fighting on the street and in front of his children, they drove off in the vicinity of the Hempstead ghetto, heavier action on their minds.

"The Cooles drove home from the movie theatre, packed into the backseat like sardines in a can," Oona said. She remembered, too, how she was as miserable as she'd ever been, but also proud. Still, she didn't know why she thought of it that way now; because when she remembered the incident more clearly, when she replayed it a couple hundred times over, it was a prototype of the old man's behavior, and Oona was left with a more deflated and empty feeling than pride. It was more like a burning shame, a feeling of not belonging, of *always* fucking up, of being outcast. Being outcast meant not coming from Long Island, even though you lived there; meant not being a part of the suburban drone of Nassau County. It meant they were from Brooklyn, not from Long Island. They were never from Long Island, or at least they never felt as if they were from there because the Cooles never fit in, never were part of the suburbs, its landscape and its social manners. So it wasn't Brooklyn; it wasn't feeling like Brooklyn that Oona was talking about. Most of the neighbors out on the Island were from Brooklyn or had a parent from there. This was feeling East New York, not like being from there, but being the place itself, the dangerous, uncontrollable, exuberant, but also unpredictable, edgy place. It was that bad attitude that got bred into the bones after a short tenure on these streets. Even now. It hung over all of them like

a shadow. Like a demon from hell. Like a sticky fluid from a
spray can.

"I can't wait to get out of here and back to Philadelphia," Elizabeth Ann said.
    "Me, I'll take getting back to Long Island," Eileen said.
    "Technically speaking," Sam said, "this is Long Island."
    "Out of Brooklyn," Eileen clarified herself.
    "Oh, okay."
    "Back to Nassau," said Oona, "out of here, away from it all."
It all sounded like the terminal Cooles.
    Then one or another of them said one more lousy thing about
their father or the family. That was it.
    "That's not a nice way to talk about your own father," Deirdre
said. "He wasn't that bad a guy after all. He had a hard life. He
was a street kid, an orphan, a ghetto monster. He didn't know
any better, either. He thought it was cool having all these kids."
    "I'll say he thought it was Coole," said Lizzie.
    "What kind of nun are you to talk this way at your own
father's funeral?" Deirdre shot back, pulling rank on her kid sister. "You ought to be ashamed of yourself."
    The sisters prayed.
    Lizzie knelt contritely in the middle of the floor and prayed:
"Father, I am sick. Of families I am sick. Of this parlor. This
head in pincers. This old neighborhood. Sick of perpetual twi-
light. Of broken windowpanes, of elevated trains. I am sick of
dreaming about East New York. Let my sisters' dreams take
hold. Let the world be nothing more than people trying to make
a life for themselves, either in the city or beyond. Stop these
windowpanes from rattling. Let no more trains pass overhead."

CURSED PROGENITORS (2)

1

AND THEN THE YOUNGEST SONS FINALLY SHOWED. AT first it was only Wolfe and Brian, but then the twins Parnell and Rory rolled in, and even, in the end, Francis, the gawky youngest. The older brothers had come back from their meal, adjourning to a basement room to smoke, drink, and talk. Soon the sisters joined them, leaving the five new ones to contemplate their dead father. That meant that all the Coole family were there except Terry, who somehow got lost as they went off in the various cars to eat. Fifteen brothers and sisters. They all hadn't been together like this since they were kids.

Some of them, like Brian and Wolfe, saw each other regularly. But no one had seen Parnell and Rory for ages, and Frankie had been missing-in-action since he left home around seventeen years old. Mickey Mack used to say he ran into Frankie downtown, but Mickey wouldn't tell anyone where he saw Frankie or where the baby brother lived. So no one pursued it. After all, they were not a close family; they were not tight with each other.

As Brian looked at Parnell and Rory, he remembered that twins ran in the family. Eileen and Nora, of course. But Grandpa Coole had several sets of twins amongst his twelve brothers and sisters back in the old country, and so did his first wife, who was a twin, too. The Coole twins, Rory and Parnell, like their aunts Nora and Eileen, were inseparable.

Rory and Parnell played CYO basketball together, forming a dynamite backcourt in the eighth grade. But they had no height, and their athletic skills peaked by high school, so neither wound up playing basketball at Wilson Park High School, where most of them went after doing eight years at Saint Aidan's, and a few before the twins doing a couple more years in the prep schools of Catholic Long Island, Mickey Mack to Chaminade, Emmett to Saint Mary's, while Jackie went off to Brooklyn and the diocesan seminary high school, Cathedral, off Atlantic Avenue, deep in the heart of the Coole family's favorite borough.

Parnell and Rory barely made it through high school, and so they never went to any of the Catholic schools some of the others attended. They took shop, auto mechanics, and mechanical drawing, and because they were no trouble like their older brothers, they passed silently along, one class to the next.

Rory played baseball one semester; Parnell was on the JV football squad another semester. But since they were inseparable—they even slept in the same double bed in the attic—neither could stand to be away from the other that long. Yet even though they were inseparable, they did not necessarily get along that well, and often one of the older boys had to go to the attic to separate them in mortal battle.

They both had dirty blond hair, muddy brown eyes, were runtish in height, but well-built, kind of like gymnasts, which is what both of them finally became, tumblers, uneven parallel bars, the horse. If one of them zoomed up a rope from floor to ceiling in gym class, the other followed with identical breathtaking speed.

When everyone became hippies on Long Island, dropping acid, listening to the Grateful Dead, and zoning out at the Planting Fields on the North Shore, watching the arboretum drip with tracers of rosy colors, Parnell and Rory kept their short jock haircuts, kept working out after high school, and, of course, joined the army together, went airborne and Rangers, and all that, coming home with wicked-looking berets cocked to a rakish slant, saluting their delighted father.

Then they went to work for Emmett; it was one of those theatrical stagehand unions run by the Irish gangsters whom Emmett knew and hung around with, and within six months, Emmett had the two Mr. Cleans blowing grass, then doing shots of whiskey with lines of cocaine. They got in trouble, were arrested. Then they disappeared. Some said it was the Witness Protection Program. Others claimed they got clean in a rehab in Minnesota—the land of ten thousand rehabs—and went out west from there. But wherever they were and whatever happened, this was their first time back east, back with the Cooles.

Then there was Francis Xavier Coole. The baby of the household. Everyone's kid brother.

X-Man was the tallest of all, a real stretch. He stood maybe six feet four or five inches tall, and was as thin as you could get, but unlike the twins and Mickey Mack, all of whom played basketball well, X didn't have an ounce of athlete in him.

He looked brainy, but he wasn't that good a student in school, even though he read books all the time. He didn't have any academic interests, and though he probably could have gone to college as Mickey Mack and even Emmett did, Frankie had no interest in college.

Drugs were Francis Xavier's true love, his calling.

Wolfie appeared like a bleached, shrunken Joe Louis, the poor white man's version, a welterweight with pale complexion, and balding, dirty blond hair. Sphinx-like face, friendly but a world of strength, misery, and grace underneath it: Wolfe was the great athlete of the Coole family, this compact dynamo.

Brian once was dark and tight, his own kind of dynamo,

though it translated into the mortal coil more than the eternal spring. He still looked good, despite what looked like a bad sunburn, even though he tanned as a kid in the Jones Beach sun. Of course, he had been utterly transformed by the fire in the Bronx; he was not anywhere related to the Brian they all grew up with. This new Brian didn't look like their brother from childhood, didn't talk like him, think like him, or even walk like him. His burnt-up body more resembled that of his Aunt Nora, whom he never met because he was too young to know her before she and Eileen ran off to California with the social worker; but the resemblance was there when Brian's older siblings looked at him and remembered their wacked-out, lonely aunt who got lit up in the basement when she shoveled coal into the furnace.

Parnell and Rory were transformed utterly, too, but in less obvious physical ways. Their changes came from inside, though when they spoke, you could tell right away that they weren't the Rory and Parnell from childhood, either. It was as if some space invaders had taken hold of these three brothers and possessed their bodies and minds, or at least that's what Wolfe thought as he did some whiskey and a few lines of coke in the back of the room, "finding my bearings," he said, explaining his absence, but instead of making his father's presence less unreal, the corpse seemed to magnify itself, so Wolfe went back for another shot and hit. The Cooles had been arguing.

"All right already," Wolfe kvetched.

"Huh?" asked Brian.

"Show a little respect."

"It's a story," added Brian.

Brian had been telling another disparaging tale about their father.

"What's it have to do with him, I mean, the deceased?" Parnell asked.

"Yeah," Rory said, "Parnell's right, what's it have to do with the old man?"

"Lots," Brian said. "Ancestry, for one."

"We ain't got no ancestry," Parnell said.

"Everybody got ancestry," Frankie spoke for the first time since arriving at the funeral parlor.

X, aka Frankie, was an extreme other.

There was no one in the family that quite resembled him, though unmistakably he was a Coole, Francis Xavier being one of the oldest of Coole family names.

Besides his unusual height, X was raillike, emaciated, his hair thin and streaked with gray, and his skin color ashen, and prematurely aged. He had on work pants, black combat boots, a beat-up Donegal tweed sweater, and a great tweed overcoat that looked as if he had been sleeping in it, and he had one gold loop in his left ear. In this shadowy light, Frankie appeared more like one of their father's relatives from the old country than this younger brother.

When his cigarette ran down, Frankie lit another off the stub, coughed, then sucked on the new one, staring off.

Brian savored the moment with his lost brothers. The young Coole boys—the last five of them—were like an entirely different family from the others, almost as if there were several families, and the five youngest boys were one of those separate tribes within the larger nations. His parents had been a world unto themselves; then came the older boys, though Wolfe and Brian had sometimes cared for Terry who couldn't care for himself. The sisters, though of disparate ages, were a unit, too. The family that Brian knew were these brothers now fortuitously assembled before their dead father.

Wolfe was the leader, followed by Brian; then the Dioscuri, the Gemini, Parnell and Rory (Castor and Pollux), the boxer and the jockey; followed by F. X. Coole, X-Man, the baby of the family, this punk reincarnation of Ichabod Crane.

Parnell and Rory were small, silent, angry, efficient, unimaginative, hard-working, lumpen, their faces as beat-up as Gene Fullmer's and Carmen Basilio's were after their legendary fights. They were like eight-round club fighters next to that sterling and athletic brother Wolfe.

Parnell said he lived out west, but gave no other information; Rory told less than that. The only clue was that they seemed to be in contact with each other, suggesting that where they did live, one was close by the other.

Brian suggested that the Gemini lived half the year in hell.

"You mean Florida?" Wolfe asked.

"Yeah," Brian said, "why not?"

"Wow, maybe Dad used to see them then," said Wolfe.

"Fuck Dad," Brian shot back.

The wonder was how this long, gangly person—Frankie X. was listed as the longest baby ever born in Brooklyn at thirty inches —had come out of so tiny a machinery as their mother's body, old Rosy being just a touch below five feet tall. Frankie was an aberration. Tall where his brothers were small and compact, thin where they were well-built, even stocky; long-haired (slicked back into a ponytail) where they were all in different stages of baldness. These were working-class Long Island guys; Frankie had an air of arty desolation, a man outside the realm of geography or class, or at least outside Brooklyn and Long Island.

"Jackie Ducks got more kids than Heinz catsup got fifty-seven varieties," Brian once heard a stevedore shout from a rig as the old man introduced Brian, Rory, and Parnell to his buddies down the piers one day, and this after years of introducing all the other kids he had to his cohorts and fellow workers.

"Fuckn Ducks," another longshoreman shouted.

"Hey, watch the language," little Jackie Ducks called out, getting angry because he hadn't had his morning drink and his lunch yet.

Fuckn Ducks, Brian thought. Fuck a Duck.

Brian was being moony and uncomfortable. He wished his brothers would show more respect for their father before they interred him forever in the cold Brooklyn ground across the hump in Highland Park, miles away in the distance, like a biblical apparition of the fallen city of Gomorrah.

The room was filled with family members, all noisy and a little angry that they had to be here to pay homage to their father. They had come to pay their respects to their late father; like him or not, they had their duties, their obligations, and even if drunk or stoned, those responsibilities would be met, so here they were.

No one expected Rory or Parnell, much less Francis, to show for the funeral.

And then, as if on cue, Frankie X. entered the funeral parlor, did not say hello to his brothers, but instead knelt in front of the coffin, praying. He blessed himself, stood, turned, and came over to Wolfe and Brian.

"What have you been doing?" Brian asked.

"Where have you been all these years?" Wolfe asked. "Who reached you to come here?"

Both questions were addressed to Frankie.

Rory and Parnell sat looking at the three other brothers in this blasé, dumbfounded way, kind of like the brothers had always been there, and probably always would be there, this was nothing unusual. They also seemed a bit punchdrunk, or maybe just plain drunk, it was hard to say.

"What do you mean?" Frankie asked Wolfe.

"I mean, where do you work? Don't you have a fuckn job?"

"Oh, yeah, sure," he said, "I make ends meet."

"Could you be more specific."

"Specific?"

"About what you do."

"Well, I do this and that."

"What else?"

"Oh, I get around, man."

"What's the use?" Wolfe asked Brian. Then he said to Frankie, "So, you're a cop?"

"A cop?"

"I heard you was a cop."

"Whodafuck said that?"

"What's it matter whodafuck said it," Brian told him. "That's what we heard."

"Hey, what happened to you?" X-Man asked. He pointed to Brian's burnt face.

Families are not subtle machines; they are more like opportunistic diseases, looking for the weak links.

"You a Westy?" Brian asked his baby brother.

"A what?"

"You know," Brian said. "That Irish gang on the West Side Manhattan."

"Never heard of them, pal."

"A priest?" Wolfe asked.

"A fuckn priest," Frankie said, laughing. "Jesus, what you guys smokn or what?"

"We ain't seen ya in years," Wolfe said.

"It wasn't that long," young Francis answered.

Wolfe counted to himself, then said, "Years and years."

"That long, huh?" Frankie asked. "Seems I just saw you guys yesterday."

"So what you doing these days, X-Man?" Brian asked.

"Doin?" Frankie asked. "I ain't doin nothn right now. I'm here. What's it look like? Jeez."

The father lay there like a stone; he lay there as he always did, even when he was alive. Mute. Aggressively silent. The past? Use your imagination, the old man might say. Frankie? Figure it out. Perhaps their father misled them all along so that they would use their imaginations, have to make up the details. In that sense, the Venerable Bede known as Jack Coole their father was a saintly man, an inspiration and even a genius, because he made his sons and daughters fill up the empty space with their anxieties and bad dreams, and finally even their creative acts.

Parnell and Rory sat next to each other, not speaking, not reacting, but listening to the other boys.

"He's kidding, right?" Frankie asked Brian.

"Of course he's kidding," Brian answered. "Wolfe's drunk enough to kill an elephant."

One of the old man's relatives, this ancient relic known as Leo McCombs, had come over from his retirement home in Cypress Hills to pay his respects to his favorite nephew, Jackie Ducks. Parnell or Rory had poured old Leo too stiff a glass of the Irish, "a ball of malt," Rory said, and this pleased old Leo to no end.

After quaffing his drink, he stared off into the great unknown, then returned to the room.

Rumor had it that Leo McCombs was ninety-nine years old now, which is why Brian had asked him so many questions about the past, especially about the family line which their own father never discussed.

"Jackie's father," Leo McCombs said, meaning their grandfather, Jems Coole, "was a cold and enigmatic man, he treated your father terribly, turned the poor boy into an orphan after his mother died because. . . ."

"Did she die from a fire on 82nd Street off Broadway in Manhattan?" Brian asked, needing to know, "or was it that other cock-n-bull story about stomach cancer?"

Leo McCombs was stone-deaf and did not hear the question.

"Jems became a drunk," Leo said, "and he abandoned your father to the streets, to raise himself alone when he was no more than five years old. Of course, the Wildes, his mother Annie's relatives down on the Jersey Shore, stepped in and gave him a decent enough home and upbringing, but those scars never left your father's life, you boys should understand it about that man, his father was a brutal, cold man."

"You could say that about our father, too," Brian shot back, loud and clear for old Leo McCombs to hear.

"Heh?" the old fellow asked.

"The old man was a bit of a prick too," he went on, "cold and enigmatic, my ass, he didn't have an ounce of sympathy for any of us."

Then Brian sat.

What comes round, he thought, goes round. What goes round, comes right back in your face.

What had happened, too, was that each brother had assumed an ancient habit in this company. Brian and Wolfe monopolized the conversation; the other three listened, pretended to listen, or didn't listen at all. Rory and Parnell had a professional code of silence, almost like the old man's, that Irish equivalent of *omertà*. Yet Frankie was possessor of the deepest, most ancient silence, more akin to the silences the old man's antique relatives from Clare and Mayo brought into every Brooklyn room they sat in—kind of an ontological one. Wherein they had nothing to say, therein they were silent. They said nothing.

The Cooles were not really talkers but brooders, partakers of long silences, dramatic and often deeply philosophical, as if listening to the rotations of the moon from this whirring axis on earth, as if contemplating the music of the spheres, not the mortal tin-can rattles of this temporal existence. Here you lived so briefly and died so profoundly long that there was no comparing the bleatings of the present moment with the humming, black, eternal silence to come. The three youngest brothers were more Cooles than either Wolfe or Brian, the talkers, in that regard.

What they did by saying nothing, Brian hoped to accomplish

with a torrent of words, out loud, on the hoof, and deep inside himself, exploding through the long, black night.

If you were a bettor, odds were that none of these three younger ones would offer more than a few obligatory condolences, followed maybe by a Hail Mary, Our Father, Act of Contrition, and a sports discussion, maybe even a political one if enough booze was found, but nothing personal, thank you. Yet even if Parnell or Rory said anything, it was certain that the gangly Frankie would be like a stone, silent till the end.

No matter what Wolfe said, Brian would indulge himself in a fitting eulogy to send off his father into the Great Unknown, into the whirring spheres of the crumbling cosmos, and, who knows, if God were all-loving as some claimed, then maybe all Jackie Ducks (little Lee Coole) would have to do was a few million years of fire and torture in purgatory, not the everlasting flames of hell.

Now they were back to talking about what Brian had been saying earlier, comparing his dead father to the legendary Cooles of old, the warriors, revolutionaries, and the poets.

Wolfe Tone Coole interrupted Brian.

"Enough," he said. "Enough already. This has nothing to do with the old man."

"It has everything to do with him," Brian protested.

"Nothn, bro."

"Huh?"

"Show a little respect, he's your father."

"It's a story," Brian said.

That's when, miracle of miracles, Frankie spoke. Even Rory and Parnell sat up to listen.

"I was working down at the Wilson Hills Golf Course," Francis said, sucking on his cigarette for security. "My ass was dragging from working on the greenskeeping crew all day, a really long one that started before dawn, getting the greens ready for a big tournament that day, and it ended when my partner and me set up the fairway sprinklers, and it was really late at night when we finished because we couldn't turn on the sprinklers until the last golfers were out."

From the earliest days the Cooles had worked as caddies or greenskeepers at the Wilson Hills Country Club. When they were twelve or thirteen years old, they caddied during the summer months. Some of them like Mickey Mack and Francis X. worked as greenskeepers after high school. Big Jackie Wackie used to caddy at the Wilson Hills, then lose his loop money playing five-card poker with the caddy-shack bums and gamblers, get drunk on cheap wine, and, on rare occasions when he won money, go off to play the ponies at Roosevelt Raceway (the trotters) or Belmont or Aqueduct (the thoroughbreds). Rory and Parnell were busboys in the clubhouse, picking up big tips from the millionaires and learning about cockfighting and boxing from the Puerto Rican and Dominican kitchen workers. Emmett had worked the pro shop with the supercaddies and the golf pro, and Patrick once worked one day as a waiter, but he wound up spilling water on a blue-haired lady while he flirted with her beautiful-looking granddaughter, a high debutante from Roslyn Estates, and was quickly fired, sent back down to the caddy yard where he belonged.

Wolfe produced a bottle of King Cotton muscatel, opened it, and poured.

"Like Cana," he said, "I've saved the best until the end."

But nothing about these terminal family rituals reminded Francis of Cana; instead, his brothers' remarks brought him back to life, back to the present, and in the present, sitting in front of his father, Frankie did not think about wine because his father never drank the stuff, but instead he was reminded of that biblical story about the loaves and fishes, and how they multiplied to feed a horde.

No matter how poor their father, he always had money to

drink, and no matter how broke, he managed to get a few rags on their backs, and, more importantly, to come home nightly with a few bags of day-old Horn & Hardart rolls and pastries. He always managed to steal a box of filet mignons off the *Queen Elizabeth,* the *Constitution, United States,* the *Leonardo,* or *Michelangelo,* ocean liners that docked at the midtown piers where he worked.

Looking at his father, Frankie forgot the nonsense Brian was saying about famous ancestors; instead the youngest Coole brother drilled his attention on his worthless progenitor, and instead of horns of plenty in the New Testament, he was reminded of wrathfulness and patriarchy; he thought of Abraham and Isaac, the story in the Bible that made him lose sleep, the story that put sweats on him.

"To the old man," Wolfe said, raising his drink, but neither Brian nor Frankie, neither Parnell nor Rory responded by picking up their drinks and saluting their father.

Francis X. Coole took something out of an inside pocket of his coat, opened a bottle of Crazy Horse malt liquor, slugged on it, and passed it over to his brothers. Then he spoke.

"Real hot, muggy Long Island midsummer night, about nine o'clock in the evening, the lightning bugs floatn around the backyard, the sound of kids playn and screamn, a sparkler shinin in the night here or there, once in a while a firecracker goes off, you get the picture, right? The old man is sittn at the dining room table in his short-sleeve undershirt, readn his papers and doin the monthly bills, the old lady is off for t'ree days on a novena with her lady friends, and all the kids are out.

" 'Where's Fuzzy?' I ask, because I don't see the cat anywhere. 'Did one of the kids let the cat out by mistake?' I ask him, but he's out of it, he ain't present really, and he don't even look up to acknowledge me. After a while I tell him, come on, Dad, let's call it a day and go to bed, and I take him upstairs, help him out of his pants and flop him into his bed, and then go downstairs.

I'm too tired to get drunk, even though the head greenskeeper gave me the next day off, and I could have gotten trashed in one of the local joints on Hillside Avenue before comin home. No one ever carded me because I was so tall, they just presumed I was legal.

"So I pour myself some lemonade, but it's warm, and I go to the freezer above the refrigerator to get some ice cubes, and I reach around this frozen blob, not a chicken, not a rack of lamb, not venison somebody got huntn last winter upstate. Who knows what it is? Too big for hamburger meat. Too small for a ham or ribs. Then I realize what I'm looking at.

" 'Fuzzy,' I say. Somebody froze my fuckn cat.

"When I ask the old man, he's too groggy and out of it to know what I'm talkin about, but over the next couple of days I piece together what happened.

"He came home in a bad mood the night before, and without the old lady or none of the girls there to make him dinner, he didn't have anything to eat, and the cat hadn't been fed because I was late gettn back to feed it, so it kept whinin and mewn and purrn, curln around his leg, and the old man, everyone knew, couldn't stand the idea of pets, even hated 'em, and, drunk, in a blackout, he picked the cat up by the tail and threw it inside the freezer, just to quiet it down, he said later, a couple of days after the incident, threw it in the freezer just to shut it up, not to kill it, he said, but he forgot where he put it, thinkn he opened the back door and let it out into the yard, he sat down at the dining room table to read his paper and do the monthly bills, all that time Fuzzy was freezn to death, mewn and cryn inside the freezer.

"So I picked up this frozen cat, stiff as Arctic shit, and dug a hole in the backyard and buried poor Fuzzy. That's when I decided that I was bookn out of this nuthouse the first chance I got."

"Nice," Wolfe said. "I always figured Fuzzy got smart and went and found himself a nicer family to sponge off of."

"I've got somethn ta top that," Brian said.

"We've all got stories," Rory said, more enigmatically.

Parnell added, "If I had a nickel for every crumby fuckn story this family told."

But then like his twin, he fell silent, not about to share any of them.

Frankie sat brooding on his tale, but already the brothers were on to other matters.

"Terry's homeless," Brian said. He asked the twins, "Did you hear where he lives?"

"In a bus," Wolfe said.

"What?" Frankie asked, annoyed.

"Terry," says Wolfe.

"Yeah?" Francis X. asked.

"He lives in a fuckn abandoned bus. Out on the Island. A fuckn school bus. Terry. No wonder everyone calls him Psycho. He is a psycho."

"You and Brian used to always indulge him," Parnell said.

"Yeah," Rory agreed.

"We don't indulge him anymore," Brian said. "But he's our fuckn brother, whattaya expect, he can't take care of himself."

"I got Terry in the union once," Wolfe added. "You know what he does? He left the fuckn delivery truck running in the middle of traffic upper Broadway Manhattan. Goes into a Blarney Stone, and gets drunk. When he comes back a few hours later, the truck is gone. So are his packages. A few days later, the police find the truck stripped down in the South Bronx. A mere shell. A fuckn shell. This, a thirty-thousand-dollar panel truck. Nothing left. No windshield, steering wheel, wheels, engine, seat."

"We get the picture," Parnell says.

"Anybody know where the *baretroom* is?" asks Rory, standing and holding his crotch.

Brian pointed to the door behind the casket, and Rory trotted off, whizzed, flushed, and came back.

". . . truck-bed lining, bumpers, headlights," Wolfe says, "all of it gone. But they didn't fire Terry. He's my brother, they figure, Wolfie's the best we got, maybe his fuckn brother will come around. Maybe he'll shape up. So they give him another panel truck, this one an old beat-up one. Hey, they ain't stupid, I mean, they ain't gonna *entrust* him with another thirty-thou panel truck. The same fuckn thing happens, he leaves the engine running, goes into a saloon, comes out a few hours later, the fuckn truck is gone. So they put him on desk work at the airport. He sleeps at my place in Queens Village, ten minutes from Kennedy, I make sure he doesn't drink too much the night before, make him turn off *The Tonight Show* to sleep, wake him at six, drive to fuckn work. I drop him in front of our work site. 'Are you okay?' I ask him. He says, 'I'm okay, Wolfe.' Says he's goin for a cup of coffee."

"What the hell's the point of this?" Brian asked. "You ain't sayn nothn."

"Huh?" Wolfe asked.

"I was talkn," Frankie said.

"You were talking?" Brian asked.

"Yeah, I was telln you guys about Fuzzy the cat when Brian interrupted me and then Wolfe interrupted me."

"Business as fuckn usual," Rory said, but not to them, rather to his twin brother.

Parnell nodded.

"You were talkn?" Wolfe asked Francis Xavier.

"Yeah," he said, "I was telln you about Fuzzy the cat."

Brian said, "Who gives a shit about Fuzzy the fuckn cat?"

Wolfe looked like he was going to punch Frankie in the face, cold cock the son of a bitch.

Then he said, "I'm a Teamster, I drive fuckn trucks, I work for a living by the seat of my pants. Out at the airport. Kennedy. What the old man used to call Idlewild—almost to the very end. Fuckn guy. I don't have the problems with him that the others had. I respected my father, and he treated me good. Of course, his life got easier the older he got, the kids grown, the house empty, it was just me and Brian who hung in there, and so did some of the girls. You want a good story? How about your brother Brian's story? Huh?"

"Brian?" Rory asked.

"Wolfe's always had a hard-on for Brian," Parnell said. Then: "Ever since we were kids."

"Well, maybe he don't have a hard-on for him no more," responded Rory. "Maybe since we been gone, he don't have a hard-on for the kid."

"He's got a hard-on for him all right," says Parnell.

"I'll give ya a hard-on," Wolfe said. "No offense, but you guys left home, Brian and me stayed, we toughed it out, we helped out the family, saw the old man mellow, watched Mom—Lord have mercy on her—get old. Brian's not a complainer, and I think you'd all agree that he's the handsomest one in the family."

"Terry," Frankie said.

"Terry's a psycho," Wolfe shot back.

"He's still the best looking."

"Isn't," Wolfe declared, and it was final. "And Brian's probably the smartest, too."

"Mickey Mack," Rory shot back.

"He's no Mickey Mack," said Parnell.

"Yeah," Wolfe said, "but if Mickey Mack were here, and Brian were absent, you'd probably say he was no Brian. Mickey Mack's not even a Terry Coole. No offense, but fuck Mickey Mack, if you catch my drift, fuck him."

"What?" Frankie said.

"You heard me."

"What did Mickey Mack ever do to you?" Francis of X. asked.

"That's just it," Wolfe said. "I'm a workn kind of guy, I drive a truck, I ain't got fancy degrees, MFAs and MAs and whatever other Ms and As that fuckn cocksucker earned, I'm a simple honest, upstanding. . . ."

"Full of shit," Parnell muttered.

"What?" Wolfe asked.

"Grandiose son of a bitch," Rory agreed.

"Huh?"

"Brian's a great guy," Wolfe Tone said.

"You make it sound like I was the one who died, Wolfe," Brian said. "Besides, I've had a lot of problems with the old man the last couple of years of his life. We weren't on speaking terms. There's a lot about me you don't want to know about."

Wolfe Tone was a man of the earth, nothing more; he had no machinations for the finer reflections as Brian did. There was not an abstract bone in him, everything real, here, now, practical, solvable, and if life were buoyant, it was because of this. Life was a set of things, tools, food, family. There was almost a kind of engineering to it, almost like driving a truck. Less than being a *shabbes goy* like Mickey Mack or their Uncle Jack Moody, Wolfe thought of himself as an honorary pisano, a lesser don, a soldier in a mob crew, a goodfella, but also not a bad guy, a man with a sense of order, that of family, of home, of things to do, obligations, duties and responsibilities. As high as he might get drinking or taking drugs, like the old man, he would never miss a day of work.

So when Brian spit out, "We don't have anything in common anymore," Wolfe had to think.

Was his brother right? They had grown apart, it was true, but didn't they still have something in common?

Everyone called Wolfe the seventh son, because Andrew had died in infancy, but if you asked Wolfe, he'd tell you that the seventh son was Brian, that all the luck, good and bad, that could be found in the world was upon Brian's shoulders.

Christ, Brian should have gone to college first, not after the fire department, and got himself a job teaching in a college. They never should have let him go in the navy and then the fire department. He would have been better off driving a truck with me at the airport, Wolfe figured.

"Did you see who the Yankees got in the off-season?" Wolfe asked.

"I'm a Mets fan," Brian told him.

"That's right," Wolfe said, playing dumb. "I root for the Jets and you for the Giants."

"The world champions."

"Once upon a time."

"Give me Bill Parcell's two championships over that team the Jets had with Joe Namath."

The Nets? No, Brian was a die-hard Knicks fan, always was, even in the early days, before the Pearl, Clyde, Dollar Bill, Big Dave, and Willis.

"How about them Rangers?" Wolfe said.

"Huh?" Brian asked.

"You hate hockey, don'tcha?"

"Sort of," Brian said.

"Well," Wolfe said, smiling. "There."

"There?"

"You said we had nothing in common."

"We don't."

Brian looked at the other three brothers; none of them had anything in common.

"Hockey," Wolfe said.

"What about it?"

"We both hate it," says Wolfe.

"Yeah," Brian says, not sure what all this meant.

"Well," Wolfe beamed. "We have that in common."

"What?"

"We both hate hockey."

2

The room fell quiet after they stopped bickering, and because they were not the talkers in the family, no one picked up the slack. Each stared straight ahead, looking at their dead father. Brian stared at the faux stained-glass windows, thinking about Lizzie, and that look she gave him when he arrived. He realized that she hadn't seen him since the accident, hadn't known that Brian would look so bad. After all, they used to say he was the best-looking one of the bunch, a black-haired, dark-eyed, romantic type. Or maybe Lizzie looked at Brian because of that time long ago. What could he do? Apologize? He wasn't responsible for it, was he? It was human nature, curiosity, his own naïveté, wasn't it? It used to bother Brian for years, but then he forgot about it until this evening. He had to get on with his life. What went on between Lizzie and Brian was the last thing on his mind when he lay in the hospital bed, month after month, one skin graft after another. ("They done fried the skin off the white man," Brian heard a black EMS driver say as they eased him on a gurney into the ambulance, just before losing consciousness.) But Brian was no longer a white man. Now his skin was too florid to be white. He used to look in the mirror and shout, "Look, up on the tenement fire escape, it's a bird, it's an assassin, it's a mugger, it's a rapist or thief. No, it's Lobsterman!"

Rebuilt to the tune of three million dollars, courtesy of the City of New York, the mayor's office, and the fire department, not to mention hospitals and rehabs and physical therapy in Connecticut, and the insurance companies, benefactors, the blue-haired old ladies who came to visit to give him comfort, the nuns and priests and Franciscan monks, the social workers. But not Brian's children, not his wife; they got out of it long before that roof gave in. They were gone. So he had lots of other things to think about besides dipping into Lizzie's underwear when they were kids, lots to worry about besides that nun—"that *fucking* nun," he called her—down in Philadelphia.

Then: "You want to hear stories."

"What you say?" Rory asked.

"I got stories that'll knock your socks off."

"Keep 'em to yourself," Frankie said.

But, then, because they had grown up on non sequiturs as if they were the only form of discourse, Rory said, "The old man should have been buried in Florida next to his wife."

"You guys should have realized that he was senile," Parnell interjected, "when he changed his will."

"Meaning?" Wolfe asked.

"We're not even Brooklyn people anymore," Rory said. "This was a big mistake to have this here."

Brian had to smile because he was tempted to say the same thing only moments earlier, and he was glad to know that one of his brothers felt the way he did. His home, the second story of a brownstone in Park Slope off Prospect Park, was maybe only a fifteen-minute drive from here on the other side of Eastern Parkway.

The flames had dried up all the liquids in his body; there were no tears, no sweat, he even had trouble peeing.

Bitterness was overrated anyhow. Those three young brothers were bitter, but who cared? Not Brian. Bitterness seemed almost like a suburban indulgence, not a real urban blight like his own emotions had become.

Shame and guilt were bigger, oh, not over Lizzie, thought Brian, he had no shame about putting his finger inside his sister's underpants, rubbing that wet ball of flesh, and watching her ooze and wiggle, squirm with guilty pleasure, Please, stop, she begged him, but he didn't want to stop. He wanted to go further, pull down his pants and shove something else inside of her, but then the doorbell rang or the telephone rang, he couldn't remember which, it was that long ago, and didn't matter anyhow, fuck it, fuck her, that little cunt of a nun. But that wasn't shameful, wasn't sinful, wasn't guilty. The shame and guilt went deeper than one incident. It was as big as that house on Long Island, bigger, maybe the size of this neighborhood, and that's why he didn't like being here. Less than being dangerous or reeking of crime and poverty, East New York was full of shame. He could smell it inside of this funeral parlor, and unlike the rich or middle class who were always innocent until proven guilty, Brian knew that the poor were never innocent, only less guilty until proven more guilty, and that the stink of shame had something to do with that, too, and that's when the real shame sets in. Bitterness was just another kind of taste compared to shame and guilt; it was no match at all. Fly away, fly away, he thought, let me out of here, let me escape through the rooftop, out of the flames and into another time, out of the world, lifted in a white gauze of light from the smoldering ruins of the grocery store in the South Bronx, south of Tremont Avenue, just like this place, husks of buildings, hollow-eyed inhabitants, packs of stray dogs, the landscape of the city, of the new imagination, into the house of shame and guilt.

So Brian dreamed about anything but his family—anything but his father, dead or alive.

Besides, Brian had only superficial details about his own father, facts he could fit on a postage stamp.

"You thinking about the old man?"

"Yeah."

"Me, too."

"He wasn't so bad."

"Not bad at all."

"But tell the others that."

"They won't listen."

"They wouldn't believe you."

"Think us nuts."

"Worse than that."

"Much worse."

"Crazy, ain't it?"

"Very crazy."

"What's it all supposed to mean?"

"Yeah."

"Yeah."

"Wasn't that bad."

"A hard life."

"Hard life."

"Can't blame him for his choices."

"Yeah."

"Yeah."

"Yeah."

A woman screamed outside the stained-glass windows that fronted onto Broadway. It sounded like Aunt Augusta, like she might sound, sexy and tough, booze-breathed and tobacco-kissed, shouting at the top of her lungs, "Fuckn Jackie Ducks, fuckn Jackie Ducks, fuckn Jackie Ducks." But, of course, that was not what the woman outside said. "Fuckn Jackleen sucks, fuckn Jackleen sucks," she said, and it was not Aunt Augusta but another ghetto kaddish by a displaced cantor, a black woman, not that crazy Irish lady.

Even if the younger brothers didn't belong on Long Island, and never did, never would, that didn't mean, all of them agreed, that they belonged back in East New York.

"Christ, this place gives you the creeps," Rory said, standing, pacing, looking at his watch.

"Fuckn Dad," Parnell said, "what a fuckn guy!"

"Keep it down!" Wolfe shouted.

"What I say?" Parnell asked.

"Fuckn Wolfe," Rory told his twin, "always bustn hump right until the very end."

Fuckn Wolfe.

Home was that yellow stucco house of umpteen children and seven rooms, the screen and storm windows mismatched, the garage falling down, car parts and bicycle parts and even cars on cinder blocks in the yard until the town gave them a summons, all the pressure of the haves upon the have-nothings, wishing his nights for a Cadillac Coupe de Ville or a swimming pool in the backyard, and then saying, upon receiving a hand-me-down suit that once belonged to Wolfe that once belonged to Terry who got it from Paddy who was given it from Mickey Mack who got it from Leland or Emmett or some well-off Rockville Center cousins, fuck it, Brian thought, it don't mean nothing. Let the rest of them have East New York, he used to think. Give me Key West. Yet, how or why, he didn't know, all of these recollections brought back the upstairs rooms in the stucco house in Wilson Park, and Brian saw himself, unburnt, tanned, hair slicked back, sleeves rolled up on his short-sleeved colored T-shirt, the Nassau County version of John Garfield, and Lizzie asleep in her parents' unmade bed.

The others had gone off to a family picnic at Heckscher State Park, cooking hot dogs and hamburgers, drinking beer in the hot sun, fighting among themselves, crashing their cars, the children fighting and screaming until a park ranger asked them to quiet down.

But here was Brian; here was Elizabeth Ann.

She was feverish, and his mother had asked Brian to sponge her down every fifteen minutes, and she lay on the bed in her skimpy bikini underpants and a training bra, hardly a womanly figure yet. He was not a man yet either, but only imagining himself into that posture.

Her fever spiked and she was nearly delirious, and Brian decided to investigate, so he pulled her underpants down to her ankles, and then ran to the window and looked outside. Only children from across the street playing ring-a-levio, and no parents anywhere, and all his family at the state park with his mother's relatives roasting marshmallows by now, but still hours away from coming home.

He ran up into the attic, and grabbed his sack of marbles, the giant ones, the transparent ones, the colorful ones, and one by one, he shoved the marbles up his sister's cunt, trying to determine, before she came out of her delirium and screamed, just how many marbles he could fit into that hole.

Sixteen, he remembered, though no big ones, only the small transparent ones, and the rest the even smaller kind, and maybe the cunt could have taken more marbles but he got scared, thought he heard the door open and so ran, forgetting to remove them, so that Lizzie woke—or at least got up—and went to pee in the bathroom, and then these marbles began to fall into the toilet bowl, one by one by one, she screamed as he sat trembling in the attic, and came running down, asking her what was the matter, but she would not tell him, and later, after she calmed down and he hoped she might think it was an hallucination, she still would not tell him what happened, though in the meantime, he dug the marbles out of the toilet bowl, washed them in the sink, put them in the sack and hid them in the attic, just as he heard the old Dodge Dart pull up and the kids come grumbling inside, their father shouting that they were ungrateful and their mother's face red with sun and booze, Brian told them that Lizzie was delirious, and Rosy a nurse checked her temperature and said it was 104, and what a good boy Brian had been, and how she only wished all her children could be as good and helpful as Brian had been.

Lizzie, delirious in her parents' bedroom, screamed out, "The pig, the pig, the pig, the pig. . . ."

Instead of a sister, there is a gash, the heated circle of sex; instead of a father, there is a thumbnail profile of a ghetto drunk, a dockside brawler.

The young brothers Coole sat in mourning, alone and apart.

If they had nothing, Brian at least had his fantasies. It was the only way to survive in the Coole household, that noisy, dirty, crowded, damp, congested, chaotic, fulminating place that seemed so heartless and cruel, but maybe was just heartbreaking and indifferent. One scar healing on top of another scar. The ripped sofa and secondhand furniture, the sticky peanut butter-smeared place mats and the broken-down stove and refrigerator and the backed-up toilet, the tiny closets and the basement filled with old papers and broken, heelless shoes, one skate, golf clubs with wooden shafts, rosaries and prayer books, Cheerios and Maypo, filthy towels and dirty underwear, and pants so old that the seat shined. Then the roof caved in on the grocery store in the South Bronx, off Tremont.

Frankie drank from a half-pint bottle of whiskey which he took from his overcoat, but this time he didn't pass it around. This was a one-man bottle at best. He seemed agitated and ready to leave, yet kept standing around, walking up to his four brothers, then to the coffin, then back to them, and so on. He lit one cigarette after another. Finally he sat down next to Wolfe and Brian, but stood up immediately again.

He pointed with a burning cigarette.

"What I am is my own business," Frankie said. "I survive. I get by. I'm going to say this once, and then I'm out of here, so listen up, especially you, Brian, Mr. Fireman, because it's why you became a fireman, why the old man asked you to do it, the fire in his house as a boy, the fire that burned up his sister Noreen, the fire that went off on our porch."

"Our porch?" Brian asked.

"After the old man did in Fuzzy with the big chill in the freezer," X said, "I decided to exact my revenge upon him. A few nights later, he came home drunk as usual, but this time he passed out in that bedroom we had out on the porch off the dining room, you know, that room where Leland, Emmett, and

Mickey Mack used to sleep when they lived at home, and every-one, once again, was not in the house, Mom at the church across the street, making another novena, the boys playing basketball at the playground, the girls off with their friends, I soaked a bunch of rags with gasoline and tossed the shit right next to where he was sleeping, then lit it and started off to bed myself, angry like a pig, but not giving a shit if I died too, let me, I thought, I'm just another worthless kid in this family, son of that worthless fat pig on the porch, so I lit up the place, him in it, and me, what did I care?

"Then I started to get a bad conscience, so I got a blanket and went onto the porch and pounded out the flames, woke him and dragged him out into the yard where I hosed him down, and it was like a miracle, only his clothes were singed, but he wasn't badly burned except for these blistery scabs that developed on his arms, the side of one leg, and his neck, but not bad at all con-sidering, and he couldn't figure out what happened since he was drunk, and although he didn't smoke, I showed him the hookah pipe and told the old man he must have been out of his mind drunk, because he had been suckn on a fiery hookah, and a spark must have dropped on the floor and set off the blankets he slept on, and as far as the gasoline was concerned, the can had been on the porch, why, I don't know, but that's the Coole family, right? Gasoline can on the porch next to the bed. A baby goat in the kitchen. A bicycle wheel next to the dining room table. A line of underwear drying in the livn room. That's the family, right? So he didn't question any of it, and, Jesus, bro's, I felt so bad because the guy kept thankn me for savn his life, I had just tried to off the motherfucker, and here he is thankn me for savn his life, I couldn't believe it, and I felt this small, and like a real shit.

"I didn't stay around after that, finished out my job at the Wilson Hills that summer then disappeared into the city with-out finishn high school, got a GED years later, and haven't been seen until this day, only here I am and there I go, because I'm out of here."

Francis Xavier, the youngest of the Coole pod, did a kind of wise-guy salute to his father, palm to side of head, flicking his arm at him, but instead of saying something like *Boffongoolo,* he said, "So long, Dad, sweet dreams, and no hard feelings," and then nodded to the rest of the family and stepped out of the funeral parlor and onto Broadway, there either to find a gypsy cab to take him back to the city or to walk a few blocks to the subway station and head back to the city that way.

Brian stood and went up to the coffin. Parnell and Rory kneeled. Wolfe had already kneeled in front of the coffin, saying silent prayers for their dead father, using a short-timer rosary bead from Ireland (this link of ten balls, not the whole shebang). The younger of the two brothers, the dark one, the one with the lineage of the black pig in his blood, just like his old man, he looked at his waxy-faced father, bleached of his humanity, the bile drained out of him, this lifeless thing. So many times when Brian was a boy his father came home *dead drunk.* Now he was, what, drunk dead, or maybe, drunk drunk, then dead dead, after which there is no coming back to dance the fandango in the kitchen.

He tried to imagine his father, young and enthusiastic, maybe even a touch good-looking with jet-black hair like a Cuban singer, that great Keltic nose like one of the goombahs on Eastern Parkway underneath the el·at their bocci courts—*gozzo a un culo* to you, too, Mr. Coole, *doozy potz*—even a touch of seriousness about his eyes, like the intellectual Jewish boys on the other side of Fulton Street.

Ah, that Seamus is a real shnook.

The shammes?

Wha?

The shammes at the synagogue.

What kind of sheeny are you, anyhow?
What kind of hymie are you calln me a sheeny?
I'm talkn 'bout Jackie Ducks.
That shlemiel!
That's the one.

Then he saw his mother, small, cute, good-looking, too, maybe even a touch beautiful, the wild Irish rose (they all loved alcohol of the rose variety), with her million-dollar smile, and that pompadour on her head, just like the movie stars, and her open-toe high heels, and this tough little guy in his sport coat and his two-tone shoes, dancing with her at a beer garden on Bushwick, the band playing "Blues in the Night" or "You Made Me Love You." For laughs, they lindied around the dance floor to "Deep in the Heart of Texas." They got engaged, quickly married, even faster than that, pregnant and with child, and then another one, and soon they lived, not in Brooklyn, but Washington, D.C., Jackie Ducks a sailor in the U.S. Navy.

Outside, he heard gunshots, then sirens; the elevated train rattled past, the windows shaking, the floor vibrating. It could not be East New York if it didn't have that agitating el.

Brian thought of his father's huge head. The old man, though he wanted to project a know-nothing countenance, had attended Georgetown, where he studied to be in the foreign service, but then had to come home when his father grew ill, and take care of him. Though he seemed like a reader of the *Daily News*, he really preferred the *New York Times*, his one daily indulgence all his life, and his one regret, before dementia set in, of living in a retirement village in Florida—you could not always get the *Times*, either delivered or at the local store. His other extravagances were a penchant, nearly gone berserk, for ordering magazines, *Sports Illustrated*, *Time*, *Newsweek*, *U.S. News and World Report*, *New Republic*, even once the *Nation* until he decided it was a commie rag, as he did *Newsday*, which, worse than being pinko, he considered anti-Catholic and anti-Irish. How he came to this conclusion, Brian never knew, but he was passionate about it until the end, when he retired south with his lady.

But, seeing his father now, Brian thought of something else. "Thank you," Brian said, and then under his breath, "cursed progenitor."

In another room, Emmett kibitzed with some younger brothers by the beer kegs, saluting the world with a big glass of Irish whiskey. Jackie Wackie, the former holy terror of the Coole household, sat quietly; he no longer drank, so was one of the celery soda drinkers. In the back of the room and in the corners, several sisters and brothers smoked dope or did lines of cocaine.

"Brooklyn," Mary Grace said.

"What?"

"The Coole family," she went on.

"We're no longer inextricable from the borough," Leland said.

"But still synonymous with this neighborhood," Rory added.

"The crazy Irish," Brian laughed.

"The wacky Cooles," said Wolfe. "The lunatics of East New York."

They were all one, at one—one big family, happy or otherwise, though more often than not, just otherwise.

At a table in one corner, Eileen spoke with a gaggle of sisters. "I can still picture the shitload of distant relatives—the Moodys with their Brooklyn accents and the Cooles with their counties Mayo and Clare speech—not to mention the stream of friends from the docks and the airport, friends from the gin mills, in Brooklyn, down the piers in Manhattan, cronies from the saloons in East Wilson and Wilson Park along Hillside Avenue."

"Yeah," one of them said.

A few of the boys came over.

"Yeah, yeah," Parnell muttered.

"She loves you," says Rory.

"What?"

"The Beatles."

"The Beatles, what?"

"She loves you, yeah yeah."

"Oh, yeah."

"Yeah."

"Yeah, yeah, yeah," Leland said.

"Yeah, yeah," sings Wolfe.

Besides the Cooles, the cousins and distant cousins, the old aunts and uncles from the old country and the ones from the borough itself, the old friends and acquaintances, there were others who had come to the wake, too. Bakers, caddies, cops, private eyes, insurance brokers, gamblers, bookies, priests, ex-priests, Franciscan monks, and waiters from chophouses in downtown Brooklyn. They were generally little potbellied men just like the old man—all the people who came to pay their last respects to Inspector Coole. Though some were—like the ex-jockeys—little and skinny. There was even a retired giant from the Ringling Brothers Barnum and Bailey Circus, a fellow the old man helped through customs once. Even a few of the old Italian gangsters from East New York were there, and a couple of the wise guys from the piers, which flabbergasted Rory and Parnell because the old man never said a kind word about "the goddamn guineas," as he always called them, though it was one of his contradictions that he spoke a beautiful Italian (Florentine accent). Even a few Cuban wise guys from the neighborhood showed, not so much for the old man, but because he was the brother of La Bella Eileen (aunt, not sister), wife of the late Jorge Panaqua, the darling of the Cubans still.

"Hey, Jorge got crazy when he was a prisoner of war in North Korea and later Manchuria," one of these Cubans told Rory, but

Rory didn't know what the guy was talking about since Jorge was dead before the young kids could remember him.

Brother Jackie Wackie and Jorge got along great because both of them loved to dance.

"I liked the way Jorge dressed," Emmett told the younger brothers when they asked him about Aunt Eileen and Jorge.

. . . his yellow slacks, his silk shirts, his pointy black shoes, his slim belts buckled on the side of his pants. You could not think of that Brooklyn killer the Umbrella Man—that fifties teenager dressed in stovepipe black pants and pointy black shoes, purple shirt and slick thin black suspenders, black cape and hat—without also seeing Uncle Jorge, duck's ass haircut, gold chain on neck, pack of Luckies in shirt pocket. Also, Emmett liked him because he ruffled the old man like no one ever saw before or since. The old man just never knew how to handle Jorge Panaqua.

"Not that we care," Parnell told Emmett earlier.

"We don't give a shit about Jorge Panaqua," Rory said, putting in his two cents.

Jorge Panaqua had died, after all, decades earlier. That was yesterday, and years ago, yesteryear and the years before that. That was history, not the evening news, not what was happening. This was no longer a funeral but an Irish wake.

What was so remarkable now was not how crazy the Cooles were, but how tame they now seemed. The calmest of all appeared to be Jack, the genuine lunatic, unlike the rest of them, amateur nuts and part-time hitmen.

Jack's madness escalated in the army, shock treatments, Florida, more shock treatments, New York lockups, tranquilizers, mood alterers, mood stabilizers, anti-psychotics ("Well, sure, I'm anti-psychotic too, aren't we all?"), still more shocks, pills with spacy names like Elavil and Halcion, spooky pills like Stelazine ("Hey, Stella!"), and things that were lighter than air—like lithium.

Lithium was his latest salt, and seemingly the best operating of everything he had taken previously.

Parnell spoke with Eileen.

"They say Jackie's been on the lithium for close to fifteen years now," he whispered. "It shows by his hugeness magnified double, his big frame and body retaining more water because of the salts."

"So what?" she said, snapping a wad of bubble gum.

"What?" Leland asked.

"Nothn, bro."

Jackie was the least of problems nowadays; Rory and Parnell had heard that he hadn't had a drink in over twenty years, and the dryness cut out 90 percent of his aberrant behavior. Still, Jackie was pissed off at the family from years ago, also twenty years back, when each one of them had done something he didn't appreciate or approve of or took all wrong.

And here the Cooles sat, a few sober, out here in Lourdes parish, where the ghosts of the Coole family were greatest, not staring each other down, but edgy and shifty. It almost was as if they had really been assimilated like everyone else, that the passage from Brooklyn ghetto to the eastern suburbs had been accomplished; they had become a part of the postwar diaspora, and everything was going to be all right. They would live happily ever after, working for the government, just like their father, and retire, if not millionaires, with benefits and enough money to get a little condo on the west coast of Florida.

Jack was now as big as an East New York gangster. Fat Tony Salerno, Vincent "The Chin" Gigante—not to mention lesser-known hoods like Shifty Fazulli, Bloody Cochran, Chicken-Heart Pollo, and Wormy Worth (all extremely fat East New York men)—Sidney Greenstreet, Orson Welles, Marlon Brando—all these names came to mind looking at their aging brother, the eternal bachelor.

Outside the street is not so noisy, even sounds a bit peace-ful, if that is possible in this part of the world. The el rattles past every couple of minutes; cars screech their brakes or honk their horns outside. It's still the ghetto; nothing is going to change that. Nothing here was ever neat or tidy, which is why this is where the old man wanted his bones interred. He liked the dangerous, messy unpredictability of this place, liked the ache and pain it gave off like a hum.

So Eileen watched her oldest brother mumble into his hands and cry. She said to Mary Grace, "This was part of the place, too, even though I never seen Jackie Wackie cry."

"Know what you mean," Mary Grace agreed. "Saw him get crazy. Saw him go crazy."

"Watched him turn psycho."

"Watched him wig out loony."

"That too," Eileen answered. Then: "Witnessed his anger. His rages. His raging diatribes against womanhood and mankind."

"But never saw him cry."

"Exactly," she said. "Saw Emmett cry over a broken bottle of whiskey, a line of drugs sneezed away." Then: "Heard about him crying when the old man had broken a bat across his back when he was a teenager, but was too young to remember that, and the old man had mellowed out by the time we were grow-ing up, he wasn't the terror the older ones described."

Mary Grace had seen her mother and sisters cry. Knew she was a crybaby herself up until she became a hardened child of Coole. Saw Paddy cry. Saw Wolfie and Terry cry. Saw every brother she ever had—and even saw the old man—cry. But never Jackie Wackie, never Leland Jack Coole.

Parnell's stomach cramped, and just where his rib cage turned into a wishbone, he had a tight feeling himself. This is it, Parnell thought. Brother Jack was back, and you do need Jacks or better to open. Or to close. He thought of the other brothers, their hawk noses, their cowish teary eyes, black as pitch, like blackberries. They all had slack jaws, hangdog shoulders, pot-bellies, flat feet, lard asses, the clones of Jack Coole. But Jackie Wackie was the prototype, and biggest of all the big men in the family. He wasn't tall. Maybe five-eight or five-nine. But he was big. Not like the song either: *He ain't heavy; he's my brother.* "He's heavy, Jackie, *and* my brother," Parnell told Rory.

"He's dead," Eileen finally said to Jackie.

"We live on, so to speak."

"We're alive, sure," Mary Grace said.

"I can see that," says Jackie. "You've done a fine job, girls."

But he said it like Oliver Hardy, saying it as though they had "made a fine mess." Perhaps they were all being overly sensitive. The funeral parlor, after this night, felt like a hall of mirrors at Coney Island. Eileen kept hearing one brother picking up where another brother left off a conversation, a eulogy, a remembrance, or a remark. They could not stop. The funeral had opened the gates, and now they would speak and speak and speak. Mary Grace had told Eileen, "I can't differentiate one brother from the other."

What she heard was a collective foul tongue, but also the hugging, swatting of backs, stamping of feet, rocking in the pews like a congregation of Holy Rollers, the final cadre of sons and daughters to mourn their father.

"This is not new to me," Jackie said. "This is not new. This is not the first death I've had to tolerate, and it won't be the last. Grandfathers, aunts, grandmothers, uncles, cousins, even siblings. Then the old lady. Rosy. What's the big deal about this one being a father? Our own time is not that far down the road. We could go tomorrow via stroke or heart attack."

"That never happens to Cooles," Parnell reminded him.

Then Rory interjected, "It's always our teeth or livers."

"True," Leland agreed, "but we could go tomorrow, hit by a bus, shot by a bullet from a raging jealous husband, or choking on a stray fishbone on Friday night."

Jack mentioned Grandpa Moody's death, the first dead body he ever saw, and the first time he had to endure this barbaric ritual of laying out the corpse for viewing, for friends and relatives to gawk at the deceased. He remembered the chill and fear he felt when he touched Grandpa Moody's cold, dead hand.

But that was in another life practically. Now their dead father was fading into memory. Now they sat in the dark parlor, with the funeral director anxious for them to leave. Rory's knees shook a bit, as did his hands. He guessed he was exhausted, and finally beat. He wanted to get back to the southwest and assume his old personality, the one the government had given him years ago, and his brother Parnell to join him in the next town over, both of them employed by the state government doing road repairs.

"This was it," Mary Grace said to Eileen. "But I just don't want to get up and abandon Jackie. We were so close once upon a time."

"You and Jackie?"

"Me and Jackie."

"I can't picture it."

"Believe it," she said, "he used to drive me into the city to hear music concerts at clubs, rock and roll, blues, mainly blues, but also rock, and sometimes jazz."

"Leland?"

"Yeah, Leland."

"Can't picture him and you friends."

"We were," she said. "Now we're like strangers. Still, we aren't fightn; we stood our ground but acted like siblings for the first time in a bunch of years."

Years full of scoring and making runs and dying slowly from their familial addictions, Jackie's to booze and madness, Mary Grace's own to booze and drugs and probably madness, too, though it never occurred to her until that moment alone with her wacky oldest brother that she might be one of the craziest in the Coole family.

"I used to think I was the sensible one," she laughed.

"You?" Eileen asked.

"The only anchor in this sea of free-floatn anger."

"At least us girls had our heads screwed on straight," Eileen put in.

"Wacky kids," that's what their father called all of them. Wacky, indeed.

Jackie Wackie: the oldest son and the last of the Jacks, a long line of holy lunacies. Jackie, the bachelor, was not about to become a progenitor, and so he sat there like a Mohican more than a Coole, more than a Jack Coole. He was literally the last of this run, the last of a line, a kind, the last of them all.

In some respects Parnell was closer to—was more influenced by—him than his parents or the other brothers and sisters. Parnell didn't have to invent Jackie whole cloth as they did Grandpa Coole because the old man refused to tell any of them about his father or even his own childhood and adult life. With Jack, you only had to observe and record. All you had to be was a tabulator, a recorder, a calculator of this life. "I'm Parnell," Parnell said, redundant to the core, "the real black pig."

"Go on," Rory says.

"You mean Terry," Brian says.

"Terry?"

"He's the real black pig," Wolfe agreed. "The dark hair, the dark eyes, the skin coloring, his temperament, he can't fit in, a complete misfit, not an outlaw, just an outcast. Emmett's the outlaw type, the black sheep. Terry is something else."

"Yeah," Brian nodded with agreement.

"Jack's a kinda pig," Rory offered.

In a rare moment of disagreement, his brother Parnell shook his head, no, no, no.

He said, "Jack's a bear, a black bear, a grizzly—he's Beefy, don't you remember his nickname from the old days? Beefy. He's a bear."

Then across the room.

"If you hated this family," Mary Grace said to Eileen, "you hated yourself, because you're one of them. One of us. If I hate them, I hate myself."

"Okay," her sister agreed. "But so what?"

"Which I sometimes do. Admitted. Sometimes I do hate myself, and that is probably when I sound like I hate them," she told Eileen.

Eileen looked as if she had no idea what her sister just said, or why.

"What you thinkn?" Eileen asked. "Penny for your thoughts."

"Nothn," said Mary Grace.

"Go on."

"You know."

"The old man?"

"Sort of."

"Family?"

"Yeah."

"I hear ya."

There once was a time when all of it was so unreal, Eileen nearly saw their lives as a kind of movie. But then she came to see there was no moral, no dramatic closure, nothing so neat and tidy.

Eileen could not hail a cab in Manhattan without thinking first that maybe her brother Emmett might be the driver. Could not watch a baseball game without imagining that Wolfe could have been the leading star. Could not visit a museum without thinking that this place is incomplete because it has no paintings by her brother Paddy. When she walked into a dive on Long Island she always imagined that Terence would be sitting at the end of the bar, drunk and homeless, waiting for her to save him. If Hare Krishnas approach her at an airport, she used to want to ask them if they knew her sister Oona. She wanted to tell fashion designers that her sister Sam was once part of that world. After coming back into the country from being away for a time and passing through customs, Eileen had to bite her tongue because she wanted to tell the man checking her baggage that Inspector Leland Coole was her father. (Eileen once did this in Chicago after flying back on a red-eye from Tahiti and when she told the customs inspector this, he isolated her and her boyfriend and went through all their baggage extra carefully.) Why do I think of this now? she wondered.

Their lives had been imprinted by this place, even as the family tried to prosper and moved out eastward on Long Island.

Eileen said: "I feel, strange, almost at home here."

In another life Jackie and Mary Grace would be tooling on the subway into Manhattan, heading toward Washington Square and south of it to Bleecker, the Mills Tavern, that Bowery dive in the Village, brother Leland's favorite place to drink when he still drank. But the Mills was gone; it was now a pizza parlor. Even the Bowery was no longer lumpen, but artist lofts and young, violent drug dealers, waiting to shanghai anyone who came along, to gull them out of their money and their lives, even. In the old days, Lee shouted, *Vee vill drink champagne under the villows, monkey face,* while a bar patron told him, *Shut up, ya lug.* He begged for more sweet wine, his life, to wit, smelly, gray-molded, smoky, latrine perfumed, unhealthy, cowardly, forgotten, forgetting, unsavory, lost and never found, hopeless. His name was Jack Coole. By the morning—again his sister reminisced about something that had never been hers, but only a memory through her siblings' stories of it, because Jack just wasn't this way anymore—he scraped himself off the concrete to order a round of scrambled eggs, bloody with catsup, and he headed into his drunken day, ending the night in a jazz club. Jasmine tea, jazzmen on reeds, keyboard flutings, drums and chop suey in Chinatown, garlic soup laced with Little Italy, hot dogs in Times Square. Then came the Sousa explosions in his head. Blood-boiling, sleepless, chemicals eternally imbal-anced, Charles Mingus on bass, Eric Dolphy on saxophone, the Five Spot Café.

"All we ever had were memories," Mary Grace told Eileen, carefully watching the brothers.

"We need a rabbi," Leland said.

"A rabbi?" asked Mary Grace, astonished.

"He's right," Rory agreed with him.

"Yeah," says Parnell. "A rabbi would be just right."

"I don't get it," Eileen said, siding with her sister. She thought of that rabbi who married Sam to Arnold Blitzer.

But the other Cooles knew that wasn't what Jack the Wack meant. They needed a Brooklyn street version of a rabbi.

Dark-haired, bushy-eyebrowed, wavy-headed—"scram, gravy ain't wavy," Smokey Stover—blue-veined, pearly skinned, camel-coated, Camel-smoking, fedora'd, money-laden, money-laun-dered, starch-shirted, wide-tied, pointy-shoed: the wise guys, the bagmen, the copman, the shylocks, the loan sharks, the kill-em-in-the-dark, shoot-em-up County Whatchamacallit gangsters, the hoodlums, the hoo-da-lums, the donnybrooksters, the crazy pad-dies, even they had their rabbis in Brooklyn, Leland had told them mournfully.

"To the old man!" Jack said, finally.

"He's dead," Mary Grace answered.

"Of course he's dead, Gracie."

"Then what?" Eileen asked.

"So what," Leland told her.

"We keep going on," says Parnell.

"Until the end," added Rory.

"To us, his sons and daughters," Eileen declared, deadpan and flat out.

"To us all," Jackie sang.

"The survivors," said Rory.

"Hardly that," said Parnell.

"Those who were left behind," Jackie intoned.

"The leftovers?" Mary Grace asked.

Jack the Wack hung his head between his humongous thighs, and if he had on a yellow suit and a bopping hat, you would have sworn he was a big-time hip-hop grand master slam.

Our Lady of Perpetual Sobriety, watch over us!

When Eileen came around again, she realized that Jack had been speaking, mumbling and muttering, but eulogizing, or maybe just making an observation.

Jack sounded craziest when he talked about his military experience, and now he spoke to them about that, the armed forces time, he called it, the court-martial, torture, given twenty-five shock treatments, put in a basket, and shipped back home. It took him a lifetime to get to know his father, but in the end he didn't know him at all.

"It was not even the alcohol that did anything to us," Eileen pontificated, but only Mary Grace listened. "It was their very name which damned them. Alcohol only exaggerated a condition that preexisted. Or at least that was how I saw it after watching a program about ACOA on television."

"I saw that one too," Mary Grace said. "I really liked that cute weight lifter from Jersey."

"That was another program," says Eileen.

"About the AA stuff and all. . . ."

" 'Nother program, sis."

"Oh."

When Mary Grace looked at Brian's face, she wondered once again if anything had ever gone on between him and Lizzie. But how did you broach it? Or, why even bother to broach it?

"Anyone see Terry?" Brian asked.

"Terry?"

"Yeah," Wolfe said, "probably blacked out somewheres."

"Maybe he left," Mary Grace said.

"Terry?" Parnell asked.

"Fuckn Psycho," Rory laughed.

"Where's Terry?"

"Dunno."

"Dumb bastard."

As they filed outside, they saw the sparks from the el, heard the clang of the train cars above, the shouts from the projects across Broadway on Mother Gaston Boulevard. Car horns, screeching brakes, hip-hop and guaracha sounds, boombox sounds, sounds of the city—gun shots, M-80 rockets, firecrackers, garbage cans, glass breaking, shouts and screams and cries.

TERRY AND THE PIRATES

THE NEXT DAY THEY LUGGED HIS SORRY CARCASS TO Calvary Cemetery for the burial. Everyone there, the girls and boys, except Psycho—Terry. Got him in the ground, threw on some dirt, said a few prayers.

They would drive off in all directions, back out to the Island, to Newark and the airport, across Highland Park and through Cypress Hills, into the vaporous wonders of Ozone Park, into the safety of Queens and the 'burbs, or into Manhattan and Jersey, up into the Bronx, at any rate, except for Brian, away from Brooklyn.

Now that their father was dead and gone, out of sight and out of mind, they focused on their missing brother Terry.

"Terry the Mooch," Jack the Wack said.

"Fuckn Terry."

"What a psycho!"

"He forgets to show up on the day of his own father's burial."

"His absence from the fiftieth was bad enough."

"But this?"

"Jeez."

"He's probably passed out at the ninth hole on a golf course on Long Island or sleepn off a blackout on the subway train, too brain-frizzed to remember," Wolfe said.

And Jack was pissed at Eileen for smoking a joint at the cemetery. Luckily, he wasn't in the rented limo that she and Mary

Grace were in, because they had done a line of coke before smoking the joint outside, and the people in Emmett's car smoked crack from glass pipes, while Rory and Parnell had a car in which everyone was nodding out.

After all the others departed, Mary Grace and Eileen were walked to their car by Rory, leaving Parnell with Wolfe and Brian. They talked about their no-show brother Terry.

"That fuckn bastard, this is the last time I'm gonna put up with Terry's bullshit," Wolfe said.

"You guys indulge him," Parnell said. "Fuck 'im."

"He's helpless," Brian said. "What you want us to do?"

"Fuck 'im," Parnell said.

Rory and Parnell would catch their plane to Tucson, and Wolfe said he would drive them to Kennedy. Brian told them that he would wait a few minutes longer, then drive back to Park Slope. They all shook hands, but nothing more, and then left. Within a few minutes, there were no more Coole family left, only Brian, who lived only fifteen minutes away, but a world apart, on the other side of Eastern Parkway. Then Brian was gone, too.

The blacks didn't like to use this parlor, but when the other funeral parlors were filled with young corpses from the street wars, they had no choice but to use this déclassé white man's place. A black family inhabited one of the rooms now. There was weeping and shouting from the other room where the young black man was laid out, his family rolling and thundering with grief.

"They're all gone?" Terry asked.

"Vanished," said the assistant funeral director.

"Shit," Terry said. "I'm sorry."

Terry said that he got lost, then amended that story to say that he had been blackout drunk on Long Island, and after a bunch of drugs in a bar in Wilson Park, time vanished from his life, and there he was. Here he was.

He wore a dirty, beat-up Pittsburgh Pirates jacket. That's how crazy he was. A Brooklyn-born, Long Island-bred kid, he didn't root for the Mets or Yankees. He's a Pittsburgh Pirates fan. His hero was Roberto Clemente. No wonder they called him Psycho.

For as long as anyone could remember Terry Coole wore a Pittsburgh Pirates warmup jacket or hat. He had it on now, standing in the vestibule of the funeral parlor, wondering where everyone was. He looked the worse for wear, too, with a day's stubble on his face, his clothes dirty and wrinkled and smelling of booze, urine, and puke. Poor Terry. He could never get it together, even for his own father's burial.

His right hand was wrapped in a dirty bandage.

Once Terry was the handsomest of the Coole children, dark-haired and dark-eyed, with the soft, grim visage of an old-time matinee idol. He used to carry a guitar everywhere he went, and even wrote a few passably good songs, complemented by an assortment of Bob Dylan and Beatles and a couple of blues and folk songs. If it wasn't enough to get him a record contract or even very good gigs, he managed to sing at Tuesday night hootenannies on that other MacDougal Street in the Village and on Second Avenue for years, and in turn that always got him more girls. Terry was never without his girls, except now; now he had no girls.

No one wanted anything to do with him.

He couldn't stay sober for more than a few days at a time; he didn't live anywhere anymore, though lately he had found an abandoned bus out on the Island, right next to the Wilson Hills Golf Club. But that was gone now too.

One of the younger black men, his tie undone, shirt collar opened, came back into the room holding two bottles of Irish whiskey.

"Them Coole folks left this behind," he said.

"He's a Coole," the old man said, pointing to Terry. "I guess he's the owner of the bottles."

"Open them," said Terry. "Go ahead, we'll have a drink, get straightened out."

Then the old white-haired black man said, "Yeah, I used to know me a red-haired Irish lady named Gussy. Gussy Morgan. Now not only did her tits flow with Irish whiskey, but she had so much beer in her, when she pissed, it was pure Budweiser."

Terry didn't make the association that the old man was talking about Aunt Augusta.

"That's what they call it in Australia," Terry said.

"What they call what?" the old man asked.

"You know," Terry said.

"Son, I don't know what the hell you're talkn 'bout."

"Piss," Terry said. "That's what they call beer."

"Who calls it that?" one of the young men asked.

"Them Coole people," the old man said.

"Nah," says Terry, "the fuckn Australians."

"Down under?"

"Whatever," Terry said.

They drank. Some beer; some whiskey. They got mellow; they got down. The old man took out a harp and played, while one of his sons produced a blues guitar, which Terry played upon, dolefully, soulfully, full of feeling and rage; clumsily because of the bandaged right hand. But then, one by one, the men were called back into the parlor to pay their respects to the newly deceased young man laid out there. Terry was left alone, and it occurred to him that he had fucked up again. The others were gone, he had no money, and how was he to get back to the Island?

He went outside, looking up and down the dark corners of Broadway, wondering which way to go, back toward Eastern Parkway, sneak on the subway to Jamaica, beg some change and get a Schenk bus on Hillside Avenue out to Wilson Park, or go the other way, toward the city, take the el into lower Manhattan, and make his fortune there.

Terry thought: I should buy a gun and shoot myself. But then Terence McManus Coole realized you need money to buy a gun. You need enough self-esteem to make money in order to buy the gun that, because of no self-esteem, you use to kill yourself, but if you had the money, then probably you also had a job—maybe hit at the off-track betting parlor or won the lottery—but at any rate you felt pretty good about yourself, so probably would not buy a gun, and if you bought it, would use it for target practice, for sport, not for shooting yourself—Jesus, life's fucked.

What to do?—take the el toward Jamaica, catch a bus on Hillside Avenue and sleep near the golf course in East Wilson, or take the el in the other direction. Toward the city. Opportunity. Destiny. He could get a stake, put a few bucks together panhandling, buy a blues harmonica, and sing to the tourists around Washington Square Park, and once he had a few bucks, not squander the money on a bone to smoke, a forty-ouncer of ale to drink, some 'ludes, uppers, black beauties, Percodan, a bottle of Jack D., hell, a bottle of Robitussin, bottle of whiskey, shot of Stoli, bottle of fuckn Corona cerveza even with a lime to suck on —suck this, baby—yeah, salted glass for margaritaville express, a few limes, a few lines of—but none of that. Salt the money away, if he could try to remember where he hocked his guitar, a Gibson acoustic—and when; was it Hempstead near the bus depot or 14th Street in Manhattan, and where was the ticket? or if he couldn't get the old twelve-string out of the pawn shop, he'd get himself a nice folk guitar off Times Square in one of them music shops. Take to serenading the suaves and señoritas. St. Mark's Place. Eighth Street. MacDougal, but not this Macdougal, the real one in the Village, not this ghetto one, Jesus. He'd bring back them old days that Leland always talked about, Bob Dylan, Phil Ochs, Joanie the Phony, Dave Van Ronk, John Lee Hooker, Brownie McGee and Sonny Terry. None of that bullshit white-bread MTV crap; this would be unplugged, sure, but also unfucked up. Terry and the Pirates. Terry Mack.

McTerry. Mack Daddy and Daddy Mack. All of them would be there with him. The legends and the hallucinations. Terry would single-handedly save, by reinventing it, American music from annihilation.

Terry sat on the steps outside the funeral parlor, high once again, talking to himself, something he did now after he had a few drinks.

What did the old man used to say, *Ya pig, ya fuckn pig, Terry, look at ya.* T dribbled pablum, dribbled his ice cream, then his beer. Now he was here. Hey, let's hip-hop. Terry'll get his guitar out of hock. They'll boogie in the moonlight under the board-walk. Under the el.

Leland used to call him—no, not Psycho, what everyone called him, but—the one true black pig in the family. Look, not a gray hair on his head; not a brain in his head either. No job, no roof over his head, no wife or children—he used to say that he was the happiest man on Long Island. Well, not happy, but you know what he meant—content. Not that. No, not that. Not that. But if he had a little taste in him, a forty and a blunt, a bottle of hooch, a bone to smoke, a line of snow, and he was out there on the street doing the doojie-woojie, he'd be cool, he'd be Terry Coole, son of Jackass Coole, little Jackie Ducks, well, fuck a duck if it ain't Jack-in-the-Box, brother to the many, uncle to quite a few, and now without his abandoned school bus to live in.

Wolfe and Brian were tired of letting Terry stay with them, so he couldn't call them; and he had no girlfriend at the moment. T slept on the subway, 179th Street into the city, but then got fucked up, lost a sense of where he was, who he was, sense of identity, his esteem. He had to let off a little steam, so he got high. "Oh my," he said, "I can't believe I missed the old man's funeral and that everyone's gone, and I don't even know which cemetery up the block, must be a couple million corpses out there, and I'm not gonna walk past every headstone until I find the one belonging to Jackie Ducks." Jesus H. Tabasco-sauce, Terry thought. Blessed Virgin Mary of Snot. Knave of Sacre Coeur. Bag lady of Our Lady of Lourdes. Bag of bones from Saint Gregory's parish, from Good Counsel, from Saint Thomas Aquinas over by Flatbush and the uncle's house. Smell her tusks. Topaz earrings. Sapphire tongue. Lace undies. Garters. This is what I need, Terry thought, not this shit. I don't need the old man, we never got along, and he hated me worse than he hated anyone else.

Give T a babe from Brooklyn with a nice curl and manicured fingers, wearing a pointy bra beneath a tight-fitting pink sweater that she buttons on backwards, with a tight red skirt and black pumps, chewing gum and smoking Pall Malls and drinking beer at the waterfront dives along the boardwalk at Coney Island. Does Terry make himself clear? Let her be Jewish or Italian, not these barley-soaked Kelts. Let her speak Spanglish and wear glossy red lipstick, have fishnet black stockings and gold hot-pants on and wear a halter right out of Li'l Abner and be a Hispanic Daisy Mae. Or let her be like Tina Turner's kid sister, all lips and tits and clit and brown sugar.

Terence McManus wasn't one of the Cooles who had to grow up in the Brooklyn crap. But sometimes he wondered what it was like here. Every once in a while he'd get this fantasy in his head that he'd marry this Virgin Mary, a local thing, and they'd raise twenty kids just like the old man and old lady did, and instead of playing the guitar in bars for drinks, he'd be a cop or fireman like Brian, and amid Maria and Terry's fighting and feuds and blood-curdling arguments with each other, they'd fuck on the kitchen floor or one of these side streets here in East New York, and Terry'd have two big Irish wolfhounds to stay behind and protect her when he wasn't there.

So where was Terry anyhow?

Jesus, he was fucked up.

All the others were gone, but that did not stop Terry from seeing them still, hearing them, and listening to their banter. He kept flashing back to the funeral parlor with Jack, Emmy, Mickey, and Paddy. In their absence Terry spoke with his brothers. He might speak to them about the racing bike, but someone like Paddy might answer,"Dad drank too much sherry." Then Terry heard Emmett growl that their father never drank sherry in his life. He said, "You're thinking of the old lady." Another brother asked: "The old lady?" Then Terry heard Emmett pipe up, "You know, Mom."

"Mom," Terry said aloud out on the street. "The old lady."

Standing out on Broadway in the cool of night, Terry didn't think of the danger of this place nor of his dead father. Instead, he imagined his mother. Dear old Rosie Moody, the belle of Madison Street several blocks over into Bed-Stuy, the señorita of Marion, the dame of the Coole family in Wilson Park. Although everyone made such a big deal about the old man and this neighborhood, it was really their mother's turf. Her Brooklyn was an elegant one, not only gentrified but wealthy, white, well-to-do, as they used to say, proper and Victorian, a correct place to raise a large Catholic family with many girls, a world of brownstones and gaslights, and in their case, even electricity and not a brownstone but a colonial mansion, with maids and a butler, children everywhere.

The Moodys were one of those good, upstanding nineteenth-century families, an old name, full of culture, belief, integrity, upstandingness, goodness. In other words, whenever the old lady spoke about this Brooklyn, Terry saw it as a fairy tale, not real, certainly not resembling anything of their own experiences, in or outside the borough.

Terry realized that while he looked like his father, he really wanted to be like William Moody, grandiose and delusional, that if he had the money, he'd dress and act like his grandfather, full of swagger and style, a boater tilted on the head, while he jaunted down the street flashing his blackthorn stick. Grandpa Moody lived with the Cooles just before he died, and he used to come down to breakfast wearing his pinstriped gray suit, his high starched white collars with a bow tie, gold shamrock cuff links on his cuffs. He smoked strong cigarettes, and his long thin bony fingers were stained with nicotine. Grandpa Moody had a waxed mustache and reminded some of the Coole boys of John Barrymore, a man he claimed to be distantly related to.

Back in the Depression, just before he lost all his money, Grandpa Moody was mugged down by the Tombs in lower Manhattan. He made his fortune from haberdashery, but he was also a bail bondsman, among other businesses, and he had just bailed out a felon. The man cracked him on the head, took his money, and fled; thereafter, he did not remember anything but life in the distant past when he was wealthy and on top of the world, when he had racehorses in East Wilson, when his mansion was considered to be in one of the best neighborhoods in the borough, while most of the other Irish struggled to make ends meet in their tenement worlds. He wore a bowler hat and spats in winter, and when cars came into fashion, he always had the latest model. When Terry once imagined his own successes later in life, he saw himself showing up to events looking like Grandpa Moody in his heyday or even in his elongated senility, a tall thin hollow tortoiseshell, a pompous human artifice. But with what Brooklyn style! No red-suited Bed-Stuy pimp in his yellow Cadillac had more style than William Moody of Madison Street. No jiving hombre named Flacco with a million-dollar bank account from Colombia resupply connections and a driveway full of Cherokees and Wranglers matched old man Moody. He was all Brooklyn to the end. And what style! Terry thought.

"What fuckn style he had," Terry said aloud.

Terry went into a bodega to buy a forty-ounce bottle of malt liquor, and now sat on the edge of a locked playground on

Broadway, drinking malt liquor, smoking cigarettes, and trying to figure out where he was supposed to go now that everyone in the Coole family had gone. One by one, he remembered his brothers' and sisters' faces, then he settled on the visage of his father, not the pasty dead one he saw recently, but that vital, dangerous one who plagued him all his life. He remembered that time, oh, maybe ten years earlier, when his father first retired from customs and still lived in Wilson Park, had not purchased the condo on the west coast of Florida.

Right after retirement, Terry's old man was in the best spirits of his life. He had a fat pension, medical bennies, perks from his credit union on loans for cars, boats, and houses, and was told by his doctor that he had the constitution of a workhorse, that he'd live to be a hundred because there was not one single thing wrong with him. The old man had invited a few of the boys over for pot roast and to watch a sporting event on television.

The living and dining rooms had never looked so neat and clean, the walls newly painted, the floors sanded and shined, new sofa and easy chairs, new dining room table and chairs, old Mr. Coole's sons were relaxed, not fighting among themselves or with the world. The old man himself had taken the pledge and not had a drink for four or five months. But then the old man decided, what the hell, why not have a few, and so he went down into the basement, into the utility refrigerator, and came back with a case of beer, which got the boys rolling.

When the case was drained, a bunch of the boys went to the deli around the corner for more beer, and Mrs. Coole asked if maybe they should not have any more beer since dinner was only a half-hour away.

"Let them have a few," Jackie Ducks shouted at his wife. "They've earned it. We've all earned it."

As their father went into the backyard to work off a little steam by raking leaves and straightening out the privet bushes with his new electric pruning shears, Emmett and Paddy got into a discussion of the fights they had watched and then boxing generally, until Emmett was ranting about how to fight dirty, his specialty, and how he learned so much technique from their father, the furious little man in the backyard, mowing the lawn and trimming the privet, his brows furrowed, nostrils flared, mouth cast in a furious downward glare, the glint in his eyes as steely as flint.

Emmett said, "Dad was the one who first suggested, instead of using Endswell and the like, that a silver dollar dipped in a bucket of ice would reduce any swelling over and around the eyes, and you know something—he was right, the old bastard. He was right. A frozen silver dollar will take the bubble out of an eye as fast as Endswell."

"What the hell's Endswell?"

"Fucking Emmett. . . ."

"I don't know."

"He probably don't know himself."

"Probably in a blackout," another brother said. "Won't remember this when he wakes up in the morning."

"What's he talking about?" Brian asked, leaning over to whisper in Mickool's ear.

"You got me, kid," Mickey Mack said, unsure of where Emmett intended to take them.

"The old man taught me a lot of tricks," Emmett said, "like carrying a little dirt in your pocket in case someone wants to start something out on the street. You throw a little dirt in his eye and beat the shit out of him."

Emmett swilled on the last of his beer, waiting for one of the younger kids to get back from the deli from yet one more beer run.

"He also showed me, not just to punch below the belt, which any moron can do, but to punch a man on his hips, hitting that nerve and crippling him. Then you finish him off with a five-punch combination. I remember the last time I spoke with Dad he said, 'There's nothing like the five-punch combination,' left to the liver, right to the spleen, left or right to the heart, and then upstairs, right to the temple, left to the jaw, bababoom! baboom! Knockout! He also said that throwing the left hook to the body off the double jab was probably the most artistic thing life had to offer a man on this earth. And, you know something, he wasn't kidding. Throwing the hook off the jab is poetry itself."

These reveries and reflections were fractured by the sound of the el above, the cacaphony of the street below, and the presence of another posse.

Before Terry could make a decision about which way to go, the posse of kids from the other night, the ones who had harassed Emmett, were back, and their ringleader, the Spanish kid, mistook Terry for Emmett—one white person being like any other white person in East New York—and didn't Terry's own father, in his cups, mistake one son for another, no matter if Emmett had dirty blond hair and Terry's hair was as black as pitch? Terry and Mickey Mack might be two of the old man's favorite targets to smack around, especially Terry, he was everyone's favorite doormat, but if they weren't around, their father would duke it out with Emmett or Paddy, Wolfe or Brian, Parnell, Rory, or Frankie.

"Yo, you don't have no respect," the kid said.

"Huh?" Terry asked, dumbfounded.

"Don't play dumb with me, Pittsburgh Pirates."

"You makn fun our posse?" a jet black skinny kid asked.

They had jackets on, satin ones, that said the Bushwick Pirates.

The ringleader smacked Terry in the face, but Terry was a tolerant sort, having suffered worse indignities than this. Besides, what could they steal? He literally was penniless, had no watch nor jewelry, his sneakers were beat up and worn out, and even his Pittsburgh Pirates jacket was dirty and caked with grease, smeared and streaked, and stinky.

Terry was not considered one of the fighters in the family, but he was tough enough, had been around, and had had his share of fights. He was a big guy, in the shoulders, biceps, hands, forearms, wrists. His ankles and calves were thick, muscular, as was his chest, and even after years of drinking beer, he had only the slightest belly.

"I'm lookn for my brothers," he said.

"What?" one of the young ones asked, pushing and shoving him into an el piling.

"Hey, watch it," Terry said.

"You talkn to me, chump?" another black kid shouted, shoving Terry again, only the kid practically bounced off Terry's chest because Mr. T resisted now, and he really was one of the strongest, if not one of the most aggressive, brothers in the family.

Brothers used to say that Terry was going to explode, he'd reach a threshold for the abuse his parents and siblings dumped on him, and go skyrocketing into violent orbit. But they were wrong. He was Buddha-like; he had a great capacity for pain. He had no clue as to the danger of the moment; these kids were no worse than his own brothers, he thought.

Obviously they mistook him for somebody else, he thought. Happened all the time. No hard feelings. Probably a bad drug deal, an outstanding loan. Terry would be on his way.

"Not so fast," the ringleader said.

The ringleader grabbed Terry's nearly empty forty-ounce bottle of malt liquor and smashed it on the curb.

"Fuck you, white boy," he said, poking Terry in the chest.

Two boys held Terry's arms, while a third ripped off his pants pockets with a big Buck knife. Even this posse was surprised to see that Terry had nothing, no coins, no dollars, no ID, no wallet, no keys, no key ring, no photos of family or girlfriend, no nothing. This chump was one big loser. His last pennies had been spent on the malt liquor.

"You piss me off," the ringleader said, "and I'm gonna teach you a lesson. . . ."

But before the sentence was completed, Terry bolted up the block, the direction he would take decided. He ran toward the city and the old Gates Theatre, toward the Chauncey Street subway stop, and hopped the turnstile just as the subway pulled in, the doors opened and closed before the posse reached Mr. T, and the ringleader shouted, "Next time, motherfucker," but Terry knew there would be no next time. This was it with him and East New York.

He caught a late-night subway, doing his invisible act so that no one bothered him. He disappeared into the graffiti and aluminum train cars, into the hemorrhoid ads and the ads to learn English in six weeks, the Apex Institute ads and the AIDS hotline numbers. He tried to imagine a lifetime away when he was a boy riding this train line with his brothers, and the wicker seats on the train cars, some of the cars painted red or yellow or dirty brown, and the ads for Miss Rheingold and Miss Subway, oh what foxy babes they were, but it was too long ago, and he was too young to remember, or what he did recall was only that false reminiscence, another family member's stories that Terry had co-opted for his own.

Terry was glad he was headed into the city, to Manhattan, the land of opportunity, into the Village, where they'd appreciate his flair for the guitar, his pleasant Irish tenor as he sang folk songs, his charming banter between the songs.

He sat back and relaxed, not paying attention to the stops the train made or the announcements the conductor broadcast on the intercom.

Shit, where was he now, for Terry couldn't remember what he was thinking about. His brain was all fuzzed up and scuzzy. Had to detox, clean up, get straight. To hell with his father now; he had to figure out where he was and who he was, and why. Maybe it was time to make some changes. He wasn't lithiumated like Jack, but he was boozed out and burnt up and fizzling, not like a short fuse as he always supposed, but a long fuse that now was just about to—what? Maybe it was time to reveal the real Terry Coole, he thought.

Terence McManus Coole weeped.

At first, he just sniffled, but then the snot rolled down his nostrils and over his lip, his chest felt cramped, a tightness was about to explode in his head, and his eyes opened up like water jets, and the tears flowed down his cheeks.

But he was not crying for his father.

He thought of his brothers and sisters.

As he cried on the train, he did not notice that the other passengers stood and moved away from him, first to the other end of the car, but then into other cars.

What a bunch of bastards all of them were, Terry mumbled to himself, and then aloud to the passersby: "What a bunch of bastards!" Even the good ones in the house, Paddy and Mickey Mack, tortured Terry, those two not exempt from the misery the Cooles inflicted on this brother.

"Let's kill Terry," Paddy suggested, blond-haired, blue-eyed, an altar boy with an angel face.

"Let's," Mickey Mack said, stocky and with a brown-haired pompadour and crooked teeth. Paddy pinned Terry and Mickey Mack applied the coup de grace.

"What color is he?" Paddy asked.

"Too soon to tell," Mickey Mack said, "I just started applying the pressure."

Terry gasped and kicked. His legs were the strongest part of his body, and if he located one of their frames, he knew he could disable one of them for life.

"You have to hold the pillow on his face until he turns blue," Paddy said.

"He's a little red in the face," Mickey replied, pulling the pillow off momentarily, while, unbeknownst to these two young

American sportsmen, Terry furtively sucked a resupply of air.

Mickey Mack and Paddy, of course, were no slouches when it came to torture. They were aware that he probably stole air when Mickey checked the facial color, and so he applied the pillow harder.

"Is he green?" Paddy asked.

"I thought you said he's supposed to turn blue," Mick shouted. "Make up your mind, will ya?"

It was good to get them fighting. They had their differences. If the feud grew strong enough, they might even forget about their baby brother and go at each other. Mickey was stronger and tougher, Paddy faster and sneakier. The big one was good in a quick thrashing, while Patrick had stamina like a beast of burden, wearing down his opponents over the long haul.

"Green or blue, it don't matter."

Mickey Mack removed the pillow quickly and put it back before the kid could get air.

"He's red."

"Keep applying the pressure," Paddy said. "He'll be a dead man before too long."

His lungs burst and Terry felt his head dry out like a grape evaporating into a raisin in the sun. His voice was muffled, he kicked wildly, hoping to make contact.

"Boys!" their mother called from downstairs. "What are you doing up there?"

"Nothing, Mommy," Mickey called, pressing hard with the pillow.

"Well, come downstairs for some peanut butter and jelly sandwiches."

They left.

Terry lay on the floor, sucking in air. Brain cells were gone, he knew, but at least he was alive.

It left Terry Coole no choice. He could only like his sisters. He wept buckets at his mother's funeral and wake, but no tears for the father. That's the way it was. The way it would be. Now and forever. All of them placed too much emphasis on the father, he thought; their father wasn't that important in the end. Another long-winded, beery, insensitive lout. All the things his old man called Terry were now shot back at the father. Bum. Rotten bum. Lazy bum. Stinkn little bastard. Fuckn shit. Dumbbell. Shit for brains. Hopeless. Psycho.

Psycho.

He figured that within a half hour, the subway would cross over the East River via the Willie B. Bridge and into Manhattan. But he had not been paying attention. He hadn't realized that to elude the posse in East New York, he boarded a train going in the opposite direction from Manhattan, and without knowing it, instead of going to the Village, where he wanted to be, Terry was headed home, back into the heart of Long Island, out to Jamaica, and the last stop on the train, and the old hunting grounds where the Cooles used to live.

"Let us praise only women's bones," he said.

He didn't realize where he was until the conductor announced that it was the last stop, and he found himself in the pitch of night underneath the elevated train stop in Jamaica, too many hours away from the city, where he wanted to be, his opportunity, he thought, escaping him. He didn't even have money to take the bus out to Nassau County and the golf course to sleep. He began the slow walk east across Hillside Avenue, about ten miles to walk before he'd get to Wilson Park.

Aloud, he said: "I like women better than all those crazy brothers and that insane father."

The women and men looked away, staring into store windows at posters of Michael Jordan, at the headlines on the evening editions of the paper.

"Take my mother," he said. "Now *there* was a woman."

He stood and walked down the street.

He shouted it.

Old Terry, good old Terence McManus Coole was on a buzz, a tear, a rip, a roll, a waddle, a shenanigan.

"Fuck the old man," he said.

Rose, he thought.

Ah, Terry. What a psycho he was. . . .

"You pig," a woman on Hillside Avenue shouted at the reeling, mumbling Terry. "You fuckn pig, why dontcha shut the hell up?"

"Rose, Rose," Terry called.

"Ya lousy bum," the street lady called out, then lunged past him.

"Rosy . . ."

"Ya lousy rotten bum!"